"You want inside the house, right? Maybe we can make a deal." Dario's voice was husky

Cassidy couldn't hide her desperation to search for the jewels. "Yeah."

"And my dad wants you to drop your claim on the place."

"True," she said, wondering where he was headed with all this.

"Sex."

She blinked. "Sex?"

He nodded. "You can stay in the house all week and search to your heart's content, but only on the condition that you'll be my sex slave."

Her heart was beating a fast tattoo, and it had very little to do with the fact that the world's best-looking man was standing a mere foot away. "Are you serious?"

"There's one more thing."

His gorgeous dark eyes had settled on the bed. The hotel room seemed dimmer now, but only because night had fallen. Moonlight was streaming through the windows.

"What's that?" she asked in a whisper.

"The sex starts now."

Blaze™

Dear Reader,

I admit to being a fan of stories about cold cases. The older the mystery and colder the trail, the more intrigued I get. A second thing I love is reading about sexy cops, so it was only natural that I'd eventually put these two things together for Harlequin Blaze.

Oh, and before I forget—a third thing I love is a superhot romance! So, quite simply, the idea for *Cold Case, Hot Bodies* came to me when I put all my favorites into one steamy love story. When an old case involving a haunted property is reopened, a descendant of the harmed party finds herself wrapped in the strong arms of the law. That's the "hot bodies" part. And what could be better than that?

Enjoy!

And thank you so much for reading! It's what keeps me writing.

Very best wishes,

Jule McBride

COLD CASE, HOT BODIES

Jule McBride

TORONTO • NEW YORK • LONDON
AMSTERDAM • PARIS • SYDNEY • HAMBURG
STOCKHOLM • ATHENS • TOKYO • MILAN • MADRID
PRAGUE • WARSAW • BUDAPEST • AUCKLAND

ISBN-13: 978-0-373-79359-4
ISBN-10:   0-373-79359-6

COLD CASE, HOT BODIES

ABOUT THE AUTHOR

Jule McBride is a native West Virginian. Her dream to write romances came true in the nineties with the publication of her debut novel *Wild Card Wedding*. It received the *Romantic Times BOOKreviews* Reviewer's Choice Award for Best First Series Romance. Since then, the author has been nominated for multiple awards, including two lifetime achievement awards. She has written for several series, and currently makes her happy home at Harlequin Blaze. A prolific writer, she has more than thirty titles to her credit.

Books by Jule McBride

HARLEQUIN BLAZE

For Kathryn Lye, editor extraordinaire,
for helping me mind my p's and q's,
and for knowing how to wrestle commas,
semicolons and everything else, too.

Prologue

December 1890

GEM O'SHEA GLIDED her hands beneath her lover's shirt, feeling his nipples contract. It was exactly the kind of well-made shirt she'd sewn in sweatshops when she'd first come from Ireland, and her lips curved into a smile against the linen. "Do you remember when you first...*bought me,* Nathaniel?"

He grinned, his eyes catching light through the carriage window, from one of the gas lamps lining the dark river road. "I don't believe I do."

But he couldn't have forgotten the night she'd presented herself at Angel's Cloud, in New York's notorious Five Points neighborhood, determined to sell herself to the highest bidder. "Should I remind you?"

"Of every detail." He urged her closer, between his legs, and the satin dress she'd worn to the wedding bunched between them, an unwanted barrier. She brought her mouth to his, and the taste of wedding cake invaded her senses.

"I had too much champagne," she whispered.

"You won't hear me complaining."

Heat surged through her limbs despite the cold. Everything but passion vanished as Nathaniel deepened the kiss—the pounding hooves on the cobbled road, the rushing of the

East River's wild currents, the crack of the driver's whip. Hungrily, her fingers opened the studs of his shirt. Just as quickly, his tongue swept inside her mouth. Heat exploded as she stroked his chest hair, and she felt it catch on the backs of her rings—beautiful rings that were gifts from him, just a few of the countless jewels he'd given her over the years.

As desire took her, Gem thought of another kiss, the one they'd just witnessed at the altar between her and Nathaniel's son, Mark, and his young bride, Lily Jordan. With the memory, her arms swept around Nathaniel's neck, and she wished with all her heart she could marry him. How many nights had she lain awake, knowing her heart's deepest desire would remain an impossible dream?

She dropped down, moaning against his chest, her tongue searing a nipple, his answer a sound of need as he grasped her hand, urging it into the folds of his trousers. Soon they'd be at Angel's Cloud, where countless warm beds waited—either in the hidden rooms, or in the bawdy house, or in the rear building where she'd lived—but she wanted Nathaniel now. Her body was burning all over, just as it had the night they met.

She'd been desperate then, still speaking with a brogue so thick that most American natives couldn't understand her. She'd rarely even kissed a man, but she'd heard other, less reputable girls talk at the sweatshop, claiming men paid them for sexual favors, and because she'd been determined to earn her mum's passage from Ireland, she'd soon found herself standing on the shell-strewn floor of a Five Points bawdy house.

"Two hundred dollars," a man had called.

She'd nearly fainted. When he'd stepped from the shadows, his sparkling blue eyes had captured hers, then she'd recognized Nathaniel Haswell. He'd gotten his start as a self-made, import-export man, a buyer and seller of whatever prospered, and he owned acres of real estate on Manhattan Island. His picture was always in the papers. Without ceremony, he'd grabbed her hand and hauled her toward the stairs, and she'd foolishly blurted the first thing that had come to mind, "You're married!"

He'd turned to stare, the set of his mouth incredulous. "Don't tell me that bothers you?"

"Of course not," she'd managed quickly. All the men in Angel's Cloud were probably married. "In fact," she'd added brazenly, "I do prefer it, sir."

He'd continued toward the room. "And why might that be?"

"No messy attachments. I'm a professional, you know."

"I see," he'd returned as they reached the bedroom. "Experienced at this sort of thing, are you?"

"Indeed," she'd enthused, the pulse at her throat ticking madly as he'd shrugged out of his jacket.

She'd been trembling all over, still scared of the rowdy men downstairs, her head pounding from cigar smoke. Her throat had tightened as Nathaniel undid his trousers, and she'd considered running, but she'd thought of circumstances in Ireland, and of her mum, then of the poor girls still working in the sweatshop, scarcely earning a wage to buy adequate food. Her stomach growling, she'd taken a deep breath, stared boldly in the general direction of Nathaniel's private parts, then she'd plunged on. "Why, I've been to Angel's Cloud many a time, sir."

With a yank, he'd brought her against his chest. "You're a virgin if I've ever seen one."

"No, sir!" she'd protested, tears stinging her eyes.

"What are you doing this for?"

She'd been so surprised at his demanding tone that she'd started crying, then the whole story had tumbled out. She'd lost her father in Ireland, and her mum had been left behind, trying to work land that could no longer grow potatoes, much less anything else.

Nathaniel had comforted her, and she'd cried harder, then his lips had settled on hers, nibbling at the beauty mark beside her mouth, and within the hour, they'd made love. Ever since, she'd been his mistress, and his alone. He'd arranged for her to keep accountancy books for Angelo Donato, at Angel's Cloud, earning far more than she had making shirts, and for her to live on the upper floor of a building behind the bawdy house, removed from the rowdy clientele. She'd benefitted from being Nathaniel's lover in other ways, too. He'd given her jewels, and most important, brought over her mum who'd died due to natural causes on American soil. He'd given her a son, too. Twenty-three years ago her reputation may have been lost, but she'd fallen in love.

"Can you stay tonight, darling?" she whispered.

When he didn't respond immediately, Gem imagined trouble was brewing on the home front. Long before she'd met him, he'd been carousing in Five Points, searching for the love his wife withheld. He was an honorable man, though, and did as Isme wished by maintaining separate bedrooms and attending public functions together. Isme had borne him one son, just like Gem, a boy the same age as Mark, named Dirk. The young man was reputed to be wild, even dangerous, and Gem suspected it was due to the loveless bond that had created him.

Suddenly feeling furious with herself, she shook her head in self-admonishment. "Never mind. I've no claim on you. I shouldn't ask—"

He tilted back her head, to look into her eyes. "We have a son…"

She craved more of him, though. He rarely shared a bed with Isme, but they did share a home. A real home. He could come and go in sunlight, not under a cloak of darkness. Why can't you let this be enough? she thought. Nathaniel escaped to her bed at every opportunity. He loved her. He adored their son. But she wanted times to be different! Codes of morality to change…wanted their passion to have full rein.

Something broken came into his voice. "How could you believe I'd leave you on our son's wedding night? Damn it, Gem. You're the one I love."

"Kiss me," she whispered, the depth of their passion drawing them together. Like the current of a river, it ran between them—reliable and unstoppable, so when his lips found hers once more, an arrow seemed to pierce her heart. He would leave in only a few hours! His tongue thrust deeper. She met the thrust, pushing back. The carriage was flying, bouncing on cobbles, throwing her into his arms. His hands raced down her sides, flesh seeking flesh. He moaned when his fingers stroked the smooth skin of her thighs. Grasping a garter, he opened it. As he pulled down the stocking, she gasped.

"Let's recreate the night we made our son," he murmured.

He was rocking her against his hips now, making her feverish. She shuddered from the heat in the wandering caresses of his hands. When he squeezed her thighs, she thought passion had seized him, but no…he was alarmed! Abruptly, he broke the kiss, and she craned to stare through the carriage window, but she saw only the black winter's night.

"What was that?" she whispered, hearing a rattle as she fumbled with her clothes, in case they needed to get out of the carriage.

"The wheel," Nathaniel returned hoarsely.

The carriage was wobbing, but the horses continued to run. If the carriage overturned, she hoped no reporters would find them…a town father with a woman associated with Angel's Cloud. Nathaniel drew back the curtain and leaned his head through the window to shout. "Something's wrong with—"

Before he could finish, the wheel spun away. The rear of the carriage dropped and the driver screamed. Gem thought he'd been thrown. The horses reared, rising on their hind legs, then hooves came down hard, clattering on cobbles as the animals galloped, dragging the carriage. Gem's head slammed into the seat. She could hear metal dragging on stone, then through the window, she saw sparks from the friction.

"Oh, God," Nathaniel muttered hoarsely. He was trying to grasp her waist, but his hands couldn't find purchase. Neither could hers. They were being tossed like weeds in wind. Pounding hooves raced on, and as the sound diminished, she realized the horses had broken free. The carriage was flying on its own momentum, careening toward the river.

Nathaniel reached past her for the door handle. "Somebody's tampered with the carriage. Jump!"

Had their carriage been sabotaged? If so, who had done it? And why? His words were in her ears as she realized the carriage was rushing down the riverbank. She tried to jump, as he'd commanded, but her dress caught, holding her back. Just as they plunged, she heard the fabric ripping, and as her dress gave away, Nathaniel pulled her through the open door, into the dark currents.

He was her hero. Her only love. He was trying to save

her, but the water was too cold, and she was sure they were going to die. *Not on our son's wedding day,* her mind shrieked in protest as her fingers laced with Nathaniel's. *Stay with me, my love,* she thought, but then she felt his fingers slip away.

1

"CAN YOU BELIEVE somebody called and complained about me and Sheila Carella?" Dario Donato asked as he strode through Police Plaza toward the courthouse, his long, jeans'-clad legs eating up the pavement. Realizing he was a half hour late for court, he uttered a soft curse. It was the wrong day to have to help his landlord dad straighten out legal matters about a rental property. Clapping a hand on his chest, over his heart, as if wounded, he said, "I mean, who would do something like this to me, Pat?"

"A taxpayer?" his partner suggested as he ran a hand over his buzz-cut red hair. "Or maybe you just pissed off the Fates. Anyway, the chief wants you to lay low until the complaint blows over. Pick up a couple cold cases."

"Budweiser or Rolling Rock?"

"You know those aren't the kind of cold cases he means."

No, Dario was supposed to rot behind a desk while an arsonist got away, and all because he hadn't kept his pants zipped. "You know we're going to wind up arresting a land developer on the arson case," he mused. Ever since plans had been underway to develop Manhattan's riverfront, properties near the water had started going up in smoke, then the land was sold for a relative pittance. Relative for Manhattan, anyway.

"I'm thinking Ralph Stone or Chuckie Haswell," said Pat.

They were the biggest players. Trump was too smart to get his hands dirty with arson. Dario nodded. "Seriously, are we on for a cold case later? Now I'm talking brewskies again."

"Tomorrow's good, but tonight I've got a date with Karen."

"Ah. The girl next door."

"Not every woman can live up to Sheila Carella."

"She does set a high bar."

Dario had met Sheila a month ago, when he'd busted her for unpaid parking tickets. She had big hair, bigger breasts, and always wore fishnet stockings with miniskirts and spike heels. She was kinky as hell, too, and liked to play all kinds of sex games, which meant things had been going extremely well. At least until Dario had taken her home to meet his folks. Not that he'd expected Sheila to blend seamlessly, but his mother, Bianca, had kept crossing herself and whispering, "When's my only boy going to grow up and meet a nice girl he can marry?" It didn't help that Dario knew she lit candles each morning at mass, in front of whatever saint presided over philandering sons. On the night of Sheila's visit, Dario's sister, Eliana, had kept rolling her eyes and mouthing, "It's her brains you like, right?" Fortunately, Sheila's main concern had been her lipstick, so she hadn't noticed. Or else Dario's dad's meatballs and red sauce had distracted her. Beppe Donato was one of the best cooks in Little Italy.

"I like Sheila," Dario defended as he and Pat started up the courthouse steps. When they reached the top, they flashed their badges at a security guard.

"The only kind of man who wouldn't like Sheila," said Pat as they headed inside, "is in the morgue."

"True," Dario agreed, now walking down a hallway. "But

I don't like Sheila enough to have to lay low for a couple weeks. Another ten buildings could burn. I just don't get it. Who could have complained about me dating somebody I arrested? Who cares?"

"Maybe Sheila called the boss. Did you two have a fight?"

"You have a devious mind."

"Of course. I'm a cop."

Dario thought back to his and Sheila's last date, when they'd skipped dinner and headed straight to bed, then he shook his head. "Last time I saw her, I put a smile on her face. She could have done a toothpaste commercial. She claimed multiples."

"Personalities?" Pat joked.

Dario shook his head. "Orgasms."

"Then I'm out of suspects. But don't worry. I've got the arson case covered, and I'll call if anything happens. Meantime, do what the boss ordered, and rustle up some cold-case files to keep yourself company."

"Will do." Dario splayed a hand on the courtroom door and prepared to push. "See you around, partner. And watch out for Karen. The glint in that girl's eyes says she's got diamonds and wedding cake on the brain."

There was a long pause. Then Pat said, "Uh…I have something to tell you. I proposed last week."

Dario's jaw slackened. "To Karen?"

"Yeah."

"Congratulations," Dario managed, but he felt hurt. Pat had been his partner for two years. They'd double-dated, played ball. "Why didn't you tell me?"

"I was going to…"

But he didn't think Dario would understand. Not Dario, who was still chasing women like Sheila Carella. "That's okay, partner," he said quickly. "I forgive you."

"Good. Because you're going to be my best man."

Even so, Dario was still reeling from the news as he entered the courtroom. Everyone was getting married. Even his sister, Eliana. She'd fallen for the nephew of a man reputed to have mob connections, but who was legitimate, according to Dario's sources at the precinct. Not that the information had calmed their mother's fraying nerves. For months, his parents' Mulberry Street apartment had been "wedding central," and in three weeks, Dario and Eliana's other six siblings—all sisters—would arrive from around the country for the wedding.

Now, Eliana's diamond engagement ring flashed as she waved from the front of the courtroom. With bright red lipsticked lips she mouthed, "Where have you been? Ma's freaking out!" Before Dario could respond, his sister turned to face the judge again, her black hair swirling around her shoulders like a cape.

Great. They'd drawn Judge Zhang, one of the most ponderous deliberators in the history of New York courts, which meant this informal hearing might drag on. Judge Zhang was so small that his robes seemed to swallow him, and his hair and eyes were as shiny and black as the cloth itself.

As his family scooted to make room for him, Dario noticed Brice Jurgenson on the other side of the courtroom, flanked by Beppe's furious tenants. Skinny and bespeckled, Brice had only a few wisps of white blond hair left. An attorney, as well as a tenant, he'd convinced the others to put their rent into escrow until Beppe finished repairs to the building.

Luther Matthews, a museum curator, was present, as Dario had anticipated, and he was delivering a speech about preserving the property for historical reasons. But why was Chuckie Haswell here? Because he was a prime suspect in Dario's arson case, Dario did a double take. Chuckie was short, with sandy hair and assessing brown eyes, and his suit probably retailed for Dario's annual salary. Was the realty mogul present because Beppe's property was on the waterfront? Did he know Beppe was desperate to sell, and that Luther Matthews was determined to declare the property a historical landmark, which would sour their chances of selling?

"Mr. Matthews," Judge Zhang said. "Would you mind starting from the top? We've had a disruption."

"Sorry," Dario murmured.

"No problem," returned Judge Zhang. You've come before my court many times, so I know you're a busy man, Officer Donato."

"Busy giving Sheila Carella parking tickets," Eliana muttered.

"At least I'm not marrying the mob," Dario shot back, before turning his attention to Luther.

"I'm from the Centuries of Sex Museum," Luther began again, using a forefinger to push horn-rimmed glasses upward on his nose. "As we all know, the geographical area in question, not just Mr. Donato's building, is of significance."

"Go on," urged Judge Zhang.

"The intersection where Orange, Cross and Anthony Streets once met, and where Mr. Donato's building stands today, used to be called Five Points. It was synonymous with vice. Tap dancing originated there, as well as our city's most notorious gangs. Famous travelers such as Abraham Lincoln were given tours of the neighborhood's crowning jewel, Mr. Donato's property, which was a brothel called Angel's Cloud."

"After Angelo Donato," Beppe put in, losing his patience. "My ancestor. We all know this. It's why I own the property. And since it's mine, I don't see why other people are allowed to turn it into a historical landmark so I can't sell it."

Dario's mother, Bianca, crossed herself. She felt the family's long-time connection to a house of sin was tantamount to a curse. "If you don't sell, Beppe," Dario had heard her vow many times, "your only son is never going to settle down with a nice girl. Due to this legacy, he'll be a womanizer his whole life, just like Angelo." To whatever extent this was true, Dario hadn't minded.

Luther continued, "When Angel's Cloud was first built, nearly every house radiating from Five Points was a brothel. So-called panel games were invented at establishments such as Angel's Cloud, where women would remove panels in the walls and rob male clients while other women kept the men…" Luther smiled "…shall we say, *occupied.*

"These were powerful men, too. Lawyers, doctors and town fathers. Many wives, under the guise of temperance societies, tried to shut the places down. Because of morals, yes." Luther flashed another smile. "But also because their husbands were having such a good time." Stepping forward, Luther lifted some folders and began handing them out. "I've put together a package of pictures, to illustrate why Mr. Donato's property must be declared a landmark."

"Ridiculous," insisted Beppe.

"As curator of the Centuries of Sex Museum," Luther continued, "I've learned a great deal about life at Angel's Cloud. Of particular interest is the possible murder of a woman named Gem O'Shea. Recently, her ancestors have been in contact with me, but before I say more about that, I'd like to acquaint everyone with the O'Shea family tree…" After pausing to catch his breath, he rattled off names, then listed Angelo Donato's relatives, including Dario's great-grandfather, Enrico, and his grandfather, Salvador.

"My predecessor acquired many items from Angel's Cloud through the Donato family," Luther continued. "For years, the museum has owned all the original furniture, as well as portraits of the women who worked for Angelo. Replica rooms are roped off in our museum, preserving rooms exactly as they once were. I think this proves that our relationship with the Donato family has been excellent, but now that Mr. Donato has voiced intentions to sell, we have to try to save the building itself.

"While an old bawdy house may not seem a national treasure, Judge Zhang," he concluded, "Angel's Cloud is one of the only original Five Points buildings still standing today."

"I have to sell," Beppe muttered, twirling the end of his inky black mustache anxiously. "The taxes are through the roof! Besides, I've been renting to tenants for years!"

"But now the area's been rezoned, and if the property winds up in the hands of a developer—" Luther stared pointedly at Chuckie Haswell "—a high-rise will appear in its place."

"This is what the Donato family gets for being patrons of the arts," fumed Beppe.

"Patrons of the arts?" whispered Eliana. "By contributing to a sex museum?"

"Shush," commanded Bianca.

"Of course Mr. Donato wants to sell!" Brice Jurgenson burst out, rising to his feet and shaking his fist. "On behalf of the few remaining tenants, I'm here to say the place is unlivable! Overrun with mice! Every Donato slumlord has renovated it, breaking it into ever smaller rental units, and now it's full of architectural oddities and tenants can't—"

"I'm no slumlord!" said Beppe in shock. Noticing how his father's liver-spotted hands were starting to shake, Dario felt a surge of protectiveness. His folks had wanted a son desperately, so they hadn't quit having kids until Dario came along; he'd been a late baby, behind seven sisters. Now his dad was too old to keep up with a rental property full of disgruntled tenants.

"There are strange sounds in the hallways late at night," Brice pressed on. "Very strange sounds. Loud music. Footsteps. Some tenants believe the place is haunted, and—"

"It may well be!" added Luther. "That's exactly my point. We must preserve this piece of history."

"This isn't about history!" protested Beppe. "Just mice. And that's why my son, *Officer Donato*," he emphasized, "has agreed to move in, starting tonight. He says he's going to take care of everything."

Inwardly, Dario groaned. "What?"

"I already told them," assured Beppe under his breath. "Before you came. You're a police officer, so you can fix anything."

He was hardly a miracle worker. "I'm on an arson case."

"Nope," countered Eliana. "I tried to call you earlier, and wound up talking to Pat. He said you got bumped down to desk duty because you were dating criminals, and I told Pop."

Chalk one up to sibling rivalry, but Sheila Carella wasn't exactly a felon. "She forgot to pay her parking tickets," Dario reminded in a hushed tone.

"A hundred of them?" returned Eliana.

Then Luther captured their attention. He was speaking again. "Gem O'Shea may have been the madam of Angel's Cloud, but no one's sure. We do know that her death in a carriage accident was rumored to have been a murder. She was believed to have a son, but he vanished, the father unknown. We have found a record of *his* son, however. He married a maidservant named Bridget in 1910. She had a daughter, Emma, who had Fiona, who had Erin, who—"

"Should be none of my business," Beppe finished.

"Not so," countered Luther. Erin is the mother of Cassidy Case." Approaching the bench, he showed a letter to Judge Zhang. "Cassidy forwarded a copy of this letter to the museum. As you can see, it indicates that a will existed, giving Cassidy's ancestor, Gem, all rights to the property in question."

Beppe gasped. "Who wrote the letter?"

"Clearly, the owner of the property," said Luther. "But it's signed only, 'your beloved.'"

"The property has been in the Donato family for over a century," countered Beppe.

"Cassidy will be in town next week, with part of the actual will, as well," Luther went on. "Legally, Mr. Donato may have only squatter's rights to this property, Judge Zhang."

"You say…" Judge Zhang stared down at his notes "…Mr. Case is going to be here next week, with the documents?"

"On Tuesday," Luther confirmed.

"We'll reconvene then," said Judge Zhang. "Ten o'clock."

"There's just one problem," said Chuckie Haswell, speaking for the first time. "Because my firm, Haswell Realty, had hoped to make Mr. Donato an offer on this property, we've been doing our own research." Heading to the bench, he put a folder in front of Judge Zhang. "As these documents prove, the property was owned by my ancestor, Nathaniel Haswell. Even if Angelo Donato had wished to will the property to Gem O'Shea, it wasn't his to give. He was a front man for Nathaniel Haswell. To protect his reputation, my ancestor only used Angelo Donato to conceal the true ownership of Angel's Cloud—"

"Used Angelo?" Beppe shook his head. "The first guy wants to declare my building a landmark, so I can't sell it, and now this one's saying I don't even own it." Hearing his father's disbelief, Dario winced. Beppe had hoped to use proceeds from a sale to pay for Eliana's elaborate wedding.

"As you'll see," continued Chuckie, "Nathaniel Haswell willed the property to his son, Dirk, and his wife, Isme. The original records, of which you now have copies, are still on file at the courthouse."

Judge Zhang said, "This is all the more reason to reconvene next week. Then we can take a look at whatever documentation Cassidy Case is bringing to town."

"Next week!" exploded Brice. "On behalf of the tenants, I have to protest! We've already had a cold snap, and the boiler didn't come on. And like I said, there's something fishy happening. We hear music late at night. Sounds of dancing. I'm a reasonable man, Judge Zhang, and I don't believe in ghosts, but—"

"Apparently, Officer Donato has promised to oversee the property during this upcoming week, as a favor to his father," Judge Zhang said. "That means you'll have on-site police protection until the matter is resolved." The judge's dark eyes landed on Dario. "Am I right?"

Dario bit back a sigh of annoyance. He hadn't anticipated the dovetailing cases to entail him moving into an old brothel. "Absolutely, sir."

"Then I'll see you next week. Mr. Matthews, you may inform Mr. Case."

A second later, Bianca said a quick goodbye and forced Beppe toward the door, clearly fearing he'd unleash his temper on Chuckie, Brice or Luther, and Dario took the opportunity to open the folder Luther had given him, feeling glad he wasn't going to have to hunt for a cold case to work on. He'd never heard of Gem O'Shea, much less her possibly unsolved murder, but now it looked as if he could both help his dad and appease his boss by delving into the matter.

He surveyed a picture of the bawdy house, then a photocopied daguerreotype of his own ancestor, Angelo. His hair was wild, and his piercing dark eyes held a devilish glint. Often, Dario had been told he was the spitting image of the man. When he moved on to the next picture, his heart missed a beat. Gem O'Shea, he thought, feeling a tug at his groin. God, she was hot. Untamed waves fell over her shoulders, and the ends of the curls looked like flaming tongues. They licked an ample chest that spilled from a laced-up dress that was sexy as hell. Lots of cleavage.

The picture was black-and-white, of course, but Dario would bet her hair was flame-red. Her eyes would be blue or green. But which?

Eliana chuckled. "And they say normal men only think about sex sixty times a day."

Dario blinked. "Huh?"

"What's this for you? Six hundred?" When he didn't immediately respond, she chuckled. "Since you're going to be staying in Dad's building, maybe you'll get lucky. Maybe Brice will introduce you to that woman's ghost. But be careful, little brother."

"Because?"

"Sheila Carella might get jealous."

"Who?" he teased, still staring at Gem O'Shea's picture. "I don't remember any woman named Sheila."

"You're incorrigible," his sister muttered, rising on her toes to peck-kiss his cheek. "But be forewarned. When guys like you fall, they fall hard."

Dario held up Gem's picture. "Let's just hope when I fall, that it's right on top of a woman who looks like this."

Eliana hooked her arm through his. "You really are impossible."

"But you love me," he guessed.

"In exactly the way all women love guys like you," she assured.

"How's that?"

"Completely against my will."

2

"GEM, YOU'RE A HOTTIE," Dario said late that night as he tossed back a shot of whiskey, drinking from the bottle. He'd showered in a cramped stall down an unlit hallway, deciding against using a tub in the empty apartments upstairs, then he'd put on briefs, gotten into bed and opened the file, mostly so he could look at Gem's picture again.

Her finger was crooked and her mouth was pulled into a sexy pout. She would have looked frivolous, but her eyes held too much awareness. Pain, maybe. Something that hinted at emotional depth. According to his information, she'd survived a famine and fled her country. She'd crossed the Atlantic, only to find herself in one of the world's worst slums, but she'd made a decent life, anyway.

Dario felt a magnetic pull, a sense of impending fate. Plain old lust, too. Or else maybe he'd just had too much to drink. Whatever the case, he was fantasizing about playing out the age-old cliché about hookers and cops. It had been a long night, and he was desperate for release. Pat had called about another arson case, and although Dario was supposed to be laying low, he'd visited the scene. Then, because Beppe's tenants had waylaid him to air their grievances as he was leaving court, Dario had wound up hauling in surveillance equipment to appease them.

Now cameras were arranged strategically around the

premises. At least, by the end of the week, Dario would be able to prove his pop's building wasn't haunted. When he glanced at the tripod-mounted camera placed discretely in a corner, his lips stretched into a slow grin.

With this camera, he was going to catch a woman, not a ghost. As soon as he'd called and told Sheila about the history of Angel's Cloud, apologizing since he'd be busy and unable to meet her this week, she'd said she'd never had sex in a haunted house and wanted in on the action.

"It's different," Dario had assured playfully. "And not something I can just tell you about. You'll have to come over and experience it yourself."

"See you at eight," she'd said.

But eight had come and gone. Typical Sheila. Punctuality wasn't her strong point. It was nearly midnight, and anticipation had left Dario as horny as the men who used to patronize the room where he was about to sleep.

To keep his mind occupied, he'd interviewed tenants. There was a middle-aged woman who ran an Italian ice stand, Carmella Liotella, and Chinese sisters, Zu and Ling, who shared an apartment on the otherwise vacant third floor. Brice, whose law office was around the corner, lived in the attic. Rosie, a liberal-looking single mom, was on the first floor, just beneath Carmella and opposite the apartment where Dario had set up camp. She had a crush on Brice, and an alarmingly flirtatious thirteen-year-old, Theresa, who'd been wearing skintight jeans, a midriff exposing a fake tattoo, and enough makeup that she could have been applying for a job as a madam herself.

Dario had moved in opposite them because everybody said that's where the noise was coming from. The previous tenant had left in a hurry—supposedly due to the haunting—which meant the apartment had ramshackle furnishings. Shirts were still in the closet. The tenant had been a big guy, almost Dario's size, so it was hard to believe he'd been scared off.

There were nine empty units, three per floor, discounting the attic where Brice lived—and that seemed weird, too, since Beppe was a soft touch and the rent was low. Ghost sightings increased whenever he made moves to sell, but Dario had always figured people would lodge complaints, no matter how absurd, to discourage the building's ownership from changing hands.

Still, people had left despite having rent-stabilized leases, when they'd have difficulty finding similar bargains, and the place was creepier than Dario remembered. While in the basement, putting out environmentally friendly mouse traps Eliana insisted he buy, he could have sworn the air temperature dropped abruptly. Shrugging off the event, he'd spent an hour trying to fix the boiler before realizing he'd have to buy a new one. The whole time, he'd felt as if somebody were watching him. Most disturbing, the tenants seemed genuinely scared.

"The sounds started about two weeks ago," Zu had reported. "We hadn't heard anything in a long time, about six months, but then all of a sudden…"

"Gem O'Shea is walking the halls at night again," Ling had added in a hushed tone. "Luther Matthews came by. He has a key to the place, you know. And he told us about Gem O'Shea. That she was murdered. I'm sure she's haunting us."

"Maybe trying to tell us who killed her," said Rosie.

"The music's, like, really loud," added Theresa.

"Here," Brice had added angrily, coming from the attic, and dumping a box of papers at Dario's feet. "This is everything I was able to find out about the place. Something fishy's going on. You should take a look."

And Dario had. Apparently, these old walls had absorbed plenty of lovers' whispered secrets, and many illicit back-room deals. The old news clippings collected by Brice jibed with records Dario had found in cold-case files at the precinct, as well as family materials related to the property that Beppe had kept, and that Dario had brought with him. A sheet in the police file indicated Gem had stashed jewelry in the house; an inventory list had been submitted in case of theft.

Definitely, the tenants hadn't lied about the shoddy workmanship. It was Dario's grandfather's fault, since he'd hired bad contractors. The original bar, which had been about fifteen feet long, was still in Zu and Ling's apartment. Someone had renovated it as a kitchen island. Brice's shower stall was in his kitchen, and because his wiring was inadequate, he'd run an extension cord to an outlet in the hallway.

Outside, Dario had stood on the sidewalk, surveying the exterior, and something had niggled, but he didn't know why. The building was tall and skinny, with a sharply graded roof and louvered windows. The bricks crawled with ivy, and a downstairs back door led into unkept gardens. The rear building, where Gem had lived, had been torn down long ago.

His cell rang. He clicked on. "Yeah?"

"Sorry I'm late."

Sheila sounded tipsy, a good sign. "Are you coming now?"

"There's more than one way to take that."

"Not once you get here."

"On my way," she said, giggling. "Keep the bed warm."

"I'm getting sleepy," he returned with mock grouchiness. "Are you sure you're going to show?"

"Put a key under the mat, sailor, and let Gem O'Shea wake you up."

Not a bad idea. "Done. Two pots on the porch are planted

with ivy. The key to the lobby doors will be in the one on the right. I'm the first door on the left—I'll leave it ajar." Maybe that wasn't the brightest thing to do, but the neighborhood was relatively safe nowadays, and besides, he'd put his gun under the bed.

"Given what I'm going to do to you," she was saying, "you'll think you're dreaming."

"So you have plans for the bawdy house?"

"Just call me Gem O'Shea."

She ended the call, and he grinned. "My kind of girl."

Yawning, he thrust his legs into jeans, took the key to the planter and returned. Then he found a pen, scrawled "I'm in here, babe," and taped it to the door, drawing an arrow toward the bed. The tenants were tucked in for the night and wouldn't see it. Absently scratching his chest, he stared into the open folder before transferring it to the floor, suddenly glad Eliana had reminded him to bring sheets, a blanket and towels. Without a boiler, the steam heat hadn't come on.

Where the hell was Sheila? He could sure use some body heat. After taking another swig of whiskey, he set the bottle on the nightstand, along with his wallet and badge. Checking to make sure his gun was under the bed, he switched on the video recorder.

Sheila was going to love his surprise. Pat would get a kick out of the story, too. Suddenly frowning, he thought about Pat's engagement, then pushed aside the thought. Everybody he knew might be settling down, but Dario wasn't going to let it get in the way of his own lifestyle.

Rummaging in his jeans pockets, he put some open condom packages and a twenty-dollar bill on the nightstand. Since Sheila was intent on playing Gem O'Shea, he'd pay her. As soon as she got here, he'd turn on the light, then they could make the homemade movie while polishing off the rest of the whiskey.

He smiled. He was glad he'd met Sheila. All she cared about was sex. She was like a female version of him. His other half. Taking off his briefs, he tossed them to the floor. Might as well be ready when she gets here, he thought.

A second later, he was out like the light.

"WAKE UP, SAILOR."

Husky murmurings sounded beside Dario's ear. Hot breath tickled his earlobe. His head was pounding, and he groaned when he realized he must have had way too much to drink last night. The warm whiskey had tasted great going down, burning a path from his mouth to his belly, just as surely as a kiss, but now…

Fingernails raked upward on his bare chest, then stopped to trace circles around his nipples. He groaned again, arousal catching him unaware. Music was playing, sounding faraway. Probably coming from one of the other apartments, he thought, but who was up so late? Zu and Ling said they went to bed early. Brice and Carmella had to work. And Rosie had a kid. Maybe he'd just drifted, and it was still only a little after midnight.

Weight was bearing down on him. Sheila, he guessed. He'd tossed and turned, so the sheet had tangled around his legs, and now, even if she hadn't been on top of him, he couldn't have moved. Opening his eyes a fraction, he saw only vague shadows, enough to know he wasn't dreaming. A woman was definitely straddling him.

"Finally," he whispered. Shutting his eyes again, he lifted his hands, curving them over hips. Nice, plump womanly hips. Not too skinny—he hated women who starved themselves—but not too padded, either. Just right. It was one of the many things he liked about Sheila. After uttering a lusty sigh, he smiled. Her muscles flexed beneath his fingertips as she rocked against him, her inner thighs squeezing.

She was so responsive. That was another thing he liked. Now, if she'd only move upward a tiny inch. She was a hair's breadth from where he was aching for her. So close.

Please. He thought the word as soft hands curled around his shoulders, then dug deep—now exploring dips and crevices around his collarbone. After a moment, flattened palms pressed down hard on his pectorals, feeling like heaven.

"What time is it?" he whispered, his voice barely audible over all the racket. It was hard to believe somebody thought whatever was playing was music. He slitted his eyes open, but again, saw only inky darkness. The music sounded like show tunes, maybe something from Broadway.

"Three," she whispered.

"In the morning?"

"Yeah."

No wonder he felt like hell. "Better late than never."

"Do we still have time?"

He didn't have to be at work until nine. "We can get a lot done in six hours."

"Sorry I didn't make it earlier, the way I promised."

"Me, too."

"You *feel* sorry," she whispered, the brush of her belly making clear what she meant. He was as hard as a rock. Her voice sounded deeper than usual. So husky that she didn't even sound like Sheila. She must have felt as sex-crazed as he, waiting all day for this. That's why she was talking like a sex siren from an old movie. She sounded like Bette Davis, Lana Turner and Marilyn Monroe all rolled into one. All shivery and whispery, as if she'd had way too much to drink and had just smoked cartons of cigarettes, and was offering him something forbidden. He imagined her in a black-and-white picture, wearing a slinky gown, and holding a highball glass and a long black cigarette holder.

Then he remembered she was pretending to be Gem O'Shea. That's why she'd worn a wig, too. Long strands of hair were brushing his face, teasing his cheeks and shoulders.

He rubbed her thighs, stroking them with the backs of his hands and shifted his weight, straining unsuccessfully to feel the crushing pressure of her pelvic bone against his erection. When she just missed the magic spot, he uttered a frustrated sigh. She was still in outerwear, a jacket and tight leggings, no shoes. "That's the great thing about clothes…"

"What?"

"We can get rid of them."

"That's why I came over."

Cold insteps with high arches were molding his calves, warming themselves. Threading fingers into her hair, he explored the wig and chuckled. Sheila really was great. She'd do anything to please a guy. What an imagination. "Are you ready to make up for lost time?"

"If you can forgive me for being late."

"Kiss me and I'll think about it." Splaying his fingers, he dragged them through her hair, using the strands to pull her face down to his. Her mouth was open, and it melted against his as their tongues meshed, sparking electricity that began dancing wildly down his nerves, making them sizzle at the ends. Rushing between his fingers, tendrils of hair felt like palm fronds under water, softer than anything he'd ever felt, even softer than her mouth. His hands found her waist again, guiding the movements of her lower body, urging her closer, as he brushed his kiss-dampened mouth across hers.

When the friction turned maddening, he feathered, then nibbled. Judging by her soft whimper, it was working, really turning her on. She whispered, "What do I have to do to make *absolutely sure* you forgive me?"

"This." He arched his hips, his body surging.

She pushed back, her thighs quivering, the inner flesh shaking deliciously as she scooted into the cradle of his legs and settled on the hard ridge of his sex. He gasped, a shiver ripping through him. Something in the back of his throat caught, and he said, "I'm glad you made it."

She was panting softly, rolling her hips with the dexterity of a belly dancer and grinding herself against his groin. "I can tell."

As she undulated, waves of need lapped through him. Pliable, ready lips fit to his again. Wet and promising, they clung as if she didn't want to let go. His sentiments, exactly. Tonight, she didn't even taste like Sheila. Her usual mint flavor had been replaced by chocolate and coffee, and the lipstick he'd eaten off was raspberry. Not a hint of alcohol, which was what he'd expected, given how tipsy she'd sounded on the phone.

"I tried to hurry," she murmured.

"You're here now," he whispered back.

Against his, her cheek still felt cool from the night air, making the spear of her tongue seem even hotter. It was warm and runny—like hot honey or butter or molasses. It was like lazy sunshine on a Sunday morning, streaming through a window. And it was climbing, too, just like the sun, its radiance gaining intensity and heat.

Every time she licked the inner recesses of his mouth, renewed fire ignited in his abdomen. Warmth was pouring through her leggings, like jets of liquid joy, and when she started nuzzling the stubble of his beard, roughening her relatively tender skin, Dario tilted back his head, simply reveling in the feel of her—her long legs bracketing his, her ample breasts cushioning his chest.

"Don't stop."

"Does it seem like I'm stopping?"

"No," he murmured. "But you could."

"I could do a lot of things."

"Then do them."

As she swirled hot saliva down his neck, in sloppy, looping kisses, the scratchy fabric of her jacket further aroused his nipples, chaffing until they were raw and painfully aroused. Merciless, she languidly licked his skin as if they had eternity, not just a night, then she dipped until a taut nipple was firmly in her mouth. Quick suckles made his mind fog….

He was sure he'd drifted again. He didn't know for how long. He was floating in bliss. Sheila felt so good…impossibly good. Every time they got together, sex just got better. Tonight it was excellent. Better than ever before. Right now, the touch of her mouth was torture. Every fiber of his being was starting to sing for release. Slowly, he caressed her bottom, thrilled when she kept playing with his nipples…

Then, from somewhere far off, he heard another song start, and strained his ears. He heard piano music and stomping feet. Clapping hands. A hoot of merriment.

"Give me another pint of ale," someone yelled.

"A pint for the whole house," another hollered.

He must be dreaming. Or else someone was playing an old dance hall recording. He felt unbelievably hot. Sweat prickled his nape as he shook off sleep once more, and opened his eyes. Still, only darkness. What was happening? He felt almost as if he'd been drugged. "You feel so good," he whispered.

"You're not bad, yourself."

As he inhaled sharply, Sheila's scent settled in his lungs. It wasn't the musky perfume she usually wore, but something lighter that evoked coy flirtation. As the music climbed toward crescendo, she continued nibbling that one nipple, making the other yearn for the ministrations of her mouth. She was raking teeth against the sides until fever took him, and the fire raging beneath his naval turned more fluid. A coiled spring of swirling lava became more diffuse, prickling through his veins, lazily roping into all his extremities.

"Are you going to wake up for me, sailor?"

Yawning and stretching beneath her like a huge jungle cat, he lifted his hips, the muscles of his buttocks straining. Between his legs, his heavy erection felt more than bothersome, an irksome annoyance that needed to be dealt with soon. Frustration surfaced in his husky growl. "Where have you been, anyway?"

"I got tied up."

He imagined her naked, and strapped to a bed with long silk scarves. "I like the sound of that."

"You would," she teased.

"Damn right I would," he whispered.

His eyes had adjusted, but it was too dark to see her features. He imagined her high cheekbones, the long, straight patrician nose. He wanted to see her undressed, her breasts swinging free from the restrictive jacket and whatever she wore beneath. He could see them softly bouncing as she rode him. "Oh, yeah," he whispered, another swift pang claiming his groin.

He reached to turn on the lamp, but her hand glided over his, stopping him. It was just as well. He could tape them later. Maybe the camera was even picking up some of the action, anyway. After all, he could see shadows, and it was motion activated.

He grasped a lock of hair and chuckled. Had she really

rustled up this wig just for him? This was almost as good as the time she'd let him arrest her in the shower. Or when she'd handcuffed him to bed. Or when she'd come over, wearing nothing under a raincoat.

"It feels so real."

"Of course it's real."

He rubbed the strands between his fingers, his loins still firing. As he brought silky waves to his face, another series of jolts pulsed into his bloodstream. He breathed in, finding the scent was more like shampoo than the neutral scent he'd expected from a wig.

"You're good," he murmured in admiration. She must have brought a boom box, too. That's why the bawdy-house music was playing. It wasn't coming from another apartment, after all. It was all part of Sheila's act. Slowly untying the belt of her jacket, he flicked open buttons, then pushed the garment off her shoulders and down her arms, exposing what felt like a tight cotton blouse. "I almost believe you're Gem O'Shea."

"You had doubts?"

"In my line of work, we're not known for our trusting natures."

"Can you trust me to give you the ride of your life, sailor?"

"I think I can manage that."

She started unbuttoning her blouse. In the darkness, he sensed, rather than saw, the edges open.

"You didn't take the money from the table," he murmured, his voice low.

"Paying me, are you?"

"Oh, yeah."

Clasping his hands, she brought them to her chest and placed them on her breasts. Slowly, he traced the lace edges of the bra cups she swelled to fill. She was spilling out, and thrusting her chest, too, as if begging for his touch. Her quickening breath urged him on, making him want to touch between her legs to make her climax.

As he opened her bra's front clasp, his own chest constricted. Light-headed, he swallowed against the sudden dryness of his mouth and pushed aside the cups. After licking his own fingers, he trailed slippery swirls of saliva on the distended tips of her breasts. Capturing one with his mouth, he squirted wet heat until she muttered something senseless. Her hips suddenly wrenched. As he sponged her, he lifted his hips, rubbing her until she was bucking. Her hands flattened on his chest, as if to slow him down, and her long delicate fingers curled, tugging wildly at strands of his chest hair. He leaned back on the pillow.

Her voice was husky. "How much are you paying me?"

"Not nearly what you're worth."

"Is this your first time on Angel's Cloud?"

"Yeah."

"And did you request me? Or was this just luck of the draw?"

"Absolutely intentional."

"You heard good things about me?"

"I heard you're the best."

"Hearsay's of little matter. Am I the best?"

He was about to explode and he wasn't even inside her yet. "You're convincing me of it right now."

"I didn't expect to find you like this."

"Like what?"

"Naked. In bed. And…so hard." She shivered as if to emphasize her point.

"Is that a crime?"

"Do you want me to arrest you?"

"You can keep me locked up for a long time."

The music seemed to surge then, and he gasped in protest as the heat of her lower body left his, at least until he realized she was only stripping off leggings. As soon as her legs were bare, his hungry hands sought flesh. Disappointment filled him when he found her panties still on. By the feel of it, it was a tiny silk thong with a string waistband. She straddled him again, her knees on the mattress. Just her scent was enough to make him beg for mercy.

Overcome, he grasped her back, hugging her, then nuzzled her face. The music seemed to be coming right through the walls as his tongue stroked the scanty fabric. When she flung back her head to take the pleasure, long hair whipped behind her, and when her back arched for the intimate kiss, his rigid tongue dove for her clitoris, soaking it. Using a hand to steady her, he pressed his mouth to her, making her writhe.

Not even air passed between them as his tongue did its magic, vibrating. Under damp panties, her cleft opened all the way, and both her hands raked into his hair, digging into his scalp. She moaned, then shuddering cries came in a steady stream. She was wet, his kiss was wetter, and in a second, her panties were drenched, but he didn't think she'd come yet. She was holding back.

"Come." He murmured the word against the silk. "Now."

But she only cradled his head tighter. No wonder it had taken her so long to get here, he thought vaguely. Where had she found dance hall music on such short notice? And whatever equipment she'd brought, so she could play it? She'd done all this for him—the wig, the music, the late-night rendezvous. And now he was going to make the effort worth it for her.

Curling his fingers over the string waistband, he fisted

his hand, yanking her nearer. Then he ripped the waistband. He was still tearing the panties when his mouth fell to her flesh, covering her completely. She was creaming, hot and slick, and she gasped.

Thighs braced his sides, shaking uncontrollably, her knees threatening to buckle as he tongued her, but she was still holding back. This really wasn't at all like Sheila. What had gotten into her tonight?

"What do you want?" he whispered hoarsely. "What's going to make you come?"

"You…inside…" Her utterance was broken. "I want…I want…"

He couldn't wait for her to spell out the rest. He was too swollen. Painfully thick, his erection was pulsing, and just a hair-trigger touch would make him explode. Blindly reaching, he grabbed a condom and roughly kicked away the sheet. A moment later, he grunted softly, voicing the agony only she could relieve. Quickly wrapping his arms around her, he urged her to lie beside him. She was naked and quivering, burning up.

"What?" he whispered raggedly, dragging kisses across her cheeks, willing to give her anything.

"Fuck me," she whispered softly, the words barely audible.

It was the sexiest thing he'd ever heard. At first, he wasn't even sure he'd heard right, but now his heart hammered with increased desire. The words hadn't sounded dirty at all, not like a curse, just needy. Even sweet. He'd never heard so much frustrated desire in a woman's voice. Hell, the more he knew Sheila, the more he discovered vulnerability he'd never have guessed was there, and it was starting to get to him. She was like a difficult case that never seemed to add up. This really didn't seem like the same Sheila he'd had sex with before, and it was intriguing him.

Maybe he was falling in love with her after all.

Mutterings emanated from nowhere as she molded to his body. He whispered sweet nothings in return, then peppered kisses into the wig. Urging her onto her back, he kneeled, turning her so he could gain the deepest possible access. Silken thighs parted, and his heart stuttered. Burning and throbbing, he teased her, parting the cleft with his erection. Catching drops of her natural lubrication, he stroked, wishing his own sex wasn't sheathed.

When he could take no more, he placed his hands on her thighs, parting them farther still, wishing the light was on so he could see everything. Crooking a hand under her knee, he raised a shapely leg, then everything seemed silent. It was as if the music had stopped, although it hadn't, or as if their panting breaths had calmed, although they were both breathing harder than ever.

She arched, silently begging.

He thrust hard, and she parted like a river, much tighter than he remembered. He'd never felt so big, thrusting harder and filling her. She sobbed as she stretched to take him, flinging her arms around his neck. When he was in all the way, he rocked his hips, then he rested and just felt the bliss, sighing.

Her heart was hammering against his heart. Her breath mingled with his breath. After a long moment, he withdrew and thrust again, staying skin to skin.

"Oh, yes," she whispered as something primal grabbed hold of him. Her possessive nails were dragging down his back now, and her claiming lips, teeth and tongue were suckling his neck. She was pulsing all around him, and with her first orgasm, she cried out, a wrenching twist of her body coming in tandem with a sob that shook his emotions. Her second orgasm sent a shudder through him, then palpitations. By the third, he was putty in her hands. She was cooing like a dove as he went over the edge, gasping once, his mind losing itself to darkness.

He'd never know how many seconds had elapsed. But when consciousness came again, she was still there, wrapped tightly in his arms, making sweet, soft sounds. Slowly, their breathing evened. Multiples, he thought. Now *that* was like Sheila. After a long moment, a smile tugged at his lips. "I think my hangover's gone," he whispered.

But she was fast asleep.

He laid in the dark for a long time, only now realizing that the music she'd brought had switched off. He hadn't even noticed. As a cop, he was usually very alert. On the job, he had one of the highest arrest records at his precinct, but when it came to sexy women, he always lost his head. He might be a cop, but he was a man, too.

He glanced down, unable to see her in the dark. Hair had fallen over her face, obscuring it, and since the wig wasn't bothering her, he let it lay. Maybe it was time to fess up, he thought. After all, he had taken Sheila home to meet his folks, hadn't he? And he didn't do that with every woman. Oh, maybe he and Sheila hadn't seemed to have much in common at first, but if sex was this good, surely they'd find areas of compatibility, wouldn't they?

He couldn't believe how content he felt right now. As if all was right with the world, and he'd arrived exactly where he was supposed to be. As if he was home. He didn't remember Sheila fitting quite so perfectly into the crook of his shoulder. Why hadn't he noticed before?

His smile broadened, turning whimsical. Maybe Gem O'Shea's ghost had a hand in this. Maybe Sheila wasn't the brightest, maybe she didn't get most of his jokes, and she'd never be able to keep up with him in a verbal sparring match. But that didn't really matter, did it?

Of course it didn't, he thought now. It was amazing how only an hour of sex could change a man's thinking about a woman. Earlier tonight, before he'd gone to bed, he hadn't even been thinking of Sheila as a potential mate. But now...

With her, sex was hotter every time. Tonight had been the best by far. She'd gone to so much trouble to please him. She had to be crazy about him. In the morning, he'd make a huge move and tell her he felt the same way, he decided.

And then he slept.

3

DANCE HALL MUSIC was playing again. As soon as Dario registered it, he bolted upright. "What time is it?" he asked, glancing toward the beside clock. When he saw only a whiskey bottle, he realized he was at his pop's building, not in his apartment in Battery Park. As he registered that the sunlight from a front room looked bright, the events of the previous night came rushing back in a barrage of hot images, but the bed was empty. The doorway to the outer hall, which he'd left ajar for Sheila, was wide open. "Sheila?"

As he stared toward the shut bathroom door, he heard a soft whirring sound. The camera was working, which seemed impossible at first, then he recalled that it was motion-activated. This and the other cameras he'd borrowed from the precinct were used on stakeouts, so maybe it had recorded last night's activities, after all. He hoped so. Even shadows of what happened between him and Sheila would be worth watching this morning. His sitting up in bed must have activated the camera again. He'd never have heard the soft whir over the music.

"Sheila?"

No answer.

That strange bawdy-house music was still sounding. It was loud and coming from…

"Under the bed?" That was weird. And where was his cell, so he could check the time? Squinting, he reached a hand under the bed. His gun was beside the cell. As he lifted the phone, he smiled. So that was the source of the music. Sheila had changed his ringer.

"Cute," he whispered. No doubt, she'd expected him to hear it during the day, and recall the bawdy-house music she'd played while they'd made love. Not just had sex, he thought. Last night, they'd definitely taken things to a new level. Surely, she'd want to meet after work.

He looked for the boom box she must have brought, but he didn't see it. He didn't see her jacket or leggings, and he hoped she hadn't gotten dressed. If so, he was only going to remove her clothes again. Flipping open the cell, he saw that it was only eight, which meant they had time for a quickie.

Sobering, he swallowed hard, something resembling a lump forming in his throat. Was he really going to tell her how he was starting to feel about her? Did he really feel the same way this morning? "Yeah," he whispered. "I do."

If work was calling, he'd tell Pat he'd be a few minutes late, to buy some extra time with Sheila. "Donato here."

"We need to talk."

It was Sheila.

Inwardly, he groaned. That explained why the jacket and leggings weren't on the floor. "You're home."

"That's what I want to talk to you about."

Probably, she'd wanted to change for work, and while he didn't share her impulse, he admired her for wanting to be where she was supposed to be. Under the circumstances, that showed dedication. If she hadn't run off, they'd be having more great sex.

"Thanks for letting me sleep," he said, meaning it. After what she'd done to him last night, he'd needed the rest.

Suddenly, his heart was in his throat, and his mind was racing. He was trying to frame what he most wanted to say. "I have something to tell you—"

"No," she said quickly. "I have something to tell you."

Maybe. But he needed to tell her he enjoyed last night so much that he wanted them to become even more intimate. He figured he'd better do so before he lost his nerve. "Me first. I want you to know I think you're the best—"

"Best lay?" she burst out. "And it's always you first! Have you ever noticed that, Dario?"

He almost chuckled. Last night must have affected her as much as it had him. She was nervous now, trying to push him away, and he didn't blame her. "Go ahead," he said. "Say whatever you need. Get it out of your system. And then I'll say my piece. I've been thinking about us—"

"Me, too! For the past couple of weeks, ever since we've been—"

"Making love?"

When she made a snorting sound, he frowned. "I don't know that I'd dignify what we've been doing with that phrase."

"We are explosive together," he admitted, "but I don't think that means our emotions can't be involved."

"Well, I do."

Their lovemaking must have really shaken her. Probably, she was hoping he'd voice his feelings. She needed assurances. It was what all women wanted. At least, that's what his sisters told him. "What I'm trying to say, Sheila—"

"At first it seemed fun," she raced on, as if he hadn't spoken. "Especially since Bobby and I broke up, as you know. I was so sure he'd never want to make a commitment—"

His heart had missed a beat. "Bobby?"

"O'Hare?" she queried, sounding confused. "He sits two desks over from you?"

Bobby O'Hare was a rookie. "Bobby O'Hare? From vice?"

"Yeah."

"I didn't know you dated Bobby O'Hare."

"I told you. I just don't think you were listening to me, Dario. To be blunt, you always have sex on the brain. You don't pay attention."

He was sure she'd never told him about her past relationships. "What's Bobby got to do with—"

"Everything. And that's what I've been trying to tell you. We'd been dating six months, and I was falling for him. All my girlfriends said it was too much, too fast. Maybe it was. But I knew Bobby was the one. I had such a strong feeling. Like we were meant to be, so I couldn't stop myself from chasing him. When I see something I like, I go for it."

"I noticed."

There was a long pause.

"You were saying?" he prompted.

"Well, the day you brought me in," she plunged on. "You know, for the parking tickets. Well…" She inhaled sharply, then blew out a short sigh. "The night before, I'd seen Bobby out with somebody else, and I was pissed. So, when you brought me in, I tried to be cool. I didn't even look in his direction. It must have worked, because after that, he kept calling me. But I didn't return the calls. Besides, by then, well…even when you booked me, you were coming on strong, so I guess I…"

"Go on."

"…was using you to get him out of my system. Don't get me wrong," she added quickly. "You're cute. A megahunk. Calendar quality. But you're even less the committing type than Bobby. Or so I thought."

His recent moves must have convinced her otherwise. The smile returned. Admitting his feelings was going to be so much easier than he'd anticipated, he realized. Sheila was doing all the work. "But now?"

"Bobby heard about you and me through your partner, Pat. You must have made me sound incredibly hot, because Bobby got jealous. He started sending flowers. And then he called and told me his real feelings. And you know the girl I saw him with?"

Dario could only shake his head.

"It was his sister!"

"Imagine that."

"Funny, huh?" she enthused. "One thing led to another, and, well, now I—"

Her voice cut off abruptly. On his end, morbid curiosity had taken hold. "Now?"

"Well…I know you're going to be happy for me. Bobby proposed. Can you believe it?"

As near as Dario could tell, everyone on earth had proposed lately. "You don't say."

"He gave me a ring and everything. It's beautiful, and while the date isn't set in stone, we've pretty much agreed."

"You can spare me the details."

There was a long pause. "You're not upset, are you?"

After last night? "I'm furious."

"Dario, we're friends. C'mon."

"When did this happen?"

"Yesterday."

How could she have lain in his arms last night, cooing like a love bird, when she'd known she was marrying Bobby? "When, yesterday?"

"In the afternoon."

"He gave you the ring in the afternoon?"

"Quit interrogating me. I didn't do anything wrong."

Her scent was still on his skin. She'd gotten out of his bed maybe an hour ago. Suddenly, he glimpsed something. Fishing in the covers, he held up what looked to be a sparkling blue rhinestone. "Your earring's still in the bed," he said.

"Don't worry about anything I've left behind at your place." There was another long pause. "Look, Dario, I'm really sorry. I didn't think you'd care. I mean, you have a reputation for being great in bed, but uninterested in commitment."

"We don't even know the same people. How could you know about my reputation?"

She named countless tangential connections they had through the police force. It was more than he'd imagined. Then she said, "Anyway, it doesn't matter. The main thing is that I really can't see you anymore."

"You could have thought of that last night." Dammit, her legs had been like long silk ribbons stretching around his back, wrapping tightly around his waist and stealing his breath.

"I did. That's why I didn't show."

"Didn't show?"

"I know I called. I was out with the girls, and we were doing shooters, and I thought maybe I'd come over, personally, and break the news to you then."

"Which is why you were flirting? Implying you were going to give me the best sex of my life?" Sex that, in fact, she'd delivered.

"Forgive me," she murmured contritely.

It didn't help that she'd asked for his forgiveness last night, too, while they'd been making love.

"It was the booze talking," she continued. "I admit it. I'm not perfect. But I wanted to…well, let you down easy. Not that I figured you'd care. But I thought once I came over, it would be easier to tell you about my and Bobby's—"

"But you came over and slept with me?"

There was yet another interminable pause. And then she said, "I didn't come over, Dario."

He'd had it. She'd been all over him. Licking every inch of his skin, and doing that mind-bending thing with his nipples. "Sheila, we had sex all night."

She gasped. "What?"

"I left the key in the pot, remember? And you showed up around three…"

"I don't know what you're talking about."

"What?"

"I never showed. I swear."

"Dammit, Sheila," he cursed softly, realizing she must be teasing him, the way she always did. She was good at it, too. She sounded so honest. "Quit jerking my chain." Last night her playful nature had sent his senses soaring, but this morning, he wasn't in the mood.

"I wasn't there."

"You wore a wig," he reminded, his voice turning husky. "A jacket and leggings. A little cotton blouse."

"I don't know what you're talking about."

He heard a rustle. Then a male voice. "She was here. With me."

Dario shut his eyes, unable to believe any of this was happening. It had to be Bobby O'Hare. It was as if the two men were at work. Sheila had committed a crime, and they were discussing her alibi. "Bobby?"

"Yeah."

"I don't know what's going on here," Dario began, "but—"

"Sheila and I are getting married. I proposed. She ac-

cepted. That's what's going on. She was here all night."
There was a pregnant pause. "We were awake all night, if
you catch my drift."

"I think I do," Dario managed.

Before ending the call, Bobby rambled a few lines about
how he hoped the situation wouldn't be awkward at work.

Regarding that, Dario would do his best. Still…as tal-
ented as Sheila was, she couldn't be in two places at once,
which left Dario stuck with one of the more interesting
mysteries of his career.

"Who was in bed with me last night?"

The earring wasn't much to go on. Her hands had been all
over him, and while he knew he could get a good print off his
skin, he didn't really want to explain that to the guys at the
precinct. The money on the dresser was gone, when he checked
his wallet, his money was gone, too. His gaze landed on the
camera. Maybe it, or the others, had recorded something.

He was going to use all his detecting skills to find her.
He had no idea what he'd do when he found his mystery
woman.

Time would tell.

A HALF HOUR LATER, Dario was showered, dressed and getting ready to replay the tapes. Somebody pounded on the
front door, and it swung open.

"Rosie?"

The liberal-looking single mom from across the hallway
peeked inside. "So, you heard it?"

The last thing Dario wanted to do right now was chat with
neighbors. His mind was focused on what he might see on
the tapes. "Heard what?"

Rosie's voice was hushed. "The music."

"It was loud!" Zu and Ling crowded into the doorway

behind Rosie, although Dario wasn't sure which one of them had spoken.

"I didn't sleep a wink," added Carmella.

It was as if they'd been waiting in the hallway until they heard him rustling around inside the apartment.

"And you were looking at us yesterday as if we were crazy."

This time, it was Brice.

Rosie's daughter, Theresa, edged in, squeezing between her mother and Brice. She was wearing a multilayered outfit that involved leggings, two skirts and a few jackets, making her look like a homeless waif. He guessed it was the style for teens. "It was, like, so loud," she said. "And I couldn't sleep. And now I'm going to fail my math test." She glared at Dario. "It's going to be your dad's fault if I'm held back a grade. We could sue. I just want you to acknowledge that."

"Theresa," her mother admonished.

"Well, it's true," said Theresa.

"What are you going to do about this?" demanded Brice.

"Nothing, if you don't leave me alone, so I can watch these tapes," Dario returned calmly. He was thirty, and years of working on the force had taught him how to keep his cool in tense situations. Not that he always bothered. But he didn't like being railroaded. He sent the tenants a long look.

"So, you may have found something?" Brice didn't sound angry now, only relieved.

"I hope so."

"Then we'll get out of your hair," said Rosie.

"One minute," said Dario.

They stared expectantly. He said, "The music you heard last night—"

"Didn't you hear it?" asked Brice.

He didn't want to admit he'd heard what they believed

to be some supernatural event. "I'm not sure what I heard. But I want to know if it's what you've heard in the past."

"So, you did hear it," accused Theresa.

Her mother was more pragmatic. "That's exactly how it always sounds, Officer Donato. The hoots and catcalls. The foot stomping. All of it."

"But not lately," reiterated Carmella.

"It quit for six months," agreed Zu.

"For a couple days it was loud," clarified Brice. "And then nothing."

"Thank you for your help," Dario told them.

A second later, the tenants were gone, closing the door behind them. He was still thinking about the music. If he hadn't slept with Sheila last night, then she hadn't brought a boom box. Wondering where the music had come from, he selected the tape from the machine by the bed. Shadows flitted, and while he couldn't see everything perfectly, he felt a pang at his groin.

When he checked the machine in the hallway, the test image was very clear and in color. He stared at the empty hallway. Then he did a double take. Sudden movement activated the camera. A woman passed, but too quickly. Hair, which he'd thought was a wig, turned out to be red. Encased in tights, those looked to be the same long legs that had hugged his hips like a vise.

He rewound the tape and played it again, freezing the image when she turned toward the camera. Instead of Sheila's sharply angled facial bones, this woman had roundish features, full cheeks and a soft, fleshy pout of a mouth. Instead of Sheila's long straight note, this woman's was a short ski jump sprinkled with freckles. She looked very Irish.

Everything inside of him seemed to go still, then his

heart thundered as his eyes trailed over the red hair, cautious green eyes and the beauty mark beside her mouth.

It was Gem O'Shea.

4

"LUTHER," SHE MANAGED. "Uh…*you're* Luther Matthews?" She sure as heck hoped she got it right this time.

"Cassidy, darling," he announced, waving at her with a manicured hand. "I expected you *next* Tuesday. But never mind! You're as gorgeous as I imagined. Gem O'Shea in the flesh. The same red hair and green eyes. If I don't keep you to myself, Seventh Avenue will steal you away while you're visiting and put you to work on a runway! What a pleasure!"

It was quite a speech, especially since Cassidy was still reeling from a night of sex which, until moments ago, she'd thought she was experiencing with Luther Matthews, who now seemed less seductive and more metrosexual. Not so the guy last night. Pinpricks of awareness assaulted her as images of hungry hands and kiss-bruised lips invaded her consciousness. "Uh…thanks for the compliments."

"Oh, no. Thank *you*." Luther winked, his blue eyes appraising behind horn-rimmed glasses, carrying hints of the flirtation they'd shared on the phone. And why not? She'd given him every reason to believe she'd soon be sleeping with him. Instead, she'd accidentally shared the sheets with a stranger who was still making her knees turn to water. Instinctively, she reached out a hand as if to break a fall.

"You cold?"

Still hot from last night, she thought, realizing that she'd shivered. "Fine."

"Good, because I've got a gazillion things to tell you. The Donatos waylaid me outside court yesterday and made me return my key to their property. Can you believe it? The museum's been working with that family for years and is currently putting together a diagram of the property during that particular era of history! But now we're being treated like thieves!"

She tried not to think of the money she'd taken from Dario Donato's bedside table. "That's just terrible," she managed.

"They are horrible people," Luther confided angrily. "Their son, Dario, works for the NYPD, and he's staking out the place, as if you and I might rob them. And it's your property! Well, next week you'll meet these people and see for yourself."

Given her and Dario's face-to-face, she was relieved when Luther zoomed on. "Give me a minute to finish up with a client, then I'm yours." He grinned. "And I do mean, all yours."

As much as Cassidy loathed men—the ink on her divorce decree was still wet—she'd felt an urge for sex lately. So, when Luther contacted her, like an angel out of the blue, saying he knew pertinent facts about her family history and possessed documents she should see, the new flirtation seemed like icing on a cake. He was decent looking, she saw now, the perfect person with whom to get her ya-yas out, but in a fussy black suit and horn-rimmed glasses, he wasn't her type.

Casual sex wasn't her style, either. Being a one-man woman, she hadn't noticed that Johnny Case, her ex, had been sleeping with incoming freshmen at the college where he'd taught. She'd been the last to know, and ever since, she'd wanted to assert herself, feel hot again, and remind somebody—anybody—that she could knock a man's socks off in bed, which last night had proven.

But what had she done? For a moment, items in Luther's glassed-in office seemed to slide off-kilter. Bookcases seemed to tilt, and the floor felt wobbly. She tried to tell herself last night was a dream, but her mind raced backward in time, and her erogenous zones told her it was real.

She'd thought Luther was expecting her yesterday, on Tuesday, on a flight from South Carolina. Due to a storm, she'd arrived late and gone straight to the Pierre Hotel where the Centuries of Sex Museum was to have reserved her room, but they'd never heard of her, and she'd forgotten to program Luther's number into her new cell.

Convinced she'd gotten her wires crossed, she'd hailed a cab and headed for the bawdy house at Sixty-Seven Anthony Street. After all, Luther had talked ceaselessly of declaring it a landmark, buying it from her and renovating it, then making it the permanent home of the museum's collection.

Making clear that he'd do anything to establish her ownership so she and the museum could make a deal, he'd said he was desperate to show her the place and he had a key. In turn, Cassidy had assured him she'd sell to the museum, and Luther had said he thought Beppe would sell only to the highest bidder. Even the museum couldn't outbid players like Chuckie Haswell, who'd now made his own claim.

After spending her last dollar on the cab fare, at least until she found an ATM, Cassidy had been relieved to find the door unlocked, as if Luther had been expecting her. She'd thrilled with anticipation, wondering what he looked like. Loud dance hall music was playing, and when she'd seen the sign on the door that read, "I'm in here, babe," she'd gotten the picture. He was setting up a bawdy-house atmosphere for their tryst, and he wanted her to play the role of Gem O'Shea.

A shudder shook her shoulders as she recalled the fiery onslaught of wet, deep, open-mouthed kisses that had followed as she'd straddled him. Now the tips of her breasts constricted against the lace of the bra she'd worn last night, and she became hyperconscious of the fact that she wasn't wearing panties, since they'd been ripped to shreds. The tingle became more generalized until every inch of her body was aching, and her mouth turned dry as she recalled how he'd buried his face against her sex.

She'd wanted to turn on the light and get a good look at Luther. Especially since his body felt perfect in the dark… big, broad, rounded linebacker shoulders, washboard-flat tummy, rock-hard abs, steely pecs, bulging muscular thighs. He had hands with long, thick fingers that bore out exactly what women said about the correlation between hand and penis size, too. His movements were so self-assured and controlled that he'd seemed dangerous, albeit in a tantalizing way.

When he'd reached for the lamp she'd stopped him. In the dark, wild abandon could take hold more easily, and the second he'd started stroking her upper thighs, she'd felt brazen.

When she'd awakened this morning, she'd realized the friendly goddess presiding over megahunks had decided to shine on her. The man she'd thought was Luther was lying on his back, uncovered and stark naked. Built like a house. On the phone, Luther had been a flirt but he'd seemed like the brainy type. Maybe too much like her ex, she'd thought. In reality, he was a well-honed, sculpted beauty. Even in repose, his sex was impressive, nestled in glistening black hair. He was so tall that his adorably big feet hung over the edge of the bed, and his face was framed by unruly, silken black waves.

She'd just lain beside him, staring. He'd reminded her of medieval Italian paintings of angels. His olive skin had a glow; his nose was prominent and aristocratic; his lips, which still looked swollen from kissing, seemed impossibly bow-shaped. He could have been Cupid in the flesh. Definitely, he didn't look like a museum curator—more like an adventurer—but then he did specialize in only sex-related artifacts.

As she'd surveyed every inch of his nude form, renewed heat had jolted through her, making her stretch against him sinuously, flexing aching muscles and relishing the soreness, gearing up for another experience to rival the previous night.

Already, she'd been imagining how she'd wake him…by nuzzling her face on his lower belly, then slowly licking his naval, twirling her tongue inside the perfectly shaped depression. Then she'd go lower and blow his mind. Her own was whirling, spinning fantasies of how she was going to spend spare time during her visit, having a no-holds-barred sexcapade with this fine specimen.

Then she'd noticed a gold shield.

Curious, she'd plucked it from the table. "Dario Donato?" she'd mouthed in confusion. Her heart had hammered. Hadn't Luther said the Donatos claimed they owned her property? Moving quietly, she'd replaced the badge soundlessly, then lifted a wallet and studied the cards. The license even had his picture.

He'd chosen that moment to stir, and she'd bitten back a yelp of surprise. She'd slept with a strange man! Someone she'd never even spoken to! She'd thought he was Luther, whom she'd flirted with, at least. She had to get out of there.

He was offering throaty moans of pleasure, as if he was having a hot dream about her. Moving on instinct, she'd pushed away guilt feelings and grabbed the bill on the table, knowing she had no cab fare. Trying not to think of how he'd said he'd left the money there to pay her for sex, she'd edged over the side of the mattress, snatching clothes as she'd tiptoed to the hallway.

Maybe no one would see her. Fortunately, she'd left her roller-style carry-on suitcase right inside the door. "I can't believe this," she'd whispered, panicking when she looked at the doors to other apartments. What if someone came out and caught her naked? Hands shaking, she'd wiggled her behind into the leggings, punched her arms into blouse sleeves, then jammed the panties into her jacket pocket. She was still buttoning the blouse as she lugged the case through the front door, thrusting her feet into shoes as she hailed a cab.

"Centuries of Sex Museum," she'd said frantically.

The driver was eying her blouse, and she'd realized it was buttoned cockeyed. "I can tell you're in a hurry," he'd said, chuckling softly.

She'd smirked. "Just step on it."

"Centuries of Sex Museum," he'd said drily. "Here we come."

She'd perched on a stool in a Starbucks until the museum opened, and now she felt further frazzled by shots of caffeine.

Luther hung up the phone. "All yours," he said, coming forward, the eyes still appraising. Lifting her hand, he made a big show of kissing it.

Great. She'd been leading this guy on for a month, and last

night, she'd been sure they were consumating the seduction. She withdrew her hand and forced a smile. "Nice to meet you."

"Likewise. I thought you were coming next Tuesday."

"I got the day wrong."

He looked ashen. "But your room?"

"I got my own," she assured, her mind flashing once more on the sheet that had been tangled around Dario Donato's hips like a loin cloth. "No problem."

"Here." He made another call, then said, "I've booked you a room at the Pierre, as promised." He explained that they had an upcoming court appearance with Judge Zhang the following week, then reiterated what had happened in court.

When he finished, she said, "Why don't you show me around?" She hoped she sounded businesslike.

"Sure. First, do you have the documents?"

Nodding, she wondered what Dario Donato would have done if he'd realized the papers were within his reach. Was he honest? Devious? Of better character than her ex?

She could feel Luther's eyes on her backside as she leaned. He thought she was a dish, which was going to make things difficult. "I brought the part of the will that I have, as well as old love letters. Regarding the ownership of the house, they may not be of interest, but I brought them, anyway. My great-grandmother passed the things to Granny Fiona, and she gave them to my mother, Erin Magee."

Hesitating, Cassidy felt suddenly unwilling to relinquish the papers. They were brittle and delicate, brown at the edges, a testament to how many generations had handed them down. Until Luther's first call, the family stories about Gem O'Shea had been just that—stories. Gem was thought to have been a madam who'd been given jewels by her lovers, and Granny Fiona had spun stories about her at Cassidy's bedtime, always against the protests of Cassidy's mother. "Quit filling her head with nonsense," Cassidy's mother would complain.

But Cassidy would plead until Granny Fiona described the dangerous ocean passage, the hard-scrabble life in Five Points and Gem's time as an escort. According to the tales, the jewels remained hidden to this day. Maybe that's why Cassidy had become a jeweler, opening her own shop. Even now, she believed the lost jewels existed, and the stories had sustained her through a lonely childhood, after her father had abandoned her and her mother.

Now the package of papers in her hands were the only proof she possessed that Gem had really lived. Her breath caught as she offered them to a stranger. "This is all I have."

"Excellent."

With care born of handling rare objects, Luther took the pages to his desk. Compelled to follow, she edged behind him as he took out a magnifying glass.

"Hmm," he said.

"Hmm, what?"

"Some of the papers we have indicate that Gem had only one lover, not many. I'll get a professional handwriting analyst to study these immediately if you don't mind."

She was grateful for the help. "Not at all."

As Luther continued his perusal, her thoughts drifted to Dario Donato. He'd looked like a god. So bronzed that he could have been glazed with hot sugar, and hard all over. Slow heat wended into her belly, and a pang of craving stirred her blood. Oh, she'd thought she'd known everything about sex. She'd been married for five years, after all.

But now, she got it. She was a dreamer, sure. But she had

a pragmatic side, and she'd always wondered how people lost their heads over sex, giving up marriages and jobs. Thanks to last night though, she understood. She'd have followed Luther to the ends of the earth.

Of course, he'd turned out to be Dario.

Her enemy. Dammit, why did he have to be associated with the one family who wanted to profit from her birthright? Worse, Johnny Case had left her in debt, so just last week she'd lost her second greatest love, her business. Unless the Five Points property was declared hers, she was in trouble.

"Huh?" she suddenly said.

"Being of full age and sound mind," he was murmuring. "Revoking all other wills and codicils made by me at any time…authorize and empower to bequeath the residence at Seven Anthony Street to Gem O'Shea…" Pausing, he sighed. "I wish more of the signature was intact."

"Me, too."

"The last letters could be an *l,* or maybe a *p.*"

It was hard to tell, since the paper had been torn in half.

"Wonder where the other half is?"

"I wish I knew."

"Do you really want to keep it locked in our safe?"

"That would be great." Carrying her heritage around in a suitcase had been nerve-racking. As he locked away the papers, she said, "I appreciate all you've done."

"You're helping us. If we can prove you own this building, then it's ours."

She tried to ignore a twinge of discomfort. Luther was starting to make her feel used. Would he argue for the Donato's case, if he felt that would help his museum? Did he care about the truth? "I'd like to see the roped-off rooms."

If the property was hers, then the items now in the

museum hadn't been the Donato's to sell, but so far, no one had broached the subject, and she wasn't about to do so. She wanted to keep things simple. Declaring the property hers was the first step.

As Luther placed a hand under her elbow to guide her, she recalled how the slightest brush of Dario's skin had solicited shivers. Just his breath, or the stir of air as his body passed hers, had made her come unhinged.

Pushing aside the thoughts, she whispered, "Wow," when she saw the main exhibit. "This was how the house looked?"

"The parlor room. We'd like to get the original bar, but it became part of a kitchen renovation."

"You're kidding."

"Unfortunately, no. It's the kitchen island in one of the apartments."

"The Donatos wouldn't let you take it?"

"Tenants have said they need it. But once you're recognized as the owner, all that will change."

Once more, she felt a proprietary twinge. Still, she'd never have been informed of her claim if it hadn't been for Luther. Vaguely aware he'd left her side, she curled her fingers over the velvet ropes protecting the display and studied the original Asian carpet. It was easily an inch thick, barely worn, and woven in swirling patterns, the dyes still vibrant after a century and a half.

She laughed softly when music started, then shuddered. Spiders could have been dancing to the show tune, doing the cancan on her vertebrae. "A player piano," she said huskily. It was what Dario had played last night. She even recognized the song. But why had he been expecting a woman to show? Clearly, he'd known the legend and had expected his visitor to pretend to be Gem O'Shea.

Her heart skipped a beat. Had the woman he'd expected really *been* a prostitute? Immediately, she rejected the notion. A man who looked like him would never have to pay.

"We found old sheet music on the property years ago," Luther was saying, pulling her attention to the present. "We had it recorded and play it in the museum."

It, too, was evoking memories. She saw Dario's shadow looming above her, his body moving rhythmically, a huge, hot, dry hand cupping her knee, raising it so he could push deeper inside her. A frenzied rush had assaulted her as he'd entered her. Suddenly, she was sure he'd look for her. A hand flew to her ear, and she realized an earring was gone. Before she must have subconsciously registered that she'd lost it. Had she left it behind? Or was it in the cab? Even if he found it, he'd have no idea who she was….

She felt a surge of power. In a flash fantasy, she imagined toying with him…calling and flirting with him on the phone. She'd drive him crazy with the need to know who she was. Huskily, she'd remind him of what they'd done. Ask him to take off his clothes. Tell him to touch himself, but pretend it was really her…

Blinking, she wondered what had come over her. She had to quit thinking like this. Dragging her attention to the room again, she took in a well-upholstered settee. Two high-backed, hand-carved chairs covered in blue velvet. A claw-footed gaming table. The original marble mantle had been preserved, and on either side, ornate candlesticks loomed. "I expected it to be…"

"More lurid?"

"Yeah."

"Showing your ankles was a big deal back then."

Seven portraits graced the walls, and the subjects were showing more than ankles. Some raised dresses to their thighs, or wore only corsets. "You can tell the pictures were hung exactly like this," she suddenly said in surprise.

"It's as if the paintings are one, isn't it?"

The first woman was looking at the hand of the second, who pointed to the third. That woman's scarf picked up a trail, seemingly flowing out of the painting, only to turn into a riding crop in the next picture. Any viewer following the trajectory would eventually be looking at Gem O'Shea. "I do look like her," she couldn't help but say.

"You have her hair and eyes," Luther said.

"But not her jewels." Gem's near-naked body was dripping in diamonds, emeralds and rubies. One ornamented hand fingered the strands of pearls looping her neck, the other hand pointed at the floor while Gem's eyes stared at the exact spot. "Wonder what she was looking at?"

"Who knows?"

"Whatever the case, the jewels are real. She must have been wearing them when she was painted." Cassidy sucked in a sharp breath, pointing. A man was standing behind Gem, almost lost to shadows.

"Angelo Donato. The reason the Donato's think they have a claim to the place."

He looked like Dario. She looked at Gem again, and a strange feeling came over her, almost a premonition, as if history were repeating itself.

She couldn't have been more relieved than when Luther spoke, saying, "Let me show you the rest."

After she'd seen the other rooms, she found herself standing in front of a framed newspaper article. "Mr. Ambrose Collier," she read aloud, "the driver, vowed he'd checked the hansom's wheels earlier in the evening. When they disengaged, he was thrown. According to Mr. Collier, an act of sabotage must have occurred. He swore Miss

O'Shea was his sole passenger, although an onlooker claimed two people appeared to be inside. Miss O'Shea's body was retrieved from the East River yesterday."

"So it may have been an act of sabotage?" she murmured.

"Maybe." Leaning, Luther took her hand.

She pulled away. "I should head for the hotel."

"So, you were just leading me on?" He was eyeing her with an urbane expression, as if sex was something he could take or leave, like dessert after a filling dinner.

"Not really. At the time I thought…but then I just…" If she'd met Luther last night, she'd have felt attracted. Now, she just wanted to catch a cab back to the old bawdy house, take off her clothes, and climb into bed with the enemy.

"You just?"

"Something's…uh, come up."

"Come up?"

The something had been gorgeous, hard and attached to the body of Dario Donato. "Yeah. My divorce," she added. "You know. I haven't quite…"

"Healed? I understand." He paused, shifting gears. "While you're here, you'll want to find out as much as you can about the property," he said, all business. "That's understandable. But steer clear of the Donato family, okay?"

Once more, those huge hands were curled over her breasts, squeezing. "Okay."

"They feel their claim is solid, and letting the courts handle everything is our best bet."

And yet she wanted to feel Dario Donato's hands stroking her skin again. Luther was smart, however. She had to do the right thing—for herself. She had to be brutal, as tough as nails. "I just want to establish my ownership. That's my goal."

"And we want to make the building an historical landmark."

As long as their goals coincided, that was fine. She settled for a nod.

"Steer clear of the Donatos," he repeated. "The son's a cop, and he can probably be ruthless."

She thought of his searing mouth. "I bet," she managed.

"Chuckie Haswell is going to be another problem," Luther continued, oblivious that a shot of liquid fire was now arrowing to her core. "He's got a lot of pull. It's my personal belief that he's forged papers to make it look as if he has a claim to the place. He'd go that far."

She was still thinking of how far she'd gone with Dario.

"Isn't he afraid of getting caught?"

"Chuckie will do anything to cash in on the new development opportunities around Manhattan. He wants to build a high-rise on the spot."

She'd barely heard the answer. Panicked when she'd left 67 Anthony Street, Cassidy was just now starting to wonder how Dario had felt when he'd awakened to find her gone. He'd have the glass slipper of an earring, a few hickeys on his neck, but nothing more. "I'm forewarned."

Luther's eyes drifted over her blouse. "If you change your mind about…"

She wouldn't. "Sure."

"It'll take you years to trust men again, right?"

Centuries. Realizing honesty might not be in her best interest, she batted her eyelashes. Dario Donato might have turned her head last night, but during this week, there was no room for error. "I'll call if I need anything."

"Maybe we can have dinner before meeting the Donatos at the courthouse."

She nodded. "Thanks for the tour, keeping the documents for me and the room."

"You'll like the Pierre."

"It's—" Oops. She'd almost given it away—he didn't know she'd gone there last night. No more than he knew she'd wound up having the best sex of her life with a Donato. "Always been on my list of places to visit."

"It's the missing ninth wonder of the world."

Silently thinking she'd discovered that last night, she offered a final nod, grabbed her suitcase and let Luther escort her to a cab. As it pulled into traffic, she found her cell, punched in information for a number, then called.

A woman answered. "Chuckie Haswell's office."

"Cassidy Case for Mr. Haswell."

"I'm sorry, he's…"

"Please let him know I'm in town and making claims against the property located at 67 Anthony Street, which he feels is his."

"Uh…you'd better hold then."

The line clicked immediately. "Mr. Case," he began, as if they were old golfing buddies.

"Mr. Haswell," she returned, making her voice extra-throaty. "I'm in town, staying at the Pierre, and I realized you and I have some similar interests. Care to meet for a drink? Say, my hotel. Six?"

If she was interpreting the pause correctly, she'd just blown the realty mogul away. In the past twenty-four hours, she'd been doing that to a lot of men. It felt good, too. Exhilarating. She was regaining her personal mojo and getting Johnny Case out of her system, hopefully forever. Dark and forbidding, the taste of Dario Donato's skin had been just another truly sensuous temptation. Better than chocolate and white Russians—her favorite drink.

But over. Finis. A one-night stand.

Chuckie Haswell had finally recovered from realizing she was a woman. "Six it is."

"I'll be the girl with red hair and a rose in her teeth," she continued in a breathy voice. Using her thumbnail, she tapped the off button, feeling a rush of satisfaction. "Keep them guessing," she repeated to herself. "A job well done."

As the cab pulled in front of the Pierre, she was thinking that her lapse with Dario Donato was unfortunate, since she couldn't afford to dwell on the delicious experience. She had to recover from it. Forget it, entirely.

After all, Johnny Case had taught her cold, hard life lessons about money and betrayal, and no more men were going to steal what was rightfully hers. As it was, all the inventory had been removed from the cases of her jewelry shop, and unless more money materialized, she'd lose the store. This week, she was going to have to play them all. Luther Matthews, Chuckie Haswell, Beppe Donato, and most of all, his son, Dario.

Sixty-Seven Anthony Street was hers.

None of the men cared about her, only their own interests. So be it. Reaching into her suitcase, she pulled out a letter she hadn't bothered to give Luther. "You know where the jewels are kept, my beloved," she read aloud softly. "They're in the house, in our special place. As long as the house stands, they'll be safe…"

"Look out boys," she added as a uniformed bellman opened the cab's door. The house was hers, and so was everything in it. As she stepped onto a sidewalk under a green awning, she acknowledged that she didn't only look like Gem, but she possessed her spirit.

"Consider me the ghost of Gem O'Shea," she whispered.

5

DRINKS WITH CHUCKIE HASWELL led to a dinner he'd probably thought was romantic, judging by how disappointed
he'd looked when Cassidy left him at the Pierre's front
doors instead of inviting him upstairs. His attraction had
given her an edge, and otherwise, she'd laid her cards on the
table, emphasizing the importance of the documents she'd
brought to town. Chuckie had evidence that his ancestor, not
Angelo Donato, had owned the building, but she could
prove it had been willed to Gem.

"By whom?" Chuckie had asked.

"I have a week to find out," she'd returned. "And I will.
If your ancestor, Nathaniel, really owned the property,
maybe he was Gem's lover."

"He was a respectable man."

"That's what they all say." She'd flashed a smile, thinking
of her ex. "Anyway, the Donatos are a wild card," she'd
pressed on, remembering just exactly how wild. "If you
can prove the place is yours, fine, but if you can't, consider
championing my cause. I only want the house for a while.
It's…sentimental."

"And you'll sell?"

"Maybe exclusively to you, if you help me stake my
claim. Because of the Donatos' squatting rights, and the re-
sistance of the historical society, I'm your best bet."

"When will you sell?"

"As soon as the tenants leave," she'd said, improvising since she wanted to search for the missing jewels. "I'm a small-town girl, so I'd hate to see them inconvenienced, and I want to make sure no work's done on the property until they're out."

"Brice Jorgensen holds the longest lease," Chuckie had said, more aware of the situation than she. "He's gone in six months." He'd paused. "You want me to give up my claim, and spend next week proving you're the rightful sole heir?"

"It's in your best interest."

"You're persuasive, and I'll think about it," he'd conceded. "In fact, you're exactly the kind of go-getter I'd love to have working for me."

Cassidy hadn't exactly taken that as a compliment, but she'd had to strike the best deal for herself, even with a bottom feeder. It was her only chance to jumpstart her business and move on. She tried not to dwell on the potential loss of her adorable store, located in the heart of her town's most popular strip mall. And now every single display case was empty, since she'd sold inventory to pay off her ex's debts. The store had been her dream, fueled by nights when Granny Fiona had plied her with stories about Gem.

"Relax," she coached herself, as she stepped off the elevator. Round one was over. She let herself into the room, and as her feet sank into thick carpet, she sighed with relief. Yesterday, she'd traveled, her night with Dario had been physically charged, and today had been tiring. She couldn't wait to strip, put on her nightshirt and drink the tea she'd ordered from room service before coming upstairs.

Looking around, it was hard not to feel a backlash of guilt, though. This was a far cry from her rustic two-bedroom cottage in South Carolina, with its wild acre of land, wide plank floors and beamed ceilings. Jewels had been her life, but usually she sold small diamonds, engagement rings for regular folks, often kids just getting out of school. Here, she was overwhelmed by opulence. In the mirrored bathroom, she'd bathed in a tub big enough for five, complete with pulsing water jets and an inbuilt bubble dispenser. The main room was more understated, but it, too, had been made for presidents, not a small-town shop owner who'd been married to a teacher at a local college.

Lifting a remote, she clicked a button that said Entertainment Center. Apparently, a menu on television also controlled the music. After scrolling to Classical, she selected a composer whose name she didn't recognize and clicked again. Soft piano music filled the room, coming from surround-sound speakers that had been tucked out of sight. Suddenly, she chuckled. The place reminded her of bachelor pads in movies where, with the touch of a button, a bed appeared, music was piped in, and the lights dimmed. All design features were calculated to lead to sex.

A king-size bed was tucked tastefully into an alcove but within view of velvet-curtained windows overlooking Central Park. One of the walls in the main room was mirrored, and armchairs had been placed on either side of a fireplace. Closer to the door, a table was covered with chintz, and even from here, she could smell fresh flowers from the vase on top. A gift basket contained condoms, lotions and oils.

Suddenly, she ached to use them, and damned Dario Donato for doing more than recharging her body; he'd put a spark of fire back inside her heart. Maybe the romantic part of her life wasn't really over, the way she'd been telling herself. Nothing more could happen with Dario, of course. She was divorced now, and might never remarry, so she had to provide for her own future, which meant getting her property.

Still, horse-drawn carriages were moving along Fifty-Ninth Street, and seeing couples inside, she couldn't help but feel wistful. Too bad marriage had been like a beautiful jewel that, seen under a magnifier, began showing all its flaws. Sex, on the other hand, would be around as long as there were men and women, she decided, thinking of Dario once more.

"How's he going to feel when he sees me in court next week?" Would some hint in her eyes give her away, when they went before Judge Zhang? Would Dario realize she'd been his mystery lover? Had he obsessed all day about their one-night stand? And who had he been expecting? He'd seemed intimate with the person, yet he hadn't realized Cassidy wasn't his...lover? Sex buddy? Fiancée?

She pulled her gaze from the carriages, realizing she was imagining her and Dario riding together, holding hands under a lap blanket. In her mind's eye, she saw the hand disengage and travel to her thigh....

Tonight, she was wearing the perfect outfit for arousing him, too. She'd been blessed with some natural assets, of course, but during the divorce, she'd raised her flagging self-esteem by going on a self-care rampage, regularly working out and giving herself facials and manicures.

After realizing her threadbare jeans and sweatshirts weren't in keeping with the Pierre's unwritten dress code and feeling determined to impress Chuckie, she'd charged the dress in a shop downstairs. It was of a skin-hugging cotton blend and had a tie that knotted under her breasts. Of bright red, the color redheads were told never to wear, it was an exact match for her hair. A tiny red bag still hung from her shoulder, and she'd worn red shoes with spike heels. Her nails, too, were bright red. She'd done her makeup to perfection, something she knew how to do because her mother, Erin, was a beautician with her own shop.

As Chuckie had eyed her, Cassidy had wondered if Dario would be equally stimulated. Now her eyes settled on the phone, and she moved toward it. Sitting on the edge of the bed, she lifted the receiver. It was risky, but she found herself whispering, "It won't hurt just to get his number." She wasn't going to really call him.

She dialed information. "Manhattan. Thirteenth Precinct, please."

The automated operator gave the number, and offered the option to dial direct. It was as easy as pressing a button with a tip of a long, red fingernail.

A moment later, his voice swept her off her feet. Her breath caught as if she'd just been sucker punched. It was sort of rusty, but not at all unpleasant. Whatever hit the back of her knees felt so fluid that she was glad she was seated. Of course, it was only a voice-mail message.

"I'll be checking my messages," he was saying. "Otherwise, you can reach my cell…."

Grabbing a pen from the bedside table, she scribbled the number on a pad. The pulse had gone wild at her throat. Every single one of her muscles felt tense.

"What would I say if I talked to him? That I had a good time?" That sounded trite, but then, she was hardly going to gush about how fantastic some strange guy was in bed. Besides, he was a cop. Maybe he had caller ID. Well, maybe not on a cell phone, she conceded. But surely he could trace her call, and then he'd come to the Pierre….

"It would take him at least a day to trace the call," she argued with herself. That would give her time to change rooms and hide from him. Or flee the city.

Knowing she'd lost her mind, she quickly dropped the

receiver into the cradle, as if she'd been burned. Bringing her feet onto the bed, shoes and all, she laid back on the sumptuous pillows, clasped her hands beneath her breasts, shut her eyes and tried to listen to the music.

But she was still thinking about him.

"Stop," she muttered.

But he was like an unwanted itch that wouldn't go away. "Like poison ivy," she continued.

An image of his naked body filled her mind. Suddenly, she ached with longing, and it was no use telling herself it was because she hadn't had sex for almost a year, since she threw Johnny out. Last night was, quite simply, the best sex of her life, and she had no idea why. They'd just screwed. It had been totally straightforward, no kinky stuff. But there was something special about him…maybe the way he smelled, or the exact tenor of his voice, or the way he moved…

"Tell me what you're wearing," she'd whisper if she called him, she decided.

"Jeans," he'd say.

"Tight jeans?" she'd probe.

She could really see him now, bare chested and dressed in worn jeans. She'd inquire, "How tight?"

And he'd say, "Very tight."

Now she imagined the material lovingly cupping him. Slowly, the powerful bulge was becoming visible under his fly, straining the zipper. "Are they always tight," she imagined herself saying huskily, "or tight because you're so hard?"

His breath was catching now, turning shallow. He was softly panting. "So hard."

"Then you'd better take them off."

She imagined the rustling of cloth, a flapping sound as he kicked off the jeans, then his voice coming through the receiver again. "What about you? Are you naked for me?"

"Oh, yeah."

"Tell me what you want to do to me."

As generalized warmth infused her pubic area, she put a hand there, her heart hammering as she imagined how he'd look, dusky and erect. A soft sound of need emanated from the back of her throat as her other hand covered her breast.

"Turn over," she imagined herself saying. In her imagination, her eyes roved over his firm rear end, his perfect strong, wide back and those huge shoulders. "I'm going to touch every inch of you."

In reality, she was cupping her own breast. When her nipples ached, she sighed and pinched them lightly, but that only make them ache even more.

"Every inch," he was saying huskily. "Is that all?"

Her belly was full from dinner and a creamy desert, and now languid warmth infused her limbs, shooting straight into her bloodstream as if through jets from the bathtub in the other room. Yawning, she felt as if she could fall asleep, yet she was becoming highly aroused.

Dammit, what had Dario done to her last night? Sex was all she could think about now. Using long fingernails, she drew patterns on her own thighs...swirling circles, then zigzagging lines. Once more, she was undressing Dario, but now he was leaning against a wall, and she was the one dragging down his zipper. He was moaning. His hips thrust outward, as if begging for the touch of her hands. She glanced up, just in time to see him raise his arms above his head, and her eyes trailed over his bare chest, from the bones of his ribcage to his bulging biceps, taking in the healthy glow of his tanned skin and muscles coated with dark hair.

"C'mon," she imagined him encouraging urgently.

Her own fingers had slipped inside the leg band of her panties. With a rush, she remembered him ripping her underclothes last night. She could still hear the soft sound as he'd tossed them away. Arching her hips, she pretended he was loving her with his hands, starting to make her climb. The music was lost. Catching her own moisture, she was captured by a dream as she rubbed the swollen nub of her clitoris. Shivering with excitement, she licked her upper lip, tonguing away beads of perspiration.

She was so far gone, she couldn't quite pinpoint the intrusive sound. She was climbing high. Almost there. So close. On the brink…

"Room service!" Hopping up with a frustrated moan, she wobbled a second on the high heels and quickly smoothed her dress. As she headed for the door, she couldn't help but glimpse herself in the mirror, and seeing that she looked totally disheveled, she silently cursed Dario again, vaguely thinking that this was all his fault.

"Just a moment!"

She swung open the door. Instinctively, she gasped and stepped back a pace. There was no tray or roller cart covered with white linen, which meant this wasn't room service. The first thing she noticed when she stared down was the man's shoes, and for a second, she thought Chuckie had come back, then she caught a flash of threadbare denim and realized her error. Grabbing the door's edge, she slammed it shut. Or at least she tried. A foot wedged in the crack as she flattened both hands on the wood and pushed. Equal pressure was being applied from the other side.

The source of the pressure was Dario Donato.

6

"WHO ARE YOU?" she demanded.

Now, that was rich. Keeping a splayed hand pressed to the door, Dario steeled himself against the raspy voice he'd heard uttering urgent cries of delight until dawn. "You're going to pretend you didn't read my badge?"

"What badge?"

This woman was a real piece of work. "You put Sheila Carella to shame," he muttered in astonishment.

"Who's Sheila Carella?"

Did she actually sound jealous or was it just wishful thinking? "The person I thought I slept with last night."

There was a long silence.

"The person I thought took my money," he clarified.

There was another long silence.

"The person who was supposed to come over and have sex with me," he added.

"You're going to have to leave," she returned flatly, "or I'm calling security."

"That doesn't seem quite fair, since you're the thief," he countered. "And besides, I *am* security."

"Not here, you're not."

She was definitely the woman he'd slept with. She wasn't protesting nearly enough, and she knew he was a cop. "I'm getting tired of talking to the door."

"You have other options."

Of course he did. With one push, he could knock her over, but it would be more civil if she invited him in. "Do you really want me to huff, puff and blow the door down?"

"I meant you could leave."

He was no expert on accents, but now he could tell she was from South Carolina, something he'd found out a few hours ago. Last night, the accent hadn't played through all the sighs. "Whatever. Just don't bother calling security. I've moonlighted at the Pierre," he lied.

He could almost hear her mind ticking; she was wondering whether to believe him. It was a tense moment, especially since the answer was no, and it was definitely the wrong time for a door to open behind him. He turned just long enough to catch a flash of silver hair and a beige blazer.

"Is there some sort of dispute here?" the woman behind him demanded.

Dario tried to pull his gaze away from door number one, but he was riveted, studying the contours carved into the wood. He was still registering the unexpected relief he'd felt when she'd first opened the door. As much as he hated to admit it, he'd feared he'd never see her again. After the sex they'd shared, why had she decided to run? Hadn't she been as affected as he?

He'd watched the tapes countless times, unable to stop himself until he'd memorized every movement she'd made while dressing—the sway of her breasts as she'd wiggled into the dark leggings, the tense expression as she'd stuffed the panties he'd torn into her jacket pocket, the trembling of her hands as she'd buttoned her blouse. Each detail was etched permanently into his mind.

All day, while he'd carried her earring in his pocket—jiggling it in his hand as he sometimes did his apartment keys—he'd wondered how long it had taken her to realize she'd buttoned her shirt crookedly. He'd stopped short of dusting his own penis for her prints, of course, but otherwise, he'd used every trick in the book to track her.

Abruptly, he turned to stare across the hallway where the elderly woman was peering at him suspiciously. "Just married," he explained.

She didn't look convinced.

He wasn't exactly a people pleaser, but even he hadn't been immune to the snobby stares in the lobby as he'd cut across it wearing jeans, a black T-shirt and a denim jacket. The woman looked like an Upper East Side type. She probably thought he was a gang member or something. "From out of town," he added. "Honeymoon."

Accepting the explanation, the woman went back inside, slamming her door. Silence came from the other side of door number one. "Let me in," he demanded.

"Why?"

"We need to talk."

"I don't talk to strange men."

He stared down at his foot, which was still wedged in the doorway. "I may be strange, but not in the way you mean."

"That's even worse," she returned. "Strange how?"

He should have guessed. Unlike Sheila, this woman would go head-to-head with him, but then Sheila had surprised him when she'd ended their relationship. "As if you care. If you'd wanted to get to know me," he pointed out, "you would have stuck around this morning."

"I'm going to have to ask you to leave."

So, she wasn't going to directly deny she knew him. Maybe there was a shred of honesty in her, after all, even if her personal records indicated she was in a world of trouble.

As near as he could tell, her husband had finally had enough of her wild lifestyle and walked.

The door behind him opened again, and the silver-haired lady poked out her head. "If you don't resolve this conflict," she informed him, her voice quavering now, "I'm calling security." She paused, drawing up her shoulders regally and added, "My granddaughter marches with Take Back The Night."

As a cop, he'd become acquainted with the marches of antirape activists on college campuses. "Believe me, the woman inside this room has been more than willing."

Since he preferred doing things the easy way, he felt torn, but he also knew he was out of options. Digging into his back pocket, he flipped open his shield protector and flashed the badge. While the woman gaped, he busied himself, wedging his thigh against the door frame, then his torso. Cassidy was surprisingly strong, though, and for the benefit of the onlooker, Dario didn't want to apply force. Using his shoulder, he nudged the door open another few inches, and as soon as there was room, he squeezed inside and pivoted. As he shut the door, he shot a final smile through the crack. "Sorry for the inconvenience, ma'am."

"Oh, dear," she said. "I'm sorry, officer."

He broadened his smile in what his partner always called his baby-kissing, public-relations smile. Then he turned his attention to Ms. Cassidy Case. As soon as he took a better look at her, he wished he hadn't. He wasn't viewing her in the cold light of day—something he could have tolerated—but rather under high-end track lighting and soft-focus dimmers that made her shimmer like a goddess. Yeah, he thought, she looked like she'd come from some distant planet dedicated entirely to sex.

"Cassidy," he found himself muttering, feeling strangely

taken aback, as if the bright red dress was a personal affront, something she'd worn to torture him.

She looked mortified. "How do you know my name?"

She was hardly a "Mr. Case," as he'd been led to believe in court. "I have my ways."

"What are you doing here?"

"Are you always this hospitable? No offer of a drink? Maybe Dom Pérignon? After all, it's the Pierre." Suddenly, he dropped the sarcasm. "Because of the directions you gave me, it took me eleven hours to get here."

"I didn't give you any directions."

"My point exactly."

"Nice to meet you," she returned, her saccharine tone calculated to make clear the encounter was anything but pleasurable. "Since you already know my name, and you're obviously such a stickler for good manners, evidenced by how you just broke into my hotel room, who are *you?*"

As if she didn't know.

"Oh, well then, let me just guess. Mr. Manners? Ann Landers's husband?" She paused dramatically. "Oh, gosh, I don't seem to have packed my crystal ball."

Even if he'd wanted to, he couldn't have spoken. His eyes were too busy, dragging down the seemingly endless length of her body. Was this really the dish he'd slept with last night? It seemed too good to be true. When he'd arrested Sheila Carella, he'd been sure he'd hit the jackpot, but this…. Realizing she was staring at him expectantly, he said, "I thought we might trade techniques."

"On?"

Lovemaking. "Breaking and entering."

"What would I know about that?"

Digging in his pocket, he pulled out the earring. For a second, he hesitated, feeling it roll in the palm of his hand, not wanting to relinquish the one item that had kept him connected to her all day. Grasping a silver hook, he held up baubles, letting them dangle, then he tossed the earring onto the bed. "Why don't you tell me?"

As if she simply couldn't help herself, she slid her eyes to where the earring landed, squarely on a pillow that still held the cradling depression of her head, and he took the opportunity to further study her.

The luxurious dress wrapped perfectly around her, as if held only by a flimsy tie. Just looking at it made him consider catching that tie between his teeth and pulling. Right now, it knotted beneath full breasts he'd fondled through the night, and her hair was really as red as poppies. The video had not told a lie. Looking disheveled, the hair feathered around her face in a haircut that must have cost a king's ransom. It seemed as if the wind were blowing, or as if she were walking along at a fast clip. In reality, she was standing so still that she could have been sculpted from stone.

"I asked you who you are," she said. "Aren't you going to answer me? At least give me some explanation for the intrusion."

"I don't grace idiocy with responses."

"But you'll make an exception for me?"

"Yeah," he said, not bothering to lift his gaze from the dress. It wasn't short—it hung right below the knee—but the recollections of his fingertips hadn't served him wrong, either. Every single curve corresponded exactly to his tactile recollection, and he went over each inch, putting two and two back together.

The legs went on for a country mile, encased in stockings that had a sheen, as if the silk had been sprinkled with gold glitter. The lower part of the dress draped her thighs, clinging, then a sloping line gracefully dropped to rounded cups of knees. Dryness hit the back of his throat as he recalled his hands curling over those knees last night...how he'd slowly pushed them apart, how she'd slowly opened for him.

By the time his gaze landed on red spike heels, he was falling into the male version of a swoon, which meant he was getting awfully hard. "Ouch," he couldn't help but whisper. He might not like her on a personal level—at least judging from all the nasty things he'd discovered about her when he'd done a background check today—but she was one helluva good-looking woman. And when had a woman's loose morals ever stopped him?

She was merely gaping, her pout of a mouth smooth, slick and moist with bright red lipstick. She hadn't budged from her place near the opposite doorjamb, which meant that she was close enough that he was smelling perfume. It made him want to burrow against her, maybe why his gaze dipped again, now to her cleavage. For a second, his face was between her breasts, and he could feel their cushioning softness against his cheek.

"You don't grace idiocy with responses?" she prompted, and he could sense her staring at him.

Coming to his senses, he slowly trailed the gaze all the long way back up her body until his eyes locked with hers. Or tried. Hers darted away as if the fireplace had just become extremely interesting.

"No," he said. "I don't."

"Were you implying I'm an idiot?"

"Take it how you will."

For his part, he felt as if someone had just hit him in the gut with a baseball bat. Breath had left his body, and bands wound around his chest. Her eyes had turned out to be shiny and green, like liquid emeralds, and he'd never seen anything like them. How they'd looked on the tape was just a faint echo, nothing more. For the split second their gazes had meshed, he felt something hard to define…like a lightning bolt had shot from her to him. He'd felt a deep connection, as if their core energies had touched.

He blew out a heartfelt sigh, his eyes on the beauty mark. Why did only the devious ones look this good? He'd spent hours discovering everything he could about Cassidy Case, and she made Sheila Carella look like Mother Theresa. Thankfully, years of practice had made him able to mask his facial expressions, and since coming into the room, he'd been doing his level best to look bored. "Have a hot date tonight?"

He was glad to see that she looked nervous as hell. She had high cheekbones, and right now, one was plagued by a slight, barely noticeable, uncontrollable tick. Her eyelashes were sandy, spiky and fluttering wildly, too, as if they were tiny wings she hoped could bat him away.

"What's it to you?"

"I think you know."

"No, I didn't have a date, for your information."

"You always dress like that for a night at home?"

"Like what?"

"In that sweat suit. Pajamas. Or whatever it is."

"Whatever it is, I'm not at home, anyway," she pointed out reasonably. "I'm in a hotel."

"You're impossible."

"I hope so."

"I bet a lot of people have told you that."

"A few."

She was determined to get rid of him, and would use any means necessary, including acting totally nuts. "You're as crazy as your nearly criminal record should have implied."

"I don't have a record."

The innocent act was wearing thin. Besides, she was too guilty to keep it up. Her cheeks had turned as red as the dress, and her carotid artery was working overtime. As he watched it tick, he realized her heart must be racing a mile a minute. Her skin was almost unnaturally pale, chalky in color like Gem O'Shea's.

Suddenly, he was thinking about how the other woman must have pleased her male clients, and he decided that there must be a gene for sexual know-how, a special DNA possessed only by some women, that Gem had passed to Cassidy.

"Look," she began again, "I really don't know what you're talking about. Or who you are. Or why you're here."

"You're one cool customer."

"What do you think I've done?"

"Besides steal the money on my nightstand this morning?"

"Oh, don't be ridiculous!"

He squinted. He had no idea what he'd expected, but it wasn't this blanket denial. "This has to be the most bizarre conversation I've ever had," he muttered, starting to get genuinely annoyed.

"If you go home, it can't continue."

"It does take two to tango."

"Then leave me to play solitaire."

"I don't see any cards." Before he thought it through, he reached for her, curling his fingers around her upper arm. She wrenched, intending to free herself, but he reacted instinctively by tightening his grip. He knew it was a dangerous mistake when he felt the tension uncoiling inside her—the leap of muscles, the rush of blood, but he was powerless to stop himself. He yanked her toward him, knowing he'd lost his mind as he dropped his voice seductively. "Looks like I'm making you nervous."

"In your dreams."

"I'm nothing if not realistic."

A shallow pant of breath teased his cheek, and her gaze was fiery when it found his. There was a thrill to the moment, something that stirred his blood and made it thrum, maybe because the circumstances were like nothing he'd ever experienced. With her, everything was new. Totally unpredictable. Besides, he knew he had the upper hand. She was attracted to him.

"We might not be in the old bawdy house again tonight," he found himself murmuring, drawing her a fraction closer, "but we are standing in a room made for sin, with a king-size bed just a hop, skip and a jump away. You might want to deny last night happened, Cassidy, but I can't get it out of my mind."

"Your mind," she echoed simply.

She was close enough now that he could feel the heat of her breath on his lips, evoking memories. "It's definitely on one track," he said.

Her lips had parted as if for a kiss. "Which track?"

"The male one."

Angling his head down, he captured her lips. Just like that. It was so easy, and immediately he felt transported somewhere far off, into a dark, heady world where everything vanished but her mouth. The night seemed shrouded in mystery. Pungent with promise. As if its magic could transport them anywhere….

She didn't fight, but she wasn't kissing him back, either, at least not until his mouth turned harder on hers, his lips firmer and more demanding, assuring her he wouldn't take no for an answer. Suddenly, he thrust his tongue, the plunge deep and forceful. Her lips parted wider, taking the heated spear, then hers pushed back, feeling urgent. Probing, he licked the contours of her lips now. As he did, fire hit his loins, and he moved his hips, thrusting.

With a gasp, she stepped back, ending the kiss abruptly with a smacking sound, leaving him breathless as he watched a hand fly to her mouth. Unexpected anger surged inside him. He'd thought about her all day. He wanted her. And he was tired of playing games. "If you think you can really wipe away that kiss, sweetheart," he found himself saying, "it's a little too late."

She swallowed hard, as if around a lump, her expression stricken. "It's you who should have thought of that."

Maybe. The kiss ensured he'd be up all night, craving another taste. "I didn't mind. I'd do it again."

"No, you won't," she whispered.

"Anytime, anywhere," he countered.

Piano music was playing—not dance hall music, like last night, but playful, single notes, all variations on the same melody. Her luscious green eyes still looked as wide as saucers. When she spoke again, the words seemed to catch in her throat. "What do you want?"

You, he thought. In bed. Right now. "Just to talk," he said, although he'd already proven that was a lie.

"About what?"

"I've been looking for you all day." All my life, an unwanted voice in his mind corrected.

"How did you find me?"

It was the closest she'd come to admitting they'd met last night, although not formally. "There are video cameras in the house." Just in case that didn't sink in, he added, "And in the hallway."

"The hallway?"

Given the crimson staining her cheeks, he guessed she was recalling how she'd gotten dressed there. "For the rest, you can thank Homeland Security."

She squinted, and it did wonderful things to her face. Her ski-jump nose lifted, and skin around her eyes crinkled.

"There are cameras all over the city, nowadays," he explained. "I tracked you from my front door, to Luther Matthews's museum, and while Luther was at lunch, I talked to his assistant." He'd studied materials inside, as well. "I found out a few things about you, too."

A steely thread wove through her words. "Such as?"

"Your husband got tired of your spending habits and walked." Only after he'd spoken, did he fully realize he'd been digging intentionally, and he was damn glad that she didn't look too broken up about kissing Johnny Case goodbye.

"You know about my marriage?"

"Some."

She was edging away from him again, and he guessed he didn't blame her, but he hadn't been about to let her get away, at least not without another kiss to remember him by. "Look," she murmured, "I want you to leave."

"And I still think we ought to have that drink."

Her lips were still glistening from the kiss; he'd licked all the lipstick off. "Why would I have a drink with you?"

"I can think of a million reasons." One was the king-size bed. "Would you rather I just shut up and kiss you again?"

She considered. Then suddenly, she spun away, turning on the spike of her heel. He watched as her whole body seemed to whirl on the axis of that slender red dagger. The gorgeous red dress swung around her, exposing heart-stopping thighs. He could only hope he was going to see whatever device was holding up the stockings.

"Don't go away mad," he found himself saying as she headed for the bar.

By the time she turned to face him, her face had composed itself into an unreadable expression. "Ice?"

He surveyed where she leaned against the bar's low-slung countertop, which came only to her upper thighs. "I could definitely use something to cool me down," he admitted, thinking he'd love to trail a cube over her bare skin. "But it depends whether you're serving anything with it."

She lifted a bottle of what looked to be good whiskey.

Leaning his elbows on the wood bar, he added, "And now, if we could just do something about your anger problem."

She didn't bother to look up from where she was pouring. "Like what?"

"Lose it. Because we've already discovered we can play well together."

"You charged in here uninvited," she suddenly began, her voice strained as she pushed a highball glass toward him, then poured herself a drink and lifted it, stopping just shy of her mouth. "And you…you…"

"Kissed you?" he supplied.

"And now you want a drink," she finished.

"Well…*you* broke into *my* bedroom last night," he returned as his fingers curled around the glass. "And you took off your clothes, and so on. I don't know about you, but I ached all over this morning." He flashed a quick smile. "It was a good kind of ache, though, if you know what I mean.

"I'll take that as a yes," he continued after a moment. "My best guess is that you slept with me as some sort of ploy, to get my father's property. So, now I guess we're even."

His little speech had gotten to her. Her jaw was slack, and with her lips parted like that, it was tempting to kiss her again. He wasn't entirely proud of it, but seeing her speechless gave him an incredible sense of satisfaction. After all, he imagined those green eyes had brought many men to their knees. Surely, he wasn't the first. So, moving with slow deliberation, he raised his glass and clinked it against hers.

"Cassidy Case," he said. "Here's looking at you."

7

HERE'S LOOKING AT YOU. Wasn't that what Humphrey Bogart had said to Ingrid Bergman in *Casablanca?* Heat was still curling between them. Sex was stinging the air. While Cassidy knew she couldn't let Dario's physical proximity unnerve her, she'd been lost to desire, touching herself and fantasizing about him when he'd arrived. She'd never expected to see him again, only in dreams, and she'd been right on the brink...but then he'd shown up and kissed her, quoting romantic movies like some erstwhile prince. Now she had to think fast.

"Given your manners," she managed to say, her lips feeling kiss-swollen, "I guess you *would* spend a lot of nights alone watching old movies."

"Not last night."

"Must have been a big break in the routine for you."

"Extraordinary."

Because her cheeks were burning, she damned herself for having such fair skin. No doubt, she was the color of ripe strawberries. By contrast, he looked so self-possessed that it was grating on her nerves. Had he really watched her get dressed on tape? And how much did he really know about her failed marriage? Not only was he killer handsome, he was a good detective, too. Not to mention Beppe Donato's son, she reminded herself. "Last night, I..."

"You?"

Was it really in her best interest to admit she'd slept with him? He knew, of course, but as long as she refused to vocalize it, she'd have him stumped.

He was watching her curiously, and his eyes did the rest of his body justice. They'd been shut this morning, but now, if he said, "undress and get into bed," she'd probably do it, as if entranced by a sorcerer's spell. The eyes were very dark, the color of bittersweet chocolate, and they were big, soulful and smoldering with desire. Framed by thick hoods of brows and surrounded by straight, barbed lashes, they were making her last shred of resolve melt.

A deep rumbling sound came from a broad chest encased in a black T-shirt that cut low enough to expose plenty of unruly chest hair. "Why'd you run off this morning? Afraid I'd bite?"

"You'd already bitten."

"So you noticed."

Her gaze drifted to his neck. "Looks like you're the one who got bit," she said, noticing the hickey on his neck.

"Must have been a vampire. I woke up alone."

"Phantoms?" she suggested.

"A helluva good dream," he countered.

"Don't dwell on it," she recommended. "You're awake now."

"I certainly am." With that, he took another sip of his whiskey.

She could have been running, given how wildly her heart was beating. "Look," she began, wishing she wasn't having difficultly breathing, and that every inhalation wasn't carrying the scent of him. "I've just rethought everything, and now, I do think honesty might be the best policy—" In fact, she'd do just about anything to get rid of him.

He interjected a grunt of disbelief, but she rushed on. "Last night, I thought you were somebody else, you see."

Unfortunately, the words didn't have the desired effect. "Why would somebody else be sleeping in that apartment?"

If he understood the one-night stand had been an accident, he'd lose interest; she was sure of it. "I didn't know it was your apartment," she insisted.

"It's not. I live in Battery Park. But my father asked me to sleep over until our conflicts are resolved."

"See? How could I have known that?"

"So, you came over to sleep with a tenant?"

"No…I thought you were Luther."

"Luther?" He stared at her. "Matthews?"

"He had a key."

He looked incredulous. "There's no way you could mix me up with Luther Matthews."

He had a point there. This guy didn't have a metrosexual bone in his body. Hoping to calm her fraying nerves, she sharply inhaled. Her lungs further filled with something that conjured Christmastime and pine forests. Ten to one, he'd showered before he'd come over. "I'd never met Luther before," she clarified.

When his jaw slackened, she realized she'd jumped from the fryer to the fire. "But you were going to sleep with him?"

"I don't usually sleep with strange men."

Now, she knew she'd misjudged him. He actually looked disappointed. "You don't?"

She shook her head.

"Under the circumstances, why bother turning on a light to make sure it's him? I mean, you'd never met him before."

"It was an accident!"

"Sorry you feel that way."

"No matter what I say, you're going to think whatever you want, anyway."

He knocked back a slug of his drink. "On that, you've got my number."

She took a sip, too, but the whiskey was strong. Just licking it off her lips made her sputter. As she replaced the glass on the bar, she wished the counter was higher, offering her more protection from him. She also hoped he wasn't noticing her hands shaking. "I'm telling you the truth."

"Why should I believe you?"

"Because I'm not lying."

A tense silence fell.

Blowing out a sudden peeved sigh, she pushed away memories of how he'd loved her body in the wee hours, and she wished questions about his relationship with Sheila Carrella weren't starting to niggle. "And whatever you heard about me is probably not true," she added. "My ex was the bad guy, and he wrecked our marriage."

"How?"

Because he looked merely curious, she said, "He slept around, spent way more than we had." She paused. "If you must know. And would you like any other information? My home address? Birth date maybe? Social security number?"

"I have all that, thanks." His eyes narrowed, and for a second, she felt as if he could see right through her, to her soul. "Sorry about your ex," he murmured after a moment.

He'd sounded genuine, and it made her heart tug. "It's not your fault," she said shortly.

"I said I was sorry, not responsible."

"A stickler with words?"

"And for the law."

He tossed back the rest of the whiskey. "So, you were going to have a rebound fling with Luther Matthews?" he guessed.

She was trying not to notice the flicker of his tongue as he tasted the whiskey on his lips, but it was evoking images from last night, all of which involved other places where his tongue had been. "Something like that."

"With no strings attached?"

"Do you always interrogate people?"

"Only if I suspect them of lying."

"No matter what I say, you won't believe me," she repeated.

"Try me, anyway." Reaching for the bottle, he poured another shot, then tossed that back with a swallow.

"Liquid courage?" she suggested. "Am I making you nervous?"

"Quivering," he assured.

She shouldn't have baited him. His expression was intense, the gaze remarkably steady. "Besides," he added. "I figured I might as well fix myself another drink, since you're taking your good old time when it comes to telling me about the jewels."

She gasped. "What?"

"Jewels. Stones. The kind emptied out of your store."

"You know about Gem's Stones?" That was the name of her shop.

"You sold the inventory to pay off your debts—"

"Maybe," she shot back hotly, acknowledging too late that she'd leaned closer to him, within reach. "But what do you know about the two jobs I worked to save the money to start that store? Or how I learned accounting and did my own books? Or built the display cases myself? And painted?"

He looked taken aback.

"My ex-husband's debts," she corrected. "Not mine."

He hesitated a minute, which she guessed was to his

credit. "Sounds like selling the inventory in your store was a smart move, but now you have no income."

Hearing him say it, she felt strangely violated. "Isn't there a law against invading people's privacy?"

"I did everything by the book."

"If not ethically," she muttered.

"The jewels," he repeated simply.

Energy drained out of her. Just as surely as if he'd taken a pin to a bubble, he'd burst her, and now she was deflating like so much hot air. How had he found out about the lost stones? Those jewels were her greatest hope, her legacy.

"I thought you were being honest," he chided.

"I am."

"Doubtful."

She eyed him suspiciously. "What do you know?"

"Everything in the precinct's cold-case files about Gem O'Shea's death. The carriage was probably sabotaged. She was killed. When they brought her from the river, she was only wearing a few diamonds, but she was reputed to have an extensive collection at home. No one ever found it."

"That was the family myth at our house," she conceded. After pausing to consider her options, she told him about Granny Fiona's stories. "My mom, Erin…she owns a beauty shop," she continued in a non sequitur. "She always told me they were tall tales."

That explained the fancy haircut, he thought. "But you don't think so?"

"If the jewels existed, I'm sure someone found them a long time ago. The idea that they've been hidden for years, untouched, is ridiculous. It's like Captain Kidd's treasure. Or Atlantis."

His voice lowered an octave, and if it wasn't for the

thread of challenge underscoring their words, she'd have taken the tone as seductive. "And your husband?"

Whatever his sources of information, they were good. "He's a college teacher, and he spends his spare time looking for antiquities, but…"

"He didn't share your ideas?"

She shook her head. "Like my mother, he just thought they were tall tales."

Dario looked formidable. "You think they're in the house."

Her gut and something in the man's eyes said honesty would benefit her, but she held back again. "What makes you say that?"

"Instincts and…"

When he held up a paper, her jaw dropped. It was the letter she'd withheld from Luther. It had been in her purse, which had been on her shoulder, which… "How did you…?"

"I spent my rookie years arresting pickpockets on the subway. I learned a few tricks."

"I'll say," she managed warily, her mind racing back to the kiss, unwanted heat spiraling through her limbs like a rope of fire. While he'd been kissing her, the man had actually taken the purse from her shoulder, searched it, found the letter, taken it out and read it. "What do you do? Moonlight as a magician?"

"Clowns. Mimes. You name it."

"You read that over my shoulder?" *While you were kissing me?*

"Yeah."

"And you think *I'm* duplicitous?"

"We'll call it evenly matched."

In more ways than one. She was sure that's what he was thinking. She was nearly as tall as he, and last night, as they'd lain in bed, skin to skin, they'd touched at all points.

As his eyes dropped down, scutinizing her dress, she instinctively sucked in her tummy, bringing a smile to his lips. Quickly, she relaxed, hardly wanting him to think she was preening. Still, no man had ever looked at her in quite this way. Moments ago, when he'd first seen her, she was sure he was going to simply grab her, force her to the floor, and start making love to her. Those dark eyes seemed almost haunted, hungry to the point of ravenous, as if he could devour her in a heartbeat. Earlier, he'd asked if she wanted him to huff, puff and blow down the door. Now, in the red dress, she felt like Little Red Riding Hood being eyed by the Big Bad Wolf.

His voice was husky. "Maybe we can make a deal."

Warning lights flashed through her system, but everything about this man made her want to ignore them—his looks, his scent, his greedy look of desire that said he was going to take her clothes off. "A deal?"

"You want inside the house, right?"

She was desperate to search for the jewels. "Yeah."

"And my dad wants the deed to the building. Whether it belongs to my family or not, the fact remains that we've managed the property for generations."

"True," she said, now speaking more cautiously, wondering where he was headed with all this, and suddenly glad he knew nothing about her meeting with Chuckie Haswell.

"We deserve to profit when it's sold," he continued.

As much as she didn't want to admit it, he had a point, and probably Judge Zhang was going to conclude that, as well. She'd hoped everything would be awarded to her, of course, but more realistically, she'd expected proceeds from a sale would wind up being split among all parties with claims. "Maybe," she conceded in a noncommital tone.

"If you were able to find the jewels, would you give up your claim on the house itself?"

Her heart skipped a beat. Was he really implying a trade?

Don't be rash, she coached herself. *Feel him out completely.* "You mean, you'd let me search for the jewels, and if I find them, I get to keep them? And your dad gets the building?"

He shrugged powerful shoulders that made her want to ask if he'd ever played football. "Why not?"

She had to be careful. "And your dad would approve this?"

"Why involve him? He just wants the building."

She'd rushed into her marriage with Johnny Case, and it had come to the worst kind of end, making her distrust her gut. Nevertheless, right now her gut was screaming yes. "If I found the jewels, and they were everything they're cracked up to be, I don't see a problem. From various sources, I've found some descriptions, not the least of which is the picture of Gem in the Centuries of Sex Museum. There were emeralds, diamonds, rubies…"

"I can go you one better."

Her heart was beating a fast tattoo now, and it had very little to do with the fact that the world's best-looking man was standing a mere foot away. "Meaning?"

He smiled, his teeth glistening. "I have an inventory list."

It was too good to be true. "What?"

"Dated 1889, the year before Gem O'Shea died. It was filed with the police, in case of theft, and later wound up in the cold-case file, which is in my possession."

"And I can see it?"

"It depends."

"On what?"

"On whether you want to make the deal."

She wanted to twist and shout, jump up and down with joy, then fling herself into his arms, wrap her legs around his waist and scream with happiness. Instead she stayed stock still. Slowly, she said, "If I really find all the jewels that are listed in the various sources," she began, "including the inventory list, then yes. I'll give up my claim to the property."

She blew out a stunned sigh at how wonderfully well this could work out, as long as Chuckie Hawell didn't step in and ruin things. Silently, she cursed herself for trying to work with him. Apparently, she should have called Dario Donato. "I get the jewels," she continued, mulling it over. "You get the house. That seems fair."

"Almost."

Already in her mind's eye, she was taking apart the place. She'd have to get a crowbar, and some other equipment. Thankfully, Johnny Case had taught her one worthwhile skill: how to dig for artifacts. Now her heart stuttered. "Almost?"

"There's a hitch."

She should have known the offer was too good to be true. "What?"

"When will you need to be in the house?"

"All the time," she managed. She didn't want to waste a minute. "And...I may do some damage," she warned. "I'll need to look behind walls, in the basement, under floorboards."

"As much renovation as the place has seen over the years, I don't think anyone will notice."

"Like I said, I'm ready to shake on it."

He shook his head, then said one word. "Sex."

She blinked. "Sex?"

He nodded. "You can stay in the house all week, but only on the condition that you'll be my sex slave."

Her lips parted in astonishment. "Are you serious?"

"As a heart attack."

He was giving her one. She considered a very long moment. "Can you define slave?"

"Nothing kinky. I'm just talking about consenting adult

enjoyment. Mine's the only bed at the house with any extra room in it, after all."

He was making this sound so reasonable. "And if I say no?"

"Then no deal."

"Let me get this straight. I have sex with you—"

"All week."

"And in exchange, I get to use your case files and search for the jewels."

"If you're nice, I might even help you look."

At some point, heat had begun flooding her whole system. Like a lightning bolt, it sizzled at one spot, then electrified her entire bloodstream. She tried to tell herself the jewels were calling her, not the man. "I don't get involved," she warned diplomatically.

"Me, neither. Confirmed bachelor. My mother's been trying to marry me off for years."

"Seriously?" she asked. "Because I hate men." As if he hadn't gotten the point, she clarified, "I mean, I really hate them."

"I could tell last night," he said drily.

"I've…decided to be alone. But this is just sex for a week, then it's over."

"Is that a yes?"

"Yes." Suddenly, her knees felt weak. "Let me get my stuff," she managed, as if all this was the most natural thing in the world. "It will just take me a minute."

"There's one more problem," he said.

When she looked at him again, his gorgeous dark eyes had settled on the bed. The room seemed dimmer now, but only because night had fallen. Moonlight was streaming into the room, through the windows.

"What's that?" she asked, her voice a husky whisper.

"The sex starts now," he said.

8

THE SEX STARTS NOW? Was he kidding? "Just like that?"

He nodded, and she watched as if mesmerized when he reached across the bar. As one of his huge, dry hands glided over the back of hers, she studied it, liking the size of it, the squarish fingers, the veins that hinted at the corded forearms that had wrapped around her last night. A thumb tucked beneath hers, and as he began rubbing a hollow in her palm, he said in a throaty rumble, "Yeah. Just like that, Cassidy Case."

Inhaling sharply, she darted her eyes around the room, realizing once more that it looked tailor-made for a sexual encounter. The lights were dim, and wide windows framed a gorgeous white-yellow full moon. The mood between them had shifted, becoming calmer. It felt like the hush before a storm, a lull on a darkening sea before gusts of gale wind.

Catching the direction of her gaze, he murmured, "Something sure put a smile on his face."

She took in the moon. "Wasn't me."

"Good. I'd hate to be jealous of the man in the moon."

She couldn't help but smile. "You're crazy."

"As a fox."

In the last moment, everything seemed to have turned on a dime. One minute, they were sparring like sworn enemies;

the next, they were people who'd already spent a night together. In the ensuing silence, something unwanted tugged at her throat, making it hard to swallow.

She reminded herself that this was just fun and games, leading nowhere significant, and yet she wondered how it would feel to make a man like him jealous. It didn't seem like an emotion he'd be inclined to feel. He was too cavalier. Easy come, easy go. He made her think of words such as ambivalence and nonchalance. Everything about him—from the heavy-lidded sexually charged gaze, to the lithe, predatory movements of his to-die-for body—screamed that he was born to satisfy many women but to stay unattached, himself.

Below the window, in the deepening twilight, carriages were still circling, carrying lovers, and she could hear the far-off clip-clop of the hooves. Time seemed to stand still. While much of the city had changed, her and Dario's ancestors would have traveled many of the streets that existed today, she realized. Had they taken walks in Central Park? Maybe together? "Gem was riding in a carriage just like that," she found herself murmuring, thinking of the woman's untimely death as she nodded toward the window. Somehow, it was as if the past and present were merging.

"What?"

"The carriages," she clarified. "Outside. Can't you hear them?"

Tilting his head, he listened, then nodded. "Variations," he said after a moment.

Was he making an implied comparison of her to Gem, and to Gem's many lovers? Her heart jump-started, beating double time, feeling almost painful now, as if it might burst out of her chest. Excitement sparked, leaping inside her, the raw energy flickering wildly like a flame in wind. "Variations on last night?" she managed. "Is that a lead-in to whatever you're going to ask me to do?"

He smiled. "Is your mind running wild with ideas about what being my sex slave might entail?"

She eyed him. "I think I can…vary things."

"I'll bet you can."

Already, she was taking in his open jean jacket and a tight shirt beneath that wasn't going to be hugging his perfect pecs for long. The tuft of black hair visible at his collar caught stray rays from the dim light and glistened. With him right in front of her, it was a lot easier to admit she'd been fantasizing about him all day. What woman wouldn't have done so? Was she really going to share a bed with this man all week?

His soft chuckle pulled her eyes to his face again. He was turned away from the light, so shadows fell over sculpted cheekbones, and the irises of his eyes looked almost black. Faint stubble coated his jaw.

"Did I say something funny?" she asked.

"I was talking about the music." The voice was lazy, as if to say they had all night to talk, but the glint in his eyes said he was thinking of other activities. "Pieces like this are called variations. The composer takes a handful of notes, then rearranges them. If he's good, he can do it for hours. Beethoven's are generally said to be the best, I think."

His thumb was still rubbing deep circles into her palm, turning her insides to mush. Now he reversed the movement, going counterclockwise. When he stopped, the thick pad of his thumb was at high noon, and when she spoke, her voice came out as a faint rasp. "Are you one of the best?"

"Depends on what I'm composing."

"Are we about to do something symphonic?"

"I'll throw in some ballerinas. Maybe a few horses and carriages for the stage."

"You're quick with answers."

"Comes from a lifetime spent getting myself out of hot water."

"I doubt water's the only thing you've found yourself in that was too hot."

"You're quick on your feet, yourself."

"My only talent."

"I doubt it."

"Maybe you're right. I must be a mind reader, because from the first, I had you pegged for the kind of guy prone to get a backside pumped full of some angry daddy's buckshot."

"Not much buckshot in the city, but I've climbed out my share of windows and down a few fire escapes."

She considered, vaguely wondering if she was putting off the moment they'd undress and get back into bed. Was she gun shy? Or building anticipation? "I thought you were a cop. How'd you wind up becoming such an expert on Beethoven's variations?"

"Don't tell me you buy into stereotypes about cops."

"I guess I do. You don't look like a classical-music buff."

"What's a classical-music buff look like?"

"Luther Matthews."

That made him smile. "And what do I look like?"

"The kind of guy who asks women to be sex slaves."

He laughed, and she decided she liked the sound. It was muted, but somehow full-bodied, coming from his chest, then catching in the back of his throat. "I only asked one."

"I feel special."

"Music appreciation," he said, his laughter becoming a muted chuckle. His thumb moved more deliberately now, and she sighed as it stretched from the hollow of her palm all the way down to the pulse point at a wrist she'd dabbed with perfume. "In college, it was a requirement."

So, he'd gone to college. The way he was rubbing her wrist was actually starting to relax her, making her feel freer to express her curiosity. "Did you have a major?"

"Besides wine, women and song?"

"You majored in debauchery?"

"Prelaw. I became a cop instead of a lawyer. You?"

"Special two-year school to study jewels. No music-appreciation courses."

"So, you know jewelry?"

"Don't worry," she returned, her eyes narrowing with pleasure as he continued caressing her wrist. "We've already established that you're never buying me an engagement ring. And in that case, I'll never be in a position to scrutinize it for the three *C*s."

"Three *C*s?"

"Carat, clarity and color."

"You learn something new every day. And it's never too late to learn about music," he offered, his fingers twining through hers. Lifting her hand from the bar, he urged her around it, and her feet seemed to move of their own accord. She felt languid, her limbs propelling her as if by magic. As she neared, he raised her hand another notch, guiding her into a graceful turn that made her dress swirl around her knees.

"You dance, too?"

"Waltz, foxtrot, tango, you name it," he assured, although she didn't believe a word. He tilted his head slightly, as if to better survey her. "But only when the woman's undressed."

"Were you always like this?"

"Like what?"

She considered. He was a type she'd met before. Flirtatious but commitment shy. If he wasn't so sexy, she might be offended by it, especially since she'd never forgiven Johnny Case for his infidelity. As much as she hated to admit it, her anger had become generalized, extending from Johnny to most men. It hadn't helped that her mother still liked Johnny. Even now, Erin Magee thought Cassidy and Johnny were destined to get back together. Finally Cassidy said, "Always after sex."

"Only since birth."

"Ever been married?"

A mock grimace lit up his eyes, making them gleam like black diamonds. "Of course not. But even the best of us can get trapped," he said sympathetically.

"I have my excuses," she defended.

"Namely?"

"Youth and stupidity."

"You're obviously not stupid." He paused. "But you are ancient."

"Twenty-seven."

He chuckled. "I hope we're having sex in the dark."

"I know," she teased, trying not to be alarmed at how much she was enjoying his company. "That way, you won't have to notice my wrinkles and cottage-cheese butt."

His smile really was a draw. Sexy and suggestive without being sleazy. "I swear I'll shut my eyes."

She was standing right in front of him, so close that their bellies almost brushed when she laughed. He had a decent sense of humor. "Why do I think you're lying?"

"Because I am."

"It would be hard for women not to like you."

"They say I'm fun, but not the kind a girl can marry."

"Perfect."

His fingers had twined, dangling by her thigh, but now he disengaged them. His eyes locked with hers, looking serious now, and he began grazing her leg with the curled ends of his fingers. Her heart seemed to be beating in her ears, and yet, at the same time, everything seemed so quiet that she felt the urge to scream. Or…

Take off my dress, she suddenly thought. Inside her, pent-up energy was clamoring for release; she needed something more to happen soon. The fingers crawling on her thigh were raising her dress hem, making her every last nerve jangle in a cacophonic sound that only she could hear, like bells clanging all at once.

"We don't even know each other," she whispered.

His slow smile was as tempting as the devil. It lifted the corners of his lips and perfect teeth gleamed in the near dark. "But you'll never be able to search my house unless you do as I say."

"My house," she murmured.

He shrugged. "Anyway, that's part of the thrill, isn't it?"

"What?"

"Not knowing each other."

"Should we promise not to talk?"

"Too late. You already know my college major."

"A deep, dark secret."

"It was. Usually I tell people I got my degree by sleeping with the dean."

"I promise not to tell and ruin your reputation. But we could stop divulging anything personal now."

"To make things more mysterious?" He studied her another moment, his gaze flickering downward, lingering on the low-cut V of her dress.

She nodded.

Just as she considered reaching for his hand and placing it on her breast, her nipples constricted beneath the cloth. Uttering a ragged sigh, he splayed his free hand on her chest, the heel of the palm landing in her cleavage, the wide span of fingers bridging her breasts, just inches from the erect tips.

"To excite ourselves," he pressed.

"Yeah."

"But there may be personal details I need to know."

"Like what?"

"Like…" Sliding his hand upward, he curled the fingers around her neck and massaged the slender column, tilting her head backwards. Knowing she was probably certifiable, she let it drop into the cradle of her shoulders, and she reveled in the sensations as he stroked more of those maddening circles beneath her ear, then on the lobe. As he charted a course from her jawbone to her chin, she shut her eyes in bliss.

"Relax," he whispered.

"I am relaxed."

"No, you're not, but you're getting there."

"Don't stop."

The whisper was suddenly beside her ear, his breath deliciously tantalizing on her skin. A shiver claimed her when the spear of his tongue dipped, dampening her ear lobe. "I haven't even started yet."

"Then start."

"Sure you're ready?"

"No."

"Ready or not, here I come."

As the thumb skimmed the hump of her chin and found her mouth, the remaining breath squeezed from her lungs. The pad probed, the nail traced, and just as she parted her lips to better let him explore, he tilted his pelvis, so their hips locked. He was getting hard. And warm…superwarm. His belly was moving with hers, their breathing in synch. Her breasts were cushioning against the wall of his chest, which was so hard it could have been made of granite.

"I didn't think I'd see you again," she managed.

"See," he said with a soft chuckle, sounding pleased, as the thumb lingered at the corner of her mouth. "You're already going mushy on me." He toyed with her lower lip until she could feel it swell, begging for a kiss. "But you wanted to?"

She shut her mouth long enough to swallow. Or at least she tried, but an insurmountable lump seemed to have lodged there. "I thought about calling," she admitted.

"Really?" He sounded pleased.

"Only for sex," she assured.

"So, you thought about me today?" he probed, the thumb pressing inside her mouth now. It wedged under her tongue and against the backs of her bottom teeth.

She whispered around it. "I had sex with a stranger. It would be weird if I hadn't thought about it."

For a moment, he said nothing, but merely glided his thumb around her lower teeth, teasing the gums. She suckled as he drew swirls on the inside of her cheek, and her hands drifted down, splaying on the sides of his legs. When she rubbed, his muscles flexed, and his hips tilted again, thrusting upward this time, making her heart stutter, as his erection probed in the folds of her dress. "Yummy," she whispered.

"Exactly what did you do when you were thinking about me today? Touch yourself…"

"Yes…"

Pulling his thumb from between her lips, he slid it under the inbuilt cup of her dress, cradled a breast and applied moisture to the aching nipple. His voice caught. "Here?"

She nodded as her hands circled his hips, then molded

over a tight behind, using it to pull him nearer as she arched. He rolled the nipple between a finger and thumb, slowly working it until her breath quickened, then his other hand sandwiched between them. Bringing the dress with it, it rose. Arrowed fingers dived between her legs, causing her to inhale sharply as he stroked. "Here?" The voice was edgier. "Did you touch yourself here?"

Gasping, she parted her legs, the spikes of the stilettos leaving the plush carpet. The backs of her thighs hit the bar, and she wished the counter were higher, so she could better brace herself. "Yes," she whispered raggedly.

He was inside the thong now, his fingers curving over her pubis, dragging through curls. He cupped her, rocking his palm, then he undulated his hand until she was shamelessly bucking. A stiff finger rimmed her opening, gathering moisture, and she buried a wet cry against his shoulder, tonguing his glowing skin. He muttered something guttural and senseless in return, then pushed a finger in, opening her. For a moment, neither of them moved. Her heart was pounding wildly against her ribs, the blood rushing in her ears.

Withdrawing the finger, he twisted his fist, soliciting whimpers. She melted as another finger joined the first and thrust together, feeling impossibly thick, filling her and making her long for his penis. Leaning over the bar, to better take the pleasure, she tasted the salty flavor of his skin, telling herself not to forget this would never mean anything more. And that meant she could do anything she wished.

Urgently he was strumming her, using a love-slick finger to flick her clitoris, and her hands pushed the jacket off his shoulders, dragging it down his arms. His T-shirt followed. He groaned as she burrowed her hands in his chest hairs, using her nails as she strained for her orgasm. "I want to touch you everywhere," she muttered.

"You have all week."

She'd explore every inch of his body. "You're just the kind of guy I'll enjoy bringing to his knees."

"Do I hear revenge?"

Maybe. For Johnny Case. For all the men she'd ever met who were this gorgeous, but who couldn't be caught. She arched to meet those magic fingers once more, shutting her eyes and swirling in dark sensations, as she said the word aloud. "Maybe."

"Go ahead. Take it out on me," he murmured, his joined fingers pushing deeper, pushing her to the edge. "Hurt me. I really want to see you try."

Suddenly, she cried out, the orgasm quick and shattering. Her hands flew to his biceps and squeezed. She realized his skin was damp now. He'd broken a sweat, and all she could think about was the basket of condoms. She curled fingers over the waistband of his jeans and unsnapped them.

As she reached for the zipper, his shudder and the flex of his hips rerouted her course, and she fondled him through the denim, his moan like music as she pressed her hand flat against his groin. A hand flattened on her belly, and he urged her to turn around. When she did, his bare chest came flush with her back, and heat flooded her as his erection probed her buttocks.

Sensing what he wanted, she leaned over the bar and found it was just the right height for what he had in mind. As she rested her belly on the cold marble surface and grasped the edge, the chill made her shiver. "Is this what you want your slave to do?"

"Oh, yeah," he said simply, his voice thick with appreciation.

"There are condoms in that basket," she managed, but her breath was shallow. Between her legs, she was throbbing. He was panting, pushing her dress upward on her back, and as she dragged it over her head, she was glad he'd seen her in it. It had been wasted on Chuckie Haswell, but this…

She heard him jerk down his zipper, then step out of his shoes and pants. "Wait right there," he said hoarsely.

As if she was going anywhere. She was shivering all over, not from the coldness of the marble now, but from knowing he was finding the condoms…knowing she was positioned to drive him wild, wearing nothing but a thong, stockings that hugged her upper thighs and stilettos.

She heard the rustle of his bare feet brushing the plush carpet as he returned. A hand settled on her neck, traveling downward with a hot caress that made each vertebrae prickle. Gingerly, he drew the thong down, and one by one, she lifted the stilettos.

"You're gorgeous," he whispered.

He leaned, the laboring pants of breath touching her lower back. Rough stubble of his skin grazed her behind as hot, dry hands reached way down and curved around her ankles, molding her calves, then her thighs. Feeling as smooth as glass, they swept over her backside as he released a ragged groan. Trembling palms urged her thighs apart, and as she parted for him, he edged closer, the burning erection finding her and pushing…

Lifting her gaze, she could see him in the mirror, his jaw slack, his eyes nearly shut in ecstacy. He was leaning away, looking down, both hands on her backside, so he could watch their bodies merge, his breath uncontrollable. He was loving this….

Her fingers tightened on the bar as his hands slid beneath her belly, the splayed fingers meeting near her naval. Suddenly, in tandem with the thrust of his hips, Dario half lifted her, half dragged her to him. Enveloped in deepening sensations, she climbed once more, let herself go as each pounding thrust pushed her nearer to the brink. She was drowning as his body covered hers, the hairs of his chest sweeping her back, his heart pounding near her shoulder, his burning mouth on her cheek. "Dario," she whispered.

Roughly, he pushed hair from her neck, then a looping string of scalding kisses rained down. "That's right," he whispered back hoarsely. "Say my name."

She tried to roll to face him, but his arms caught her, holding her like a vise, and she stilled, powerless to move, trapped by his body, but not caring. "Dario," she whispered again.

Hearing his name seemed to drive him mad with lust. His groin was hotter on her backside, and she could feel each slow stretch of muscle as he went deeper. "I'm going to come," she whispered.

An arm reached down the length of hers, his hand found hers, and he wove their fingers together tightly, then he said, "Now."

Three hard, determined thrusts of his body sent them both tumbling over the edge together. Just as quickly, he urged her to turn to face him, swinging her leg near his shoulder, so their bodies never separated. As soon as they were face-to-face, his mouth fell to hers in a tongue kiss. Her arms circled his neck, and she wrapped her legs around his waist, locking her ankles.

"C'mon," he whispered, after a moment, withdrawing from her body and discretely losing the condom. "Why don't we move? I'd hate to waste that big bed."

"Your call," she replied huskily. "I'm the love slave."

He shook his head, those gorgeous dark eyes just an inch away, studying her. "You turned the tables. I'm yours now."

"I can handle that."

"Can you?"

"Sure." But could she? As he stood, grasped her hand and pulled her toward the bed, her heart skipped a beat. As much as she'd felt determined to search the house, maybe she'd been a fool to agree to this trade-off. Could she really sleep with Dario Donato for a week and come away unscathed? For a second, she realized she'd better call it quits right now.

But then he urged her onto the plush duvet, and she hugged him again. "Since I've turned the tables, and you're my love slave now," she whispered, "there are a few things I'd like for you to do."

"Sit on my lap."

She squinted at the non sequitur. "What?"

"That way you can better give Santa your Christmas list," he said.

And so she did.

9

"WHAT DO YOU MEAN, I can handle the arson case alone for the rest of the week?" Pat asked, using a soda straw to shoot a spit wad across his desk to Dario's.

"Now, that's mature," Dario joked as the wad landed on his cold-case file. Not that he'd been reading the file. All day, he'd been drifting, remembering Cassidy in that bright red dress, imagining the wickedly sexy look in those green eyes, which had glittered like the emeralds she'd once sold in her shop.

Now that he'd talked to her, he felt bad about her losing her business. Everything she'd claimed had checked out this morning, when he'd dug deeper. While he didn't like using his badge to further his personal life—the past month had been unusual—his curiosity about Cassidy was insatiable. Her husband had put her into debt, and she'd had the class to clean up his mess, but it had cost her a business she'd loved. It was a story he'd heard many times on the job.

"Men can be pigs," he muttered.

"Come again. That sounded like girl talk."

"Nothing."

"I heard you, but I don't get it. Did you grow a heart overnight?"

"No. And I'm as lazy as ever. The boss took me off the arson case," Dario reminded, returning to the topic his partner had initiated, his eyes drifting over Pat's spiky red hair and streetwise getup—worn jeans, a fake tattoo and an earring. "Because of my transgressions with Sheila Carella, remember?"

"How could I forget? But you've been anxious to stay involved, and night before last, you came to the scene of a fire."

"Do you have any new leads?"

"No." Pat paused. "Uh…rumor has it, Sheila's marrying Bobby O'Hare."

"I'd offer to be the best man, but you hired me first." Rising to stretch his legs, Dario noted the soreness of his muscles and tried to stifle a smile. He'd gotten a helluva workout last night. Definitely better than what the precinct gym offered.

He glanced through a floor-to-ceiling window. At the other end of Police Plaza, he could see a couple coming from the courthouse, where they'd just been married by a justice of the peace. The woman wore a simple white dress, and the man was carrying her, cradling her against his chest while she clutched a bouquet of roses. Emotions tugged at his heart, not that he wanted to examine them too closely.

Realizing Pat had followed his gaze, he raised an eyebrow inquiringly. Pat said, "Are you…?"

"Broken up about Sheila Carella?" Dario squinted, then laughed. "You're joking, right?"

Pat shrugged. "I heard she called you last night and ended your relationship over the phone…"

"Relationship would be a strong word, no?" Dario returned, giving up on working and tossing his pencil on top of a file about Gem. He'd left the rest at the house this morning for Cassidy. A contact at the public library was faxing over news clippings that Dario's previous research visits had missed, and which he didn't recall seeing during his stop at the Centuries of Sex Museum. According to the librarian, Gem had been coming from a wedding at Saint Andrews church when she'd died, and since the church was still standing, records might be on file, if he checked. At the courthouse, he'd copied the original architect's plan for the building, too, which he'd take home to Cassidy.

Home. As many women as he'd known, Dario had never cohabitated, and strangely, he felt a surge of excitement at the idea. "Gossip sure travels fast in precincts," he commented now, thinking Cassidy was his own little secret. "My mother's sewing circle is tighter lipped."

"Your mother's not in a sewing circle," Pat pointed out.

"Busted again," teased Dario. "It was a figure of speech."

"It's not really a rumor," Pat said uncomfortably. "So, don't worry about people knowing. It's just that, uh…Bobby asked me to say something, to…break the ice between you and him. He thinks you're hurt, so he's making himself scarce today. And Eliana's worried."

Dario wished people would stay out of his private business. He couldn't believe Bobby O'Hare was laying low. "My sister?"

"Yeah. She tried to call you this morning."

"She calls three times a day. I can't wait until she gets married. Maybe she'll start calling her husband."

"I don't know why you're complaining. I answered your phone again, and she talked to me." Pat squinted. "You must have special radar for when she's going to call, because you always manage to step away from your desk."

"Telepathy," assured Dario.

"Your sister's afraid you're going to wake up in about five years and realize…"

"I'm the only bachelor left in America?"

He nodded. "And earlier…when I told you Karen wants you to meet us for dinner, you said you had plans *indefinitely*. I mean, you're always up for dinner or drinks. Last night, you were ready to party hardy, but today, you're…"

Daydreaming about Cassidy. "Trying to turn over a new leaf. The boss wants me on cold cases this week, so I'm on cold cases."

Pat didn't look convinced. "Tell me if you're in danger of doing something stupid, buddy."

"Have I ever done something stupid?"

"When it comes to women?" Pat rolled his eyes. "Only every day of your life."

So, he really believed Dario wasn't licking his wounds over Sheila. "You're engaged a week, so you're giving me advice?"

"Sorry. I deserved that. Look…" Pat paused. "I really am sorry. It's none of my business. But you're my best buddy. My longtime drinking companion. A skirt-chaser extraordinaire. And I've learned a lot from you. Without your moves, Karen never would have agreed to marry me. Now you're going to be the best man at the wedding. So…I just want to make sure you're all right."

"Sheila Carella didn't break my heart," Dario said again.

But after last night, he was starting to think someone else might. In fact, he was half-tempted not to return to 67 Anthony Street tonight. He'd let Cassidy have the whole run of the place this week. Let her search the property to her heart's content. Give her the bed.

But he knew it was a lie. Lust would win. He'd left her a note, with directions about how he expected to find his love slave when he got home—naked, up to her chin in suds in an old claw-footed bathtub in an empty apartment upstairs. On top of the note, he left the upstairs key, condoms and a bottle of bubbles from the Pierre's complimentary gift basket.

All day, he'd been watching the clock, waiting for five o'clock. He felt like a kid waiting for the bell to ring on the last school day before summer vacation. "If you must know, I have a new running partner already."

Tilting his chin downward, Pat stared at Dario from under heavy eyelids. "You're kidding."

"Slept with her last night." To make sure Pat got the picture, he added, "She was there when Sheila called."

Pat's jaw dropped.

"Just so you know."

Looking impressed, Pat said, "I stand corrected."

"I'd offer to bring her to meet you and Karen, but she may not want to get dressed for a while."

"Anybody I know?" Pat covered his eyes. "No, let me guess. It's Sheila's big sister."

"I wouldn't," claimed Dario. "Her name's Cassidy Case. The ancestor of the cold-case murder victim I'm working on."

Pat shook his head. "The person who might be making a claim against your dad's rights to his property on Anthony Street, along with Chuckie Haswell? I thought that was a guy."

"Nope."

"And doesn't this pose a conflict for you and Cassidy?"

"We're hoping we can work it out in bed. You know," Dario said, flashing a smile. "Like Romeo and Juliet. Warring families uniting through love."

Pat guffawed. "You're serious?"

"Why not?"

"Romeo and Juliet died in the end."

Dario clucked his tongue. "I thought Karen had turned you into a romantic."

"Don't you want to try someone who's not so complicated?"

Dario saw a splash of red, the puddle of a dress on the Pierre's toe-squishing carpet, and how Cassidy had looked in the dark, silhouette in the window, backlit by the light of the full moon—her belly curved, her backside perfect, the aroused tips of her breasts tilting upward. He had to suppress a groan. It was four o'clock, which meant that she was preparing herself for his arrival, undressing and wiggling down into the tub, covering herself in bubbles. He imagined the rosy color of her breasts now, hot from the water, and how the suds would just cover her nipples….

"Dario?"

He glanced at Pat. "What?"

"I said, do you ever feel the urge to get involved in a situation that's less complex?"

Thinking once more of how Cassidy had looked last night, with her feverish, creamy skin looking flushed in the moonlight, Dario slowly shook his head. "Absolutely not."

DARIO WAS ALREADY half-hard as he entered 67 Anthony Street an hour later. Anticipation had built all day, and now he was pleased to see the door to the apartment shut. When he jiggled the knob, he found it locked, too. "Cassidy," he whispered. "You're playing the love slave to perfection."

Peeking from beneath the door, a folded note was visible. Smiling, he lifted it, figuring it would contain descriptions of whatever wild, sensual delights were in store for him. But it said: You were not here last night to protect tenants, so we have no choice but to report this to Judge Zhang. Loud music played all night, and we heard constant banging. Sincerely, Brice Jorgensen, on behalf of the tenants' association.

Thankfully, most of the tenants didn't seem to be home from work yet, but Dario could hear muted heavy-metal music coming from across the hallway, which meant Rosie's daughter, Theresa, was home from school. Probably, she'd been the one playing the music. Shoving the papers from the courthouse inside the apartment, he relocked the door and went upstairs, taking the steps two at a time, determined not to let tenants' complaints sour his evening plans.

Knocking lightly, he pushed open the door of the empty upstairs apartment, and once more, felt surprised at the vacancy. The walls were in good shape, the carpet new, and the two rooms were huge; in a city where many people lived in cramped studios, this had been a bargain. "Cassidy?"

No answer.

His disappointment took him by surprise. Suddenly, he realized he hadn't noticed any of her belongings in the downstairs apartment, either. Had she decided to renege on their contract and stay at the Pierre? Should he call? Let it go?

Retracing his steps, he went into the apartment where he was staying, walked the rooms and found a black roller suitcase tucked neatly in a corner, along with the basket they'd brought from the hotel, containing condoms and the bubbles. Which meant she was here somewhere. Feeling more relieved than he wanted to admit, he started at the top of the building, then worked his way down, until he was heading for the basement.

"Cassidy?" he called as he descended a rickety staircase.

A muted reply sounded, then scraping, as if she were dragging debris. Squinting, he made his way downward, into a dim, musty, windowless cave of a room. Something clinked, and he saw a hole where bricks had been removed, and he realized she was inside the wall. "What are you doing?"

"Searching."

As he neared, he could see her belly crawling backward, coming toward him with her delectable backside wiggling.

Steel-toed workman's boots appeared first, then oversize, baggy cargo pants, which he recognized from the closet of the apartment where he'd been staying. She scrambled to her feet, and just as he realized she looked cute as hell, relief flooded him. She hadn't left; she was his all week.

"I forgot," she said, peering down at a dirt-streaked wrist, the gesture of someone used to wearing a watch. Realizing her wrist was bare, she said, "What time is it? I was supposed to take a bath, wasn't I?"

"So you remembered."

"I don't welsh on deals."

His heart soared, and he couldn't help but grin. She was just as interested in their little game as he. She was wearing a matching khaki shirt with the cargo pants, which were hiked nearly beneath her breasts and held up by a piece of clothesline, which she'd used as a belt and tied in a bow. Her wavy hair, which had swept around her shoulders last night, now looked hopelessly tangled. She'd twirled it into something resembling an animal's nest, then skewered the mess with a barrette. Chuckling, he shook his head. "You look like you're on a safari."

She offered a lopsided grin, her green eyes sparkling, reminding him of bright sunlight on the ocean. Bringing a hand to her forehead, as if in mock salute, she made a show of peering around the basement. Finally, her eyes landed on him. "Looks like I just got lucky and caught something wild."

"Keep at it and you might get luckier."

"Then I'll call it a lotto kind of day."

"I won't mind being your jackpot."

She cracked up. "Careful. Or I might paint numbers on your balls."

"Fine by me. As long as you use edible paint." He loved

sparring verbally with her. She was sharp, and didn't act too coy, like a girly-girl. She didn't pretend to be offended by things when she really wasn't. He'd expected her to look a little nervous about what they were doing, but no one could have looked happier. She seemed entirely comfortable. "Being a love slave suits you."

"You, too." She smiled. "I turned the tables last night, remember?"

His eyes drifted over her. Every inch of her was filthy, and a tool belt, complete with screwdrivers and a hammer, was slung around her waist. She was gripping a flashlight.

"You were supposed to be waiting in the bath. Not getting grungy so I'd have to give you one."

"What?" she asked rhetorically, her eyes glinting with humor. She stalked closer, the tool belt clanking, then she poked him playfully with the flashlight. "You were expecting some prissy woman who smells like powder and flowers? You wanted to see me wearing a little apron and high heels while cooking you a big fat steak and potatoes?"

He shook his head, laughing. There was something so offbeat about her, so unpredictable. "Is that so terrible?"

"Uh-huh. Because I'm too busy to cook."

His tongue found his inner cheek and toyed with it. "You were cooking last night, honey."

Her laughter deepened. "Until everything burned."

Him, especially. But he'd never have guessed that the elegant woman he'd had sex with last night could transform into such a street urchin. "Now you look like something out of a Charles Dickens story."

"There you go again," she chided, crossing her arms over her chest in a way that only served to accentuate her breasts. "More high-brow literary references. Are you *sure* you're a cop?"

"We had to read Dickens in high school," he defended, holding up a staying palm. "After that, I swear I only read stock tips and racing forms."

"No porn?"

His eyes bugged. "A little." He paused. "God, you're nosy."

"Do you mind?"

"Not really." He yanked her close. At the contact of their bellies, she inhaled sharply, the sound attesting to what had already happened between them…and to what was about to happen again.

Not that he wasn't going to take his time and wring out every ounce of sweet anticipation. "You're giving me germs," he complained, peppering kisses over her temples.

"So, you don't like rough, working women?" she teased, bursting into a gale of giggles, clearly pleased with her own ridiculous patter. "Dirty women with tools…"

He couldn't stop laughing. "I have my own tools," he assured, tightening his grip around her waist, so she could feel one of them. Heat claimed his groin, and when their chests touched, he could feel her bra. Suddenly, he wanted to see it. Was it white and frilly? Transparent?

"Ah." She leaned back a fraction, something that made their hips lock more snugly as she whipped out the flashlight. Quickly unbuttoning his shirt, she trained the light on his chest. "You say you have your own tools. Let's take a look."

She was being incredibly silly, and he was loving every minute of it. "Not until you're clean," he protested. "I need to wash every inch of you first. Otherwise, I might get some dread disease and die."

"You're so mean," she whispered, staring up at him and batting her eyelashes. For a moment, he drowned in her gaze, taking in things he hadn't noticed before—their slanted, teardrop shape and the tiny flecks of brown in her irises. He was lost to imagination when her hand unexpectedly slid between their bodies and fondled the most intimate part of him. His temperature shot into the stratosphere. "I like how you touch me," he murmured.

"How's that?"

Her hand felt soft, but her grip was firm. Assured. "Like you like it."

Her voice was a soft pant. "I do like it."

A heartbeat later, he was so aroused he knew he couldn't wait another moment. "You're cute as hell," he found himself muttering, his voice oddly slurred as he gazed at her. "Have I told you that yet?"

She quit stroking him. "No. Do you like the outfit?"

"Almost as much as your little red dress."

"Now I know you're lying."

Slowly, he shook his head. He wasn't. No matter what she wore, she looked amazing. Definitely, she was the sexiest woman he'd ever encountered. Leaning a fraction, he curled both hands over her backside, smoothing her cheeks, exploring the crevice where her legs began. Huskily, he said, "Is there a butt anywhere in these baggy pants of yours? I can't seem to find it."

She chuckled, the sound shot through with excitement. "Do you have some kind of butt fetish? Something weird I should know about?"

He brought his lips close to hers, near enough that he could feel her breath. "Cassidy," he whispered, "I have to inform you of something."

Now she was whispering, too. "What?"

"Every man has a butt fetish."

"Oh," she said innocently. "I had no idea."

"Yeah, right." He sucked a breath through clenched teeth as her hand stroked the space over his pant's zipper again.

Using his hand to cover hers, he curled his fingers, a shudder racking his body as he urged her to apply more pressure. "Harder," he whispered.

A shuddering breath left her lips. The muscles of her fingers rippling against him. "Like this, Dario?"

"I like it when you say my name."

"You said so last night."

"Nothing's changed."

"We're still on a first-name basis?"

"Just kiss me," he growled.

"Where?"

He couldn't wait to see her mouth circling him, his hands threading through her hair and pulling her toward his groin. But he said, "On the lips."

She did, gingerly at first, then by nibbling at his mouth. "Hard day at the office?" she asked, playing the attentive homemaker.

"Terrible, sweetheart," he lied gamely.

"You're home now." She unsnapped his jeans. "Time to relax."

Blood was racing through his system. It was just a game, but it felt good. Maybe having a woman around to greet him after work wouldn't be so bad, after all. "Are the kids in bed?" he managed to tease.

"Are you afraid we're about to make too much noise?"

"Absolutely."

"I sent all our children to boarding school," she promised. "They will never return again. Or at least only on vacations. In fact, they're not even in the state of New York. And I think many people want to adopt them, too."

"It sounds like we're really alone."

"We might as well be on the moon," she agreed, pulling down his zipper.

His hand stopped her. "Like I say, I draw the line at dirty girls."

"I thought every guy liked dirty girls."

"Not tonight. I have my standards."

"I see."

Rezipping his pants, he snagged her shirt and nodded toward the stairs. "What say, I wash you off?"

As they started up, her stomach rumbled and he frowned. "Hungry?"

She looked a little guilty, and he did a double take, further considering her outfit. "It must have taken you hours to get that dirty. Did you eat?"

"I forgot."

"You didn't eat anything?"

She shook her head.

Once Cassidy Case set her mind to a task, she went for it, ignoring all distractions. "Look," he suddenly said, pausing at the top of the stairs, "my partner wanted me to go out to dinner, but I said no. Would you feel like meeting him and his fiancée?" The second he'd asked, he wondered if he'd just crossed the line into something too personal. "I mean, it's no big deal," he quickly added. "Just a quick bite."

"Why not?"

He tried to tell himself this would kill two birds with one stone—fulfill an obligation to Pat and get her fed. Still, he had to admit he was curious about how she'd get along with Pat and Karen.

"Only one stipulation," she said, turning and winding up in his arms.

Her mouth was close. Before she could continue, he bent and kissed her again, and he was pleased to find that her response was immediate. As soft as pillows, her lips crushed under his, remolding to the contours of his mouth, and the dark heat of her tongue pressed between his lips like a tiny blazing sword. When she drew away, she said, "If I'm meeting people, you'd better get me extra clean. I'd hate to make a bad impression."

"They say my tongue works better than bleach," he promised.

"You're on."

Stopping in the first-floor apartment, he grabbed condoms, the soap bubbles and two towels, silently thanking his sister once more for suggesting he bring them. Looping one around Cassidy's waist, he used it to lead her farther upstairs. A jolt of arousal shot through him as they entered the empty apartment and he locked the door behind them. The dead bolt clicked, sounding definitive, as if it were sealing their fate. By the time he turned around, she'd already located the bathroom and started running water. As he entered the room, she finished squirting in bubbles. Then she stood and turned toward him.

"Strip for me," he commanded simply.

She considered a second, then hummed the age-old stripper's song in an off-key tone that made him chuckle once more. He watched as she took a screwdriver from the tool belt. After twirling it before him as if it were a tiny scrap of panty, she tossed it to the floor with a loud clank.

"Sexy," he said, still laughing despite the fact that his voice was straining with need. Stepping forward quickly, he ran both hands into her hair. "Anything living in this nest?"

"Such as?"

He shrugged. "Small birds. Squirrels maybe."

She shook her head. "Only a field mouse."

"Let's see if I can't find him."

"For a city boy, you sure know a lot about critters."

He made a show of leaning and snorting animal sounds against her neck, until she was giggling once more, then he poked his fingers into her upswept hair, as if checking for the mouse. Finally, he unclipped the barrette and set it on the lip of the sink. A mass of red waves fell, untwining from a knot and cascading over her shoulder. His eyes roved over the tendrils now framing her face.

"Da-da," she whispered, kicking off her boots and unbuckling the tool belt, letting it fall to the floor.

For a minute, he could only stare at her. Lifting a hand, he used a finger to swipe away the mud streak that zigzagged across her cheek. She was stunning, he decided. Absolutely beautiful. Her skin was so creamy, the color of something a cat might lap up. "Cassie," he whispered.

Her lips parted with emotion he'd couldn't readily interpret. "You already have a nickname for me?"

"Do you mind?"

She shook her head, but he could see the play of confused emotion in her eyes. Already, they were going deeper than she'd bargained for, but secretly she wanted it. She wasn't going to fight. He tried to smile, to think of something to say to keep up their banter, but he couldn't. The tub was getting dangerously full now, the bubbles threatening to overflow. Unable to stand the tension any longer, he lithely leaned. In a swift motion, he tucked an arm behind her knees, then lifted her, cradling her against his chest. As she squealed, the mood broke, and he deposited her into the suds, clothes and all. She sputtered, "You're crazy!"

Quickly stripping, he kicked off his shoes. For a second, he merely stood there before her, giving her time to look her fill. When she did, her green eyes seemed to darken, turning hot and hungry. Slender fingers slipped over the lip of the tub and curled around it, as if she needed to brace herself.

Seeing that the perfectly shaped nails were still bloodred made him feel like a bull behind a starting gate. Splashing, he followed her into the water, positioned himself between her legs, then began unbuttoning her shirt. "If I'm crazy, you're making me that way," he defended, slipping the drenched shirt off her shoulders.

"Let's push the envelope," she whispered.

His breath caught when he found the bra was more serviceable than sexy. Except that it was black and made with wires that pushed upward, enhancing her cleavage. Just looking, he felt his erection flex against her slippery thigh. In his mind's eye, he was rising on his knees, bracing them on either side of her. Already aroused beyond the point of return, he imagined thrusting his hips, gliding into that deep cleavage. Her flesh would fold around him, creating a scalding hot, slippery tunnel.

He was still eyeing the bra. "I think you're cleaner with that on," he whispered.

She chuckled as he edged into her arms. His hands sloshed under the suds, fumbling with her zipper. "You want my pants on, too?"

"No way."

As he moved against her, waves of heat coursed through him, and sweat broke out, tingling on his skin, making it feel even hotter than the water. The cargo pants rolled down suds-coated thighs that felt silkier than they had last night.

"You'd better hurry," she cautioned, panting now. "Because I'm starved, Dario."

His eyes landed squarely on hers. Only now did he unhook the front catch of her bra. Bracing himself with one hand, he pushed aside the cups, the vision of her nude body making his heart do wild flip-flops. An open palm glided over her slick skin and wiped away thick white bubbles obscuring her nipples. "So am I," he managed. "And after I have my dinner, you can have yours, Cassidy."

With that, his ravenous mouth descended.

10

IN THE DREAM, Gem O'Shea was screaming, pressing her hands against the side of the carriage, looking behind her as if someone was there. Who? As Cassidy drifted, images jumbled, probably because she and Dario had lain in bed earlier, reading the files. They'd stopped only when tenants had come by to complain about last night's noise. Now Cassidy heard hooves pounding, and saw a road illuminated by gas lamps hanging suspended from iron stands. Suddenly, the horses reared; the carriage began rattling, its nearly disengaged wheel clattering, and it plunged over the bank, splashing into forbidding waters that churned furiously.

Suddenly, the scene shifted and Cassidy was nervously entering the Chinese restaurant where she and Dario had eaten with Karen and Pat tonight, then she was joking with his best friends, amazed that they were hitting it off. Karen was apparently best friends with Eliana, and Cassidy suspected she'd like Dario's sister, as well. She'd had no idea how to use chopsticks—the only Chinese restaurant in her hometown served with forks—and everyone had pitched in to teach her.

"Don't wear panties tonight," Dario had said as she'd discarded a pair of jeans and decided on a dress to wear while they were preparing to leave.

"No panties?"

"Please," he'd whispered.

"Are you prepared to beg?"

"On my knees."

She hadn't made Dario do so, but she hadn't worn any panties, either. Completely naked beneath a green silk shirt dress, she'd thrilled at the way the night air had felt, then at how easily Dario's had surreptitiously caressed her as they'd enjoyed dinner. All night, Cassidy had wondered what was happening between her and this man. Should she embrace feelings that already threatened to become more than the sexual encounter they'd agreed to share? Or run?

Karen and Pat's company had been an impediment to love-making, and it had left Cassidy chomping at the bit. To offset the feelings, she'd tried to tell herself she was only using Dario, so she could search the house, and also because she needed to do something wild, to get her feet wet after the divorce. Dario was going to keep peeling back layers, just the way he stripped off her clothes, to reveal dangerous potential she'd never guessed she had, a vein of sensual gold only he could tap.

On the way back to Anthony Street, they'd walked hand-in-hand through winding streets of Chinatown. Crowds had surrounded them, jostling and pushing them into each other's arms. He'd bought a fruit she'd never heard of from a vendor, then he'd fed it to her. Tossing away the seed, he'd hauled her into an alleyway and licked juice from her lips until they were both shivering with need.

They'd barely made it inside the apartment before they were tearing off each other's clothes. After unbuttoning her dress, he'd backed her against the door, lifting her into his arms. As their mouths met, her legs had circled his waist, and a second later, he was inside her, his jeans still on, unzipped and pushed down on his hips.

Relief had consumed her from the second they joined. He went deeper than before, the brute power of his thighs propelling him, and her pulse jagged. The demanding thrusts effected her like a catapult, shooting her to brand new heights. The next thing she knew, she was weightless and breathless, flying off a cliff.

Afterward, they'd read the files before making love again in the lumpy bed. It wasn't the Pierre hotel, but they hadn't minded. Now something niggled at her consciousness. Sighing, she tried to roll, then realized he was behind her, his breath a rumble—not quite a snore—his body warm. They'd sunk into a groove in the center of the mattress, and his chest was spooned comfortably against her back, his legs tucked so that his knees locked into hers.

Suddenly, her eyelids fluttered. They batted like wings, then opened on the dark room. Grasping the hand that had settled on her waist, she pushed it aside, along with the covers, struggling upright. "That music," she whispered. Placing a flattened palm on his hip, she shook him. From somewhere far off, a piano was pounding out dance hall music. People were hooting, shouting and clapping, stomping their feet, and tap shoes jangled in tandem, as if women were doing the cancan.

"Dario," she whispered.

He awakened as she had, abruptly sitting, his hand reaching instinctively over her and under the bed. When she realized he'd grabbed his gun, her heart stuttered. Even in the dark, when she wrenched around, she could see that he looked startled. "What's wrong?" he whispered groggily. "Are you okay, sweetheart?"

Maybe under other circumstances, she would have noticed the chiseled contours of his naked body, or the fact that he'd called her sweetheart. Just days ago, she'd been convinced no man would ever call her that again. But she was too intent on the sounds. Her heart was beating out of control, and she was rapidly blinking her eyes, hoping they'd further adjust as she reached for the light.

His hand stayed hers. "Wait," he insisted, grabbing his cell phone and flipping it open.

"What time is it?"

"Two in the morning."

No wonder she felt so tired. "This is what the tenants said they heard last night while we were at the Pierre," she continued in a hushed voice. "This music was playing night before last, too."

"I thought you brought it."

She squinted in the dark. "Why would I do that?"

"I thought you brought a boom box or something," he clarified. "Because you were pretending to be Gem O'Shea."

"You thought *Sheila* brought a boom box."

"You really didn't bring it?"

"No. Even if I had, that wouldn't explain this."

"Did you change my phone ringer?"

"No." She paused. "Could you put away the gun? It's making me nervous. Besides, since we're ghostbusting, bullets will go right through our prey."

He made no move to replace the gun, but got up as silently as a panther. Rustling jeans from the floor, he pulled them on, shoved his feet into shoes, then the gun into the waistband and said, "Don't worry, I know how to use my gun."

"Are you sure?"

He stalked close and whispered in her ear, making her skin tingle with pleasure. "I'm a man."

"Oh, please," she muttered.

"And I'm a cop," he added.

"Don't all you guys take graft?"

"Only in movies. Besides, such activities would only enhance my competency with weapons. Now, stay here."

Instead, she hopped out of bed, ignoring the flattened palm that landed on her chest and tried to push her onto the mattress again. As she fumbled for her clothes, she realized the volume of the sound was increasing. "It's chilly in here, too," she said, the cold making her teeth chatter and her nipples ache. Goose pimples broke out on her arms.

"Right. So get back under the covers. I ordered a new boiler today. By tomorrow night, we'll have heat."

It was the wrong time to figure out that three days had passed. Were she and Dario going to spend only four more nights together, before their fantasy week was over? It didn't seem like enough time.

"It's hard to tell where the music's coming from." She craned her neck. "Probably we'll get a better idea in the hallway."

"Exactly. So, like I said, do me a favor and stay in bed."

"Maybe *you're* still in bed," she returned, stepping into the jeans she'd almost worn to dinner. "Because you're obviously still dreaming. I'm not staying in here alone, listening to this racket."

As she pulled on a T-shirt, his hand curled over her shoulder, this time applying pressure. "It's probably just Theresa, the teenager across the hall. Maybe she's playing a prank."

"To make it seem like the house is haunted?" The idea calmed Cassidy's nerves. It was definitely better than the alternative. "The music sounds real," she whispered.

"It is real. There are no such thing as ghosts," he assured, heading toward the door. "Don't tell me you believe in them."

"You're starting to sound like my mother." Erin Magee had never believed in the stories about Gem. Tonight, the material Cassidy and Dario had read had jump-started Cassidy's mental juices, though, and now they were flowing faster than a river in a storm. For years, tenants had heard music that seemed to have no source, and some claimed to have seen scantily dressed, transparent girls float through the hallways. A shudder zipped down Cassidy's spine. Sidling close behind Dario, she hooked a finger over the waistband of his jeans. "If there are no ghosts, then I'll be perfectly safe."

"Unless there are bad people," he pointed out.

"Oh, yeah," she teased as they crept into the hallway together. "Carmella definitely looked like a serial killer. And Zu and Ling are probably with the mob."

"And Brice?"

"A crime of bad taste," Cassidy continued, further lowering her voice. "Mismatched socks. One black, one brown."

"That deserves capital punishment."

"But we should let him off. Rosie might be able to rehabilitate him."

"If she would. You think he's got a thing for her?"

"Yeah. Judging by how he was acting earlier, when they all stopped by."

"I thought so, too," said Dario. Reaching an arm behind him as if to shield her, he pushed open the door and inched into the hallway, his weapon drawn. As they crept toward the staircase leading to the second floor, the music seemed increasingly muted. "That's weird," he whispered when they reached the landing.

"Yeah," she agreed, glancing over her shoulder, toward their half-open apartment door. "Out here, you can't hear anything."

"The music's fainter."

"But the others hear it sometimes."

"It's coming from inside the walls."

Turning, she pivoted and headed for their apartment again. This time, he didn't stop her when she turned on the lamps. Blinking as she glanced around, she took in the high ceilings and unevenly plastered walls of the cavernous rooms. Pressing her ear to the wall, she skimmed the surface with her hands, feeling vibrations. "It's definitely in the wall," she agreed.

As if sensing there was no imminent danger from which he'd need to protect her, Dario relaxed. Despite the circumstances, she couldn't help but notice that sleep had done wonders for him, tousling dark waves of his hair so that they fell in rakish hanks over his forehead and chiseled cheekbones. His eyes were seductive midnight slits, reminding her of how they looked half-shut in ecstasy, and his chest was bare, his jeans unsnapped. Jet hair tangled between his pecs then arrowed downward, kissing the gun still tucked in his waistband.

"Really," she said. "Put the gun away."

Yawning, he shrugged, put it under the bed again, then came behind her, putting his ear to the wall. Making a fist, he began rapping on plaster as he moved toward the kitchen. Casually, he stroked her side, as if it was the most natural thing in the world. It was as if their physical relationship had gone on for years, rather than days.

He said, "Would you mind getting me the crowbar?"

She'd bought one today, just in case she needed to pry up floorboards. "Sure."

By the time she returned, he was inside a walk-in closet. "Here," she said, following him inside and ducking, but not before she rattled empty clothes hangers overhead. Reaching, she pulled a bubble cord, and a bald bulb snapped on.

Edging closer, she couldn't help but glide a hand over his back as she handed him the tool. He was tanned a deep bronze color from the summer sun, and skin that was as smooth as glass seemed to flow beneath her fingers. Still feeling warm from bed, he turned and circled his hands around her waist, drawing her flush against him.

"We have a ghostbusting mission to complete," she reminded, tilting her head toward the wall.

His slow smile was dazzling, the tilt of his lips endearingly ironical. He swayed to the music. "You haunt me."

"Not as much as your tenants will if you don't find the source of the noise."

"My dad's tenants," he corrected in a sexy murmur, kissing her. The kiss tasted luscious, and his arms wrapped around her were as warm as a wool blanket on a snowy day. For a second, she felt as secure as she had as a kid, and in a flash fantasy, she remembered how she'd come inside from playing in the snow. Granny Fiona would peel wet gloves from Cassidy's frozen fingers, then put them over the heater vent to dry and wrap her in home-knitted afghans.

Her lips broadened into a smile beneath Dario's, and he smiled back. "What's so funny?" he whispered, leaning away.

"Nothing. You feel warm."

"Only because you're used to dating ice men."

"Are we dating?"

"Sort of. We're standing in a closet, anyway."

"It's the next best thing to Aruba," she agreed.

"And that music's still blaring."

"Very romantic."

"Sexy," he corrected. "That's what we're doing here, remember?"

His free fingers traced her waist when he turned away,

as if to say they'd rather linger on her skin. With his other hand, he tapped the crowbar against the back of the closet. "It's hollow. There's nothing back there."

"Take it out."

Before she'd finished speaking, he'd banged the bar against the plaster. A hunk of drywall fell to the floor, then another. After a moment, she leaned, bringing her cheek next to his, and they stared into a black hole. The music was even louder now. "Yeah," she ventured. "It's definitely coming from inside the wall." No ghosts had floated out, either.

"Weird," he commented.

"Keep removing the wall, and I'll get the flashlight."

She was nearly to the closet door when she glanced over her shoulder. For an instant, she was half-tempted to return to him, finish undressing and pull him into bed again, the music be damned. He had an adorably tight butt and as he used the crowbar, the taut, sculpted muscles of his forearms rippled, shot through with cords of veins. Suddenly, he craned his head in her direction, caught her looking, and grinned. "Flashlight," he said simply.

"I got sidetracked."

His bow-shaped lips twisted into a smile she was coming to know very well. It was ironical, bemused, suggestive. "I tend to do that to women."

"Modest, too."

"Only if you take into consideration that I'm the hottest man in the world."

"Oh, let me pause to consider that."

"Better not. You'll be there all day."

Snorting, she rolled her eyes and headed for the flashlight. When she returned, he'd taken out enough of the closet's back wall that they could walk through the hole. "You first," she said, slapping the flashlight into his palm.

"I thought you wanted to protect me."

"There might be ghosts. Or mice. Or…"

He squinted. "Do you really believe in ghosts?"

"Sort of."

"Hmm." Making no other comment, he stepped through the hole, and she followed.

"Wow," she whispered, ducking since the ceiling was only about five feet high, and inhaling dust. The space was too narrow to accommodate them both, and she hooked a finger over his waistband again. They inched forward. The music was even louder now, but it echoed in the crawl space, so its source was difficult to pinpoint.

"The passageway feels long," she said in a hushed tone.

"I bet it runs the length of the building."

"Do you feel that draft?"

"Yeah."

All at once, the temperature had dropped, and now she could see her breath fogging the air. She tried to tell herself the gust of cool air came from outside, but all she saw was dark, cracked, cobwebbed walls. Another tingle of fear skated down her spine, feeling like spiders dancing on her vertebrae. Covering her mouth with a hand to mitigate the musty scents, she tried to joke. "Maybe we just discovered the gate to hell."

He made a spooky ghost sound.

Her mood lightening, she smacked his behind playfully. "I'm serious," she whispered. "I'm thinking of all the movies where kids find caves that turn out to be bottomless pits."

Turning, he suddenly grabbed her. Because his weight caught her off-guard, her knees buckled, but he caught her, chuckling devilishly.

"You're evil," she said in mock consternation.

"You love it."

Before she could answer, his lips were on hers again, even as the music continued. Thankfully, the fire of his mouth was transporting. It could have been five hundred years ago, or yesterday. Time no longer mattered at all. They'd stepped into a strange world, on the other side of the wall, just as Alice had stepped through the looking glass into Wonderland. Cassidy's tongue mercilessly toyed, but his was teasing her to distraction. Hours might have passed, or minutes. She felt all tangled up in knots. Her body had been tingling from head to toe, but fear and pleasure blended now, intertwining.

Suddenly, she squealed, breaking the kiss. Something near her feet had moved. "A mouse," she whispered, her grip on Dario's waistband tightening. Another scurried near their feet.

"They're all over the building," he confirmed.

"Great," she muttered.

"I put down traps. They're more afraid of us."

The only alternative was to turn back, but there was only one flashlight, so she urged him to continue searching. A moment later, they rounded a corner and the ceiling dropped. Crouching lower, she realized the tunnel had stopped cold.

"Dead end," he murmured, tapping the crowbar against the wall, lightly at first, then harder. "This one's solid," he said.

And then the music stopped.

It happened all at once, in midsong, without warning. It was as if ghosts had heard the crowbar and finally knew they were bothering the living.

Dario stared at the wall a long moment, then shook his head.

"The side walls of this passageway must have space

behind them," she persisted, as he handed her the flashlight, gesturing that he was turning around, and that she should lead the way now. "The music is right on the other side."

"Maybe. Sounds can be deceiving. The rooms are like old caverns. I'll come back tomorrow," he murmured, as she crept toward the closet again.

"Don't you have to work? As much as I hate to admit it, the idea of searching this place alone is losing its appeal. A person could die in here and no one would ever know." It was a morbid thought, and she pushed it away, but the inner walls of such a notorious building probably held plenty of secrets.

"I'll take the day off."

For her? "Are you sure?"

"Technically, I'm working, since this might lead to information about Gem's death."

She felt a rush of relief, then excitement. This was larger than her own personal obsession. With Dario's help, she'd become part of a real investigation, one that could lead to answers about her family. "Whatever expertise you can bring to bear would be appreciated."

"You know…" His voice trailed off as they emerged from the closet.

"What?"

"In the papers I brought home with me this evening, there are a stack of original blueprints for the property," he said, heading for the front door. "We haven't had a chance to look at them, since we started with the files, and now it's too late, but first thing tomorrow…" Reaching for a cardboard tube he'd left beside the door, he uncorked an end and pulled out some rolled papers. "Here," he said peeling off the top sheet.

She helped him unroll them, using the crowbar and flashlight as anchors for the corners. Kneeling beside him, she watched as he splayed his fingers, smoothing flattened palms over the top sheet. She liked his hands, she decided. They looked strong and bronze against the white paper, capable and economical.

"This one's a surveyor's map," he said, comparing it to the next sheet, "and this is the original interior floor plan. I always thought there was something weird about the building. Even as a kid. It always seemed…"

"Like there was wasted space?"

He squinted at the papers thoughtfully. "There are hidden rooms here. At least I think so." His eyes locked with hers. "Your instincts were right."

But were they right about him?

His eyes looked a shade darker now, and they were catching glimmers from the dim lamplight. For a second, she felt too open, even more naked than before, although she was dressed now. Still, there were many kinds of nakedness, and Dario Donato seemed to have just as many ways of disrobing a woman. Swallowing hard, she glanced away.

Just as quickly, he grasped her chin. His thumb fit right beneath her lower lip, and slowly, he turned her face to his again, looking into her eyes once more. For the space of a heartbeat, she felt panic. She wasn't sure what he wanted from her, or if it would be too much, or if she was ready to give it, whatever it was. And he seemed to read all those emotions in the blink of an eye.

With deliberation, he angled his head nearer. His eyes were even closer now, looking deep inside her. His mouth hovered, his breath tantalizing. Then he came closer still. Their lips grazed—once, twice. Leaning another fraction, he pressed his mouth to hers. There was no dampness now, only firm pressure and heat.

After a very long moment, he leaned away, and she blew out a shuddering breath. "Nice," she whispered.

"Yeah, but we ought to sleep."

It was the last thing she felt like doing. "It *is* two in the morning," she agreed.

Rising gracefully to his feet, he stretched down one of those impossibly long arms and offered his hand. She slid her fingers across his palm, then felt her heart swell unexpectedly as his fingers closed around hers. With a tug, he pulled her to her feet and into his embrace.

It was the wrong time for someone to pound on the door. In unison, they groaned. Dario lifted his voice, his eyes fixed on hers. "Who is it?"

"The tenants' association," Brice Jurgenson called through the door.

And then Cassidy's cell phone rang.

11

CASSIDY WAS TRYING to follow two conversations at once. "No, really, it's okay, Mom," she said into her cell, catching snippets of the tenants' complaints. Whatever Dario was saying was calming them.

"I can't believe I forgot about the time change," her mother apologized. She was on vacation in California.

"That's okay. We, I mean, I was up anyway," Cassidy managed, still staring through a crack in the bedroom door at Dario. He really did look over-the-top handsome. Tall, slender and well muscled, he had one of those V-shaped torsos that her ex had spent hours in a gym trying to create. Forcing herself to turn away so she could concentrate on the call, she glided bellyfirst onto the bed. She started filling her mother in about her own trip, deciding not to mention Dario. "There's a hearing on Tuesday. A Judge—Judge Zhang— will make a decision."

Her mother was a worrier, and now her voice sharpened. "And everything's fine with the hotel?"

Cassidy glanced at Dario's shirt on the floor. "Great. The Centuries of Sex Museum is picking up the tab, just the way they said, but I'm really glad you called my cell because I—"

Before she could manufacture a lie, her mother saved the bell by saying, "I didn't have the hotel number—"

"Which is just as well because the phones here haven't been working that well—"

"In such a nice hotel?"

"Strange, huh?" Cassidy was almost angry at herself for lying to her mother, but a second later, she remembered why she always did so.

"I wish you'd get these crazy notions about Gem O'Shea out of your head," her mother said on a sigh. "There are no jewels. And no murder. And really, honey, apparently that building has been in the Donato family for over a century, so I wouldn't get your hopes up. I mean, it's nice for a museum to try to help, but—"

"I really believe those things," Cassidy interjected, feeling herself clamming up inside. Whatever excitement she felt, her mother was the first to toss the wet blanket on top of her.

"I'm sorry," her mother said.

"I wish you could be more supportive."

"I know you always feel that way, and I'm sorry, honey, but I think it's good to be realistic. And…well, that brings me to the real reason I called."

Another tiny knife twisted inside Cassidy. Oh, she was used to the way her mother treated her, like a child, but she wished—just once—that her mother would call without an agenda, just to chat. "Which is?"

"Well, I know you won't want to hear it, but—"

"Then don't tell me!"

"Maybe I shouldn't. I mean, I wasn't going to, but now… well, I'm obligated to say something. You see, a couple weeks ago, I stopped by your house, just to check on you…"

"I can take care of myself, Mom."

"Of course you can. But guess who I found outside, sitting on your porch, wearing a cute, pitiful hangdog expression?" Before Cassidy could ask, her mother pressed on. "Johnny Case, that's who. Oh, Cassidy, I know you don't want me prying, but he's taking this divorce so hard. You were so darn mean to him, and he never could understand why. As I told you, I wasn't going to say anything. He made me promise I wouldn't, but—"

"He was at my house? On my front porch? Had he been inside?"

"Why are you so distrustful, honey?" her mother asked, sounding crestfallen. "You loved him so much, and I know he loved you. Your whole life was going so well. Everything was all figured out."

"Every time we had a fight, you sided with him."

"That's not true."

"Mom," Cassidy huffed. "I love you, but I really have to go now. It's almost three in the morning."

"I'm so sorry. I forgot. I thought it was about eleven."

Even that was too late for Cassidy. Her mother was the night owl. She sighed. "It's okay. I'd really better get back to sleep, though."

"Are you sure you're all right?"

"Fine," Cassidy promised.

"I knew I shouldn't have told you," her mother said again. "But I've bumped into him a few times. He was hoping to talk to you when you came home from work. He's so stressed about your financial problems, since he's not there to support you any longer. I mean, he said your store brought in income, but…" Her voice trailed off. "I told him all your news, though," she began again brightly. "He couldn't believe the Centuries of Sex Museum called, and that a twist of fate might change your luck."

Emotions warred within her, among them shame. How much had her mother told her ex? "Look, Mom, I really have to go now."

Relief filled her as she clicked the off button. A second later, warm hands landed on her feet, curling around the insteps. They glided upward, molding her calves and stroking her thighs, then Dario took the phone from her and tossed it aside.

His voice sounded gentle and kind. "You okay?"

There was no hiding her tangled feelings. As she rolled over to face him, she'd felt a surge of anger and dismay. "Yeah."

Propping himself on an elbow, he tucked a fist against his cheek and stared down at her, using his free hand to brush hair away from her face. "So, you didn't tell your mom that your ex wrecked your finances?"

"Eavesdropper."

"A filthy habit, I admit."

"I thought we were trying not to get personal."

"It's impossible not to when you're sleeping with somebody."

"Now you tell me." She shook her head, considering. "Mom really liked Johnny. *I* really liked him. At least at first. He was a teacher at a small college in our area, and he seemed to know a lot, and I guess Mom and I were both a little too impressed. I mean, neither of us have four-year degrees, and he was a teacher." She looked at Dario, deciding how much more to say, and suddenly, she wished he wasn't turning out to be quite so easy to talk to. "In the end, I was ashamed of misjudging somebody's character to that extent."

"You can't know a person until you live with them."

It was nice of him to say so. "Maybe. Anyway, I didn't want Mom to worry, but that backfired. She believes he was supporting me, when it was the other way around. He spent his own money like water."

"Are you ever going to tell her he was a scumbag?"

"Well, it's already been a year, and it's all starting to seem like water under the bridge."

"Only because you're in another man's arms."

"Only for a week."

Leaning, he pressed a quick kiss to her forehead, then studied her. Something in his gaze made her feel compelled to say, "My mother and I…"

"Don't get along?"

"It's not that," Cassidy said quickly. "She loves me. And I love her. But she always worries. And my dad left when I was young, so it's just me and her. Dad didn't want to keep in touch, and I let it go. Mom saw Johnny as the solution, not that he was my dad all over again. She can be a hypercritical, but she means well. She was so sure Johnny was the best thing that ever happened to me, and I didn't want to take that away from her. I wanted her to feel like my life was all squared away. When I got married, it was like she finally quit worrying about me."

"Mothers and daughters," Dario mused.

She couldn't help but smile. "You're an expert?"

"With a bunch of sisters? Uh…yeah. I could have a Ph.D. in the topic. Impressed?"

She laughed, then the laughter tempered to a soft chuckle. She was starting to genuinely warm to Dario Donato. He was quick with answers, and it made her feel good inside. Special. Heard by him. Safe.

"Like I said when we were having dinner with Karen and Pat," he continued, "Eliana and my mom are at each other's throats all the time now. After the wedding, Pop says they may never speak to each other again."

Cassidy's smile turned rueful. "Johnny used to bring up my relationship with my mother. He'd turn our sniping into something more. You know, pathologize it, like we were both nuts, dysfunctional or something."

"But it was typical mother-daughter dynamics?"

"Which *are* crazy," she admitted.

Dario shrugged. "Your ex sounds worse every time you mention him." He fell silent a moment. "He was really at your house?"

"According to Mom." She nodded agreeably, then understood what he was getting at. "Johnny's not dangerous."

When Dario didn't look convinced, she laughed again. "Now you're acting like a cop."

"How's that?"

"You look like you want to arrest my ex."

"He did leave you saddled with his debt, and my guess is, he made a decent salary. What was he spending it on?"

Her lips pursed, she glanced away.

When he spoke, the rumble came from his chest. "You don't have to tell me."

She sighed, her eyes finding his again. Something about him took away the shame of it. "Other women. Girls really. I mean, I only know about one, but suspect others. She was a freshman in his class." Her voice held a touch of bitterness. "As young and doe-eyed as I was when I sat in on his classes."

Dario looked stunned. "He wasn't just a scumbag. He was crazy, toots."

Somehow, he'd gotten a smile to tug at her lips. "You think?"

"Absolutely." He toyed with a tendril of her hair. "You were in his classes?"

"He teaches history and antiquities, and I was interested in old jewels. I supplemented my own schooling by auditing some regular college classes, and his happened to be one."

She narrowed her eyes. "I bet you're a good cop. People must tell you all kinds of things."

Ignoring the compliment, Dario shook his head. "No man in his right mind would sleep with somebody else if he could have you."

"Diplomatic of you to say so under the circumstances."

"Simple truth." A sudden, dazzling smile made his eyes crinkle at the corners. Dropping a lock of her hair, he traced a lazy finger down her cleavage, then splayed a warm hand on her belly. "Ready to get undressed again so I can prove it to you?"

Once more, he seemed to be seeing more than she'd meant to reveal. "Not before you tell me what the tenants said."

"The music is as loud in some of their apartments as here," he reported. "Rosie and Theresa heard it, but Brice said he was awakened by footsteps. Zu and Ling didn't come down. I guess they're still in bed." Inclining his head, he lasered his eyes into hers. "Now, can I restore confidence in your sexual abilities?"

She smiled, then suddenly thought of something. "They used to play panel games in old bawdy houses," she said as he began swirling circles around her naval.

"I've heard about that from vice cops," he murmured, clearly more interested in undressing her. "One woman would keep a guy occupied while another would enter the room by removing a panel of the wall. She'd steal his money, replace the wall panel, and the guy wouldn't know what happened to his cash."

"So, it would make sense if there really were hidden rooms here."

He unsnapped her jeans. "We'll find out tomorrow." He paused. "After we sleep in. Then we'll have breakfast. And then we'll demolish the house. I want to go to the church where Gem went the night she died, too." Earlier, as they'd read the files, he'd told her a librarian had found the information, and even now, she could barely believe the church was still standing. "Sounds like a big day, so I could use a nightcap."

"I polished off the whiskey night before last," he said, "so this is the best I can do." When his mouth found hers, the heat of the kiss entered her bloodstream with the strength of pure grain alcohol. Just like whiskey, it hit the back of her throat, then wended slowly into her belly, traveling to her groin before it curled up like a sleepy cat.

As he gently nudged her lips apart with his, she felt drunk with the sensation. Already, she was dizzy, spinning into a vortex, whirling into the abyss as he slowly eased down her zipper.

"Do me, too," he whispered.

Finding his zipper, she pulled it down, pushing denim over his slender hips. Now that she was in his arms again, she knew sleep would elude her. "The light," she whispered.

"I want it on," he said, sitting up and leaning his back against the wall, his arm stretching for a condom on the dresser. Circling his arms around her back a moment later, he urged her to straddle him.

He was ready and waiting, hard for her, and as she glided onto his length, he felt like scalding granite. Ripples undulated through her. The heat of his eyes matched that of his body as they roved over her breasts. She couldn't believe the heat of their passion, its ease. Raw need was a scent in the air as she settled her palms on either side of his head, using the wall to brace herself.

"We're good together," he whispered, watching her.

"Maybe too good."

"Maybe."

There was danger here, she thought, rolling her hips, grinding against him, taking the pleasure that he was so ready to give. They could take these sensations anywhere… or nowhere.

"Scared?" he asked.

"Of you? No," she lied, then she shut her eyes. The light was on, but now the world inside her mind became as dark as pitch. Desire was winding through her, tying her in knots, coiling and tangling, pulling her toward the inevitable climax. "You?" she whispered, her chest suddenly tight, her breath shallow. "Are you scared?"

"No."

But she didn't believe him, either. Emotion welled inside her and crested like a wave as she rode him. They'd started an innocent love game, but now it was weaving its own spell around them. There was no way out. From the first moment, his every glance had promised delicious sensations, and now he was making good on all his silent promises.

As he cradled her closer, she felt her heart stretch to breaking. His hands trembled, spanning her back as he buried his face against her chest, and tenderness claimed her as she undulated her hips, pulling him deeper inside, so deep that he touched her womb. Johnny hadn't wanted babies, a bombshell he'd dropped after their wedding, retracting his earlier promise to have them. Now, feeling Dario inside her, she felt the call of something she'd forgotten…a dream she hadn't remembered for years.

Crying out softly, she threaded her hands in hair that felt like silk, then she whimpered, rocking against him. He seemed to sense the tenderness in her heart now, and he hugged her close, his hands gentling, as if she was made of something fragile. *I love you.* Unbidden, the words surged to her lips, but she held them back. The impulse to say it was crazy. She barely knew him.

Or did she? Everywhere he touched her, she felt both tender and hot, and as if her heart was breaking all over again. She hadn't yet healed from Johnny, but this man was already ripping open wounds, making her want to trust again, to try at love....

His breath was shaky against her skin, his thighs straining in tandem with hers. He was unbelievably hard now, taut inside her, about to explode. His fingers turned urgent on her flesh, his release imminent. The mouth that touched her mouth was greedy, the kiss so thorough that the man could have believed it to be his very last. Why did she think she didn't know him? What more did she need to know?

They came as she and Johnny never had, at the same second. He was holding her so tightly that his arms seemed to circle her body countless times, leaving no space for a breath. She was the ball, and he was the twine. His heart was pounding against her heart, his lips capturing a sigh from her lips, and a scent rose between them that wasn't him, or her, but their joined selves.

"Now, we can sleep," he said softly, sounding satisfied, urging her lower on the mattress, to share a pillow.

She said nothing, but her arms and legs were twined around him more tightly, like vines growing around a solid tree trunk. She felt like a boat carried on a strong, sure current. That was her final thought as she tipped over the edge of a waterfall once more, into the world of dreams.

12

"Wow," Cassidy murmured in awe the next afternoon. She, Dario and their guide, a woman who'd introduced herself as Mrs. Harrison, stepped through a wrought-iron gate, then beneath the stone archway of a cloistered path, and into the interior courtyard of the church where Gem O'Shea had been the night she'd died. Huge hardwood trees with giant trunks towered over ivy that tumbled from planters, and as they walked under a canopy of sunburst-orange and moon-yellow leaves, the shade made the temperature drop.

As soon as Cassidy shivered, hugging her arms around the raincoat she wore, Dario responded, drawing her to his side. She'd forgotten how much she'd missed receiving public affection from a man. When she and Johnny had first started dating, they'd shared occasional kisses on the street, something that ended after they'd married. Often she'd wound up charging a few steps ahead, while he'd ambled behind. It was as if he was always holding her back. By contrast, she and Dario walked together as if they were one person—his strides matching hers.

Realizing she was comparing the two men again, Cassidy focused on her surroundings. "This is amazing."

"It's one of the oldest buildings downtown," chirped Mrs. Harrison, a birdlike woman with pointy features—a sharp nose and chin—and bright blue eyes that sparkled with intelligence. Looking self-satisfied, she shoved both hands into the pockets of the tweed blazer she wore with khaki slacks. "It's a hidden oasis, isn't it?" she asked rhetorically, guiding them to a door marked Office.

Cassidy had come to the city on buying trips, but she'd never seen the sites through a native's eyes, and all day, Dario had dragged her down intricate winding alleyways that would have been lost on the less observant. The cloistered gardens at the church proved to be another such revelation. While Mrs. Harrison found her keys, Cassidy glanced sideways, smiling at Dario. There was a moment of shared desire, then of intense emotional connection such as Cassidy hadn't felt in a long time. "Thanks," she whispered to Dario.

"For what?"

"Bringing me here. I didn't know places like this existed in the city."

"I could show you a million more," he promised.

"Now, have a seat, you two," said Mrs. Harrison, as she pushed open the office door, "because you're going to need it."

Inside was an oak-paneled room with floor-to-ceiling shelves crammed with leather-bound volumes. Twining his fingers through Cassidy's, Dario urged her to sit beside him on a leather sofa. Feeling their thighs connect, she sighed, suddenly transported backward in time, not to the distant past, but to this morning, when she'd awakened.

As soon as she'd opened her eyes, she'd found him smiling down at her, as if he'd been watching her for a good long while. A bag from a deli was on the nightstand. A mischievous expression on his face, he was waving a cup of coffee beneath her nose.

"Wake up and smell the coffee, huh?" Her muscles tingling as she stretched.

"Undress and you can have it," he'd bargained, his dark eyes crinkling at the corners when he smiled.

"I'm already undressed," she'd returned, smiling back.

"I don't believe you."

"You have trust issues."

"No doubt."

"See a shrink," she suggested.

"But I want to see you."

Slowly, she'd lifted the sheet, giving him a peek. Leaning closer, he'd made a show of scrutinizing her naked skin. By the time they were finished with the full-body viewing, another two hours had passed and the coffee was cold, the cream curdled on top. So, he'd taken her to a small, bustling brunch spot in Little Italy, where he seemed to know everyone, from the waitresses to the busboys and the cashier.

Unexpectedly, her throat got tight now. What was happening between them was supposed to be a moment out of time. In a couple of days, 67 Anthony Street was going to be hers, and she had to be prepared to walk out of this man's life. Had desire blinded him? In the end, was he going to be angry at her? Certainly, his father wouldn't approve of her staying in the house, much less tearing it apart as they had much of the day. They'd found nothing. Nor did Dario know that Luther was relying on her, or that she'd met with Chuckie Haswell.

Wondering if she should tell Dario, she shifted uncomfortably, reminding herself she'd done nothing wrong. Her guilt was due to torn loyalties, but she didn't owe Dario Donato anything. She had a right, even an obligation, to cut the best deal for herself.

Pushing aside her thoughts, she surveyed the room. Mrs. Harrison was lifting a plastic-wrapped package from the desk. She came toward them, her movements economical.

"After you called this morning, I went into action," she assured, excitement in her voice. "I phoned Janet Kay, the archivist at the public library, whom you mentioned." Gingerly removing the contents of the bag, Mrs. Harrison placed a white, leather-bound wedding book before them, then opened it, turning the book around so they could read.

"Gem O'Shea," Cassidy said, gasping, taking in the scroll-like script. It was the first signature. Her hands trembling, she grasped the delicate page and turned. "Mark," she continued, "and Lily."

"They were married here on December 23, 1890," Mrs. Harrison said.

"A Christmas wedding," Cassidy murmured. But why had Gem been here?

"This is a very old church, and our rectors have all been collectors, so we have rooms of materials, as you can imagine. I've done my best to organize them during my tenure as the cataloguer." Mrs. Harrison paused. "It'll be thirty-six years when I retire next year. In my experience, it's a rare pleasure when somebody wants a long-lost item. I can't give the book to you today, of course, since my superior has to sign off on transfers of documents, but if you're really..."

"A relative of Gem O'Shea's?" Cassidy finished. "Yes. I am. And I would be interested in having it. It's family memorabilia." Possibly, she'd donate it to the Centuries of Sex Museum for safekeeping. Guilt twisted inside her, and she suddenly wondered what would happen to Luther's collection if the building became hers and she sold to another buyer. Maybe Johnny Case's betrayal had ruined her. The old Cassidy wouldn't have been so afraid about her own future, nor would she have played one man off against another. She'd had more faith in herself, and the abundantly positive powers of the universe. Sex was one of those powers, too, and now as she glanced at Dario, she realized something magical was happening to her. Because of him, she was starting to heal….

"No one here's using the wedding book," Mrs. Harrison was saying. "It's just been filed away. So, I can't see why there would be an objection to your having it."

After all these years, it was astonishing to see Gem's handwriting. It made her seem so real that Cassidy could almost imagine Gem was in the room with them. Her pulse quickened. If Gem had really been in the church, then everything else might well be true, and that meant the jewels must truly be hidden in the house somewhere. Finding the wedding book was even more exciting than seeing the paintings at the museum.

Suddenly, another reality hit her. "She was here right before she died." Maybe Gem had even sat where she and Dario were now.

"Just hours before," agreed Mrs. Harrison. "If newspaper accounts of her death are accurate, anyway. And like I said, once we do paperwork, the wedding book is yours, if you want to take it. Janet passed along information from Mr. Donato, which is how I knew to look for it." Pausing, Mrs. Harrison shrugged. "Family members are always busy during a wedding, then or now, so we often safe keep items such as this. No one ever returned for it."

Dario was turning the pages, reading the names. His index finger settled on the very last line, and he blew out a soft wolf's whistle. "Take a look at that."

Cassidy leaned closer, catching the scent of his body, something pinelike and purely male. "Nathaniel Haswell," she whispered, her gaze darting to his. "Isn't that the guy who's supposedly related to Chuckie Haswell?"

"Sure is," he said, giving her hand a squeeze. "Chuckie's trying to prove he owned 67 Anthony Street."

"Obviously, Nathaniel had some relationship with Gem. Maybe he did own the property and willed it to her."

"Maybe." Dario shrugged, seemingly more concerned with the truth than his family's interests. "Maybe they were…"

"Lovers?" Cassidy asked on a quick exhalation of breath.

"That's what I thought," Mrs. Harrison interjected, her tone becoming a bit smug. "I thought to myself, now, what if Mark or Lily was Gem's child…" Quickly, she shook her head. "And then I thought, no, that seems too far-fetched."

"But why not?" Cassidy interjected.

Mrs. Harrison's beaklike mouth opened in anticipation. "Exactly. So," she continued, rising and returning to the desk, "I checked our files further. Since Mark and Lily were married here, it stands to reason that the same church would be used for other rites, such as baptism and confirmation. A service was said here for Gem after her death, too."

"It was?"

Mrs. Harrison nodded. "She's buried in a cemetery in Brooklyn. Apparently, her mother was buried there, as well."

"I can't believe this," Cassidy said with wonder in her voice.

"I can give you the address. And…" Mrs. Harrison laid a photocopy on the table. "As it turns out, Mark was her son, after all. Further records showed that Gem arranged for the wedding for her boy. The bride's surname was Jordan."

"No father's listed on the baptism record," observed Dario, scrutinizing the paper.

"True, and we'll never know who he was," Mrs. Harrison returned. "He wasn't buried with Gem, and I don't know where Lily was put to rest. Still, it's an amazing find."

"It really is," Cassidy assured, gushing. "I've heard

stories about Gem all my life. And now, it's…almost as if she's come to life."

"History does that, dear," Mrs. Harrison said. "Nothing truly dies. Ideas float for all eternity. Traces of people linger. Some say their belongings even carry their essence."

Mrs. Harrison paused. "Now for the icing on the cake. Janet Kay and I got to talking. In fact, we had so many ideas about linking our archive files that we wound up making a business lunch date. Anyway, once we had Lily's maiden name, Janet was able to go back into the archives at the public library and, as it turns out, she has Lily Jordan's diary."

Cassidy gaped. "You're kidding?"

Mrs. Harrison shook her head. "There was a push about fifty years ago—before my and Janet's time—to track down documents about the Five Points area, and bring them back home to the city where they belong. Archivists were hoping to create a more solid body of information about the immigrant populations who came here in the nineteenth century. Many were Irish, displaced by the potato famines."

Pausing, Mrs. Harrison inhaled sharply, as if to say she wasn't used to talking so much and needed to catch her breath. "Anyway, an ancestor of Lily Jordan's lived in Boston at that time, and she left a box of materials to the library when she died."

"Small world," said Cassidy.

"If you ever want a job with the NYPD," Dario said to Mrs. Harrison, "give me a call."

Mrs. Harrison laughed. Then she said, "If you head over to the library, Janet actually has Lily Jordan's diary. You'll have to read it on the premises, of course, or take the photocopy she's made for you. She told me she wouldn't have a chance to read it before you came—she had meetings this morning—so, whatever you find will be a surprise, I'm sure.

She has no idea if anyone has *ever* read the diary from cover to cover."

"She made a photocopy? And it's at the library? Right now?" Cassidy's heart was beating too fast, but there was no way she could calm it.

"It's not usually standard practice. Usually we'd look over the materials first. But this may help Mr. Donato with a criminal investigation, and you're a relative."

"Great." This was an incredible turn of events, and it was all because of Dario's connections. Feeling a rush of excitement, she sighed. This was the kind of moment that made her sure that, one day, the world's mysteries would all be solved. Wrapping her hand around Dario's biceps, Cassidy rubbed the muscle, feeling a rush of awareness as her breast pressed against his side.

"The diary's waiting for you," assured Mrs. Harrison. "Third floor. In the map room. Ask for Janet. The library's open for another hour. Uh…Janet will recognize Mr. Donato."

Other than the library, the only place Cassidy would rather be was back in bed with Dario, so the innuendo wasn't lost on her. That he and Janet Kay had been an item was confirmed when her eyes found his. Janet must have said something telling on the phone to her new friend. So, once they'd thanked Mrs. Harrison and gone outside, Cassidy said, "Another girlfriend?"

He brushed his mouth across hers in a blistering sweep of a kiss that felt as hot as a winter fire. "How many others do you know about?"

"One. Sheila."

"Sheila wasn't really a girlfriend." He paused. "And you didn't meet."

Cassidy wasn't sure she wanted to know. "And Janet?"

Dario urged her closer against his side while he considered. "I thought we weren't getting personal."

"Maybe. But when we were talking about my life, you said it was inevitable." She squinted, wishing she hadn't gone through so much heartbreak with Johnny's infidelity. "Before I meet her…at least tell me if you slept with her, so I won't feel weird."

"Knowing I slept with somebody would make you feel less weird?"

"Yeah." As soon as the word was out, she understood why. "It…makes me feel that you and I are more intimate, like you'd have bothered to let me know."

"More intimate than her and me?"

Stopping, he turned to face her, and as he did, a lump lodged in her throat. He looked gorgeous at this moment. She wished she had a camera, and could take a snapshot that would last forever. She could barely believe she was hanging around with a guy who looked this good. His dark denim jacket was unbuttoned, the collar turned up against the wind, the thick navy cotton sweater beneath bunched under her palms. Tilting against him, she looked into his eyes. As if sensing what she wanted, he lowered his head and captured her lips, and she stretched her arms around his neck, kissing him back.

When he drew away, his expression was hard to interpret, his voice rough, so low she had to strain to hear. "Would you mind?"

She didn't want to admit it. "Yeah. I mean, I'd feel funny about it. You know, about meeting her."

She sensed, more than heard, his breath catch. She could feel the bracing of his body, too, a tightness in his chest when he inhaled, the sudden flex of hands that found her waist. "We went out a few times. Came close, but we never…"

Should she believe him? She felt more relieved than she wanted to admit, although she knew her emotions were unwarranted. "A long time ago?" she persisted in mock interrogation, as a way of keeping the tone light. "Another century? Yesterday?"

"A couple years ago."

"Just asking." With that, she shrugged, flashed a smile, tapped his shoulder and turned abruptly, as if to say the answer wouldn't have mattered, one way or the other, although it wasn't true.

"Where are you running off to so fast?" he asked, following.

"The library," she tossed over her shoulder, making a beeline toward the wrought-iron gate leading to the street. A few paces later, he caught her hand from behind. She swung around, feeling breathless and sure her face was too naked, too bare. He'd seen how much he was affecting her and guessed she really liked him. Maybe she could even love him. Maybe he'd guessed that, too.

She backed up a step, only to realize a tree was behind her. Bark scraped her back as a long, leisurely arm stretched upward, his palm landing right above her head. Bringing his lips close, as if just to tease her, he didn't bother to kiss her, just let his lips graze hers. His eyes seemed too serious now, dark with emotions she couldn't fathom. Something, maybe a warning, flashed in their depths, prompting her to say, "One look at you, and I know I'd sure hate to be on the wrong side of the law."

His smile was hard to read. "Do I look dangerous?"

"Sort of."

"What are you thinking?"

"Oh, no…not *that* question," she chided. "Isn't that what people always ask when they're trying to start talking about their emotions, or the things we're not supposed to be having?"

"Like what?"

"A relationship."

"Yeah." His eyes were steady. "But I want to know."

She shook her head, wondering how much to divulge. A few days of his company had led her to want more. What exactly, she didn't know. Just more. "I like sleeping with you," she found herself saying. "Eating with you, waking up with you. Dammit," she suddenly added, her voice dropping, "you know this was only supposed to be…"

"An innocent game of shared sexual abandon?"

"Yes. But things…feel like they're spinning beyond my control."

"Beyond mine, too," he said, his voice so husky that she shivered as the finger traced a line around her lips. His mouth followed, his tongue coloring in the line he'd drawn.

"But I don't want to confuse things," she managed to protest, suddenly glad twilight was coming early. It was nearing four o'clock, but already the sky was graying and she could smell nightfall. The shadowy canopy overhead made her feel less exposed until his hand dropped to her shoulder in a caress, and her resolve to keep emotionally distant faltered.

He was watching her carefully, and as if sensing a moment of weakness, he placed both hands on her shoulders, then curled his fingers around them, so they dug into her skin, ensuring she couldn't turn away. "What's confusing you?"

"You know what I mean."

"Yeah." He stepped closer, wedging a foot between hers, forcing her to widen her stance, bracing herself as he pressed flush against her. Hard and warm and male, he drove her back against the tree trunk. His mouth was on hers then—hot, quick, wet. Responsive fire sparked in her belly, ignited and roared as her mind ran wild with possibilities.

Already, she was imagining frantic hands fumbling with her jeans zipper, and hearing the rustling sound of fabric as he pushed away her coat and lifted her into his arms. The memory of how he'd taken her against the apartment door was swift and visceral, and shudders racked her.

The church was behind them, the tree between them and Mrs. Harrison's prying eyes, and now Cassidy's hands were powerless, seized by passion that was a force in its own right. With a will of their own, they molded over his hips, traveling downward. Through rough denim, she could feel the hard bunched muscles of his thighs flinch. His hips arched, and suddenly, she felt him between her legs, the pressure of the erection making her ache. A gnawing craving filled her, and she felt strangely elated, and yet doomed. Having loved this man physically, she realized she'd always crave what they'd shared. There was no escape.

"You're not confused," he said speaking thickly against her lips before plunging his tongue hungrily again—now in a demanding thrust. "You want me. Want this."

Her hand slid between them, over the bulge at his fly. He let loose a soft moan. For a blissful moment, she shut her eyes, and her mind went blank. Just touching him flooded her with a relief such as she'd never felt. Once more, they were going to share passion…bring each other to completion. The last time they'd shared sex hadn't really been their last…

Forcing her lips farther apart, his tongue swept inside her mouth, causing her to tilt back her chin for a stormy assault. Her hand edged away, and she lifted her hips, all the while wishing they were elsewhere…anywhere that passion could have full rein. Another deep guttural sound emerged from the back of his throat as he ground against her, his movements rhythmic and purposeful, the circular pressure making her feverish.

His tongue dived once more, and hers lashed against it. As her arms circled his neck tightly, the hem of her coat swung, further shielding them from onlookers, hiding the unsuppressed surge of lust. Crushed against the tree, she gasped, parting her legs a fraction more, lifting on her tiptoes, feeling near release. Even through the clothes, she could feel his erection separating her cleft.

Her breath catching, she moved with him, the maddening friction bringing her right to the edge, need driving her.

But suddenly, he wrenched away, leaving them both shaken.

She was panting. He looked less shaken, his lips glistening from the ministrations of her mouth.

"I'm not him, Cassidy," he said simply.

For a second, she couldn't imagine what he was talking about. She was aching all over, her heart pounding, yearning for the sweet bliss wrought by the movements of his hips. Vaguely, she was aware of her own moisture, how slick and hot she felt. Frustrated desire was all she could feel, but she shook her head as if to clear it of confusion. "Who?"

"Your ex."

For once, Johnny Case was the furthest thing from her mind. "I never said you were him."

"Sure you do," he returned, his voice low, his grip on her shoulders tightening. "You say it every time you talk to me," he said gruffly. "Every time you look at me. Every time you kiss me. Every time you—" His voice breaking off, he thrust his hips again, making her sigh. "Bring your body to mine," he finished. "And every time we…"

"Have sex?"

"Make love," he countered, his lips close once more, hovering, threatening to descend, his breath slightly labored and feathering her skin.

"We don't even know each other. Not that well."

"Well enough for this."

"C'mon, Dario, let's go to the library. Okay?"

For a second, his eyes darkened, looking thunderous, and she realized he was as aroused as she and just as flinty because of it. "I thought you wanted a week of passion."

"Uncomplicated passion."

"Coward."

"You're not the kind of man who ought to say that," she shot back, her heart still beating double time, the awareness of her erogenous zones making her blind to all else. As soon as the words were out, she wanted to evade his piercing dark eyes. Since the first second he'd seen her, every glance seemed to remove stitches of her clothes, as surely as he was removing the character armor that defended her heart.

His eyes sharpened. "What kind of man is that?"

The kind who had countless girlfriends all over town. Janet, she suddenly thought. Sheila. She'd bet there were hundreds more. "The kind who never settles down."

"I thought you were finished with settling down yourself."

"I am."

"Then why should you care?"

He was twisting everything around. "I need to heal."

"You feel healed enough right now."

"You know what I mean."

"Maybe I could change."

"And you think I should be your test case?" she burst out. Why couldn't he understand? Her heart simply couldn't take any more man trouble. Not now. Maybe not ever. "After what happened in my marriage? No way. I'm more self-protective."

"For how long?" His hands were in her hair now, threading through the strands, his eyes imploring. "Are you going to keep protecting yourself, even if it stops you from exploring something better? Something real?"

"You think this is more real than my marriage?"

"Yeah."

"Why?"

"My gut says so."

"Sex," she forced herself to say, despite the telltale racing of her heart. "Plain and simple. That was our deal, Dario."

His lips parted, but she had no idea why. Was it in protest, or self-defense, or mere astonishment? Or was he about to kiss her again? The flash of heat in his eyes said he was definitely thinking about it. She doubted many women had talked to Dario Donato this way, and he seemed to be excited by the challenge.

"Just sex. So, it's really that easy for you?"

"Yeah," she lied. "Isn't it for you?"

"No."

"What about Sheila? Janet?"

"They were different."

She wanted to pretend he hadn't said it. And yet she wanted to know why. Instead of asking, she said, "We had a deal."

"I'm aware of that, Cassidy," he muttered. Without warning, he leaned, his mouth clamping down on hers again. Hands mussed her hair, and suddenly, his nails were scratching crazy circles on her scalp. They glided down her back, caressing each vertebrae, until each had begun tingling and he was cupping her backside once more. A breath sizzled, pulling through her clenched teeth as he brought her against him, wanting her to feel each inch of him again. The rock-hard, slender muscular length of his body sent her reeling. His weight, his heat, where he was hard—everything. "We need a bed, not a churchyard," she whispered.

"But that's all," he whispered back. "A bed. I'm aware of the deal."

"Good," she managed.

"Make good on it tonight," he said, leaning away, an indecipherable spark in his eyes. As he stood back a pace, she felt his body leaving hers by degrees, but all the impressions remained. Searing heat. Pine scents. Shallow breath. Aroused male flesh. He surveyed her a long moment, his eyes drifting over her, lingering on her breasts and looking hungry. Flashing a smile, as if to say he'd win this argument in the end, he turned and began walking toward the gate.

She stared at his broad back, the wide shoulders, tapered torso, perfect butt and mile-long legs—as she licked his kisses from her lips. Warring emotions claimed her. He expected her to run after him, but she'd never give him the satisfaction. She didn't want the altercation to end this way, though. What was she supposed to do? Beg his forgiveness? And for what? Not admitting she feared her growing feelings for him?

She exhaled a frustrated sigh. Raising her voice, she yelled, "Donato. Quit being a total horse's ass and wait for me."

His steps stilled. Slowly, he pivoted. It didn't help to notice the man was still hard. Oh, it wasn't that noticeable, unless a woman was looking, but she was certainly looking, and she could see the curve under the zipper of his jeans.

"C'mon," she ventured when she'd almost reached him, struggling for a light tone, despite how unsettled she felt. "It's supposed to be a great moment." She'd told him all about Granny Fiona's stories; he knew what finding the wedding book and diary meant for her. "And we may be close to solving a mystery. We did see Nathaniel Haswell's signature, after all. Share this with me."

"Sorry," he apologized, his eyes full of awareness. "I don't know what got into me."

Desire. And she'd felt it, too. "C'mon," she urged, concealing any hint of a plea. She slipped her hand into the crook of his arm and curled her fingers over his forearm. "Is our deal really that terrible?"

"I've made worse."

She feathered her lips across his cheek until she found the heat of his mouth. "Indulge me."

"That," he said, "I can do."

"It's only for a few more days. You'll live."

"You'd resurrect a dead man," he assured.

"Is that what I've done?" she couldn't help but ask. Did he really feel differently about her than other women? Had she, somehow, made sex become more than a game for him?

"Maybe."

Once more, she was glad for the twilight, since emotion welled within her. "Maybe you're doing that for me, too," she found herself saying. "So, let's enjoy it for what it is."

He nodded.

Hugging him more closely as they began to walk, she sighed in relief. They'd avoided a blowout, and things were going to be fine. Wham-bam-thank-you, ma'am. No feelings they couldn't control. No promises they couldn't keep. No shared possessions, knotty entanglements or locked chains that only attorneys could undo.

That had been their deal.

Except that she was falling in love with Dario Donato. And she was pretty sure he was falling for her, too.

13

HOURS LATER, CASSIDY glanced up from some of the photocopied sheets of the diary and caught Dario studying her. Propped against the pillow next to him, she stretched, the muscles of her shapely legs going taut, the hem of a nightshirt rising on tempting thighs. "Hmm?"

He shook his head. "Nothing." When she eyed him, unconvinced, he added, "I can't concentrate when you're beside me, half-dressed."

"You'll live."

"Better if you undress the rest of the way."

Looking preoccupied, she offered a smile, but then began reading again, becoming engrossed. Ignoring the copies in his own hand, he settled his gaze where the slopes of her breasts were visible beneath her shirt. As slow heat ran through him, his lower body tensed. Smoking tendrils curled in his abdomen like jet trails, or like residue left from an explosion of dynamite or gun powder.

The room was warmer tonight—he'd gotten the new boiler installed—but Cassidy looked warmer still. He started to reach for her, but something held him back—either seeing the joy she was taking in reading, or his own conflicted emotions.

He'd never stop wanting her. He knew that now. From their first night together, his response to her had been elemental. Like earthquakes or volcanos, summer storms or avalanches, it was an unstoppable force of nature destined to come to a halt as abruptly as it had begun. Only because she was going to walk away, though. He was just glad he'd been kicked off the arson case, so he'd had time for the adventure.

But Cassidy wouldn't keep in touch. She'd try to forget him, denying how good they'd been together. Maybe that's why he'd been seized by an urge to imprint her with memories as soon as they'd returned home. He'd grabbed the waistband of her pants and pulled her close. In the instant her mouth pressed against his, fire met fire, and in another moment, they were as aroused as they'd been in the churchyard.

"Make good on your deal," he'd challenged.

"You don't think I will?"

"Tease," he'd chided.

A lazy finger had hooked over his belt buckle. "As I said, I don't back out on deals."

"Prove it," he'd whispered, his mind already fogging, his body assaulted by visceral memory and knowing the bliss of loving her was only a breath away.

Emerald slits of eyes had found his, sparkling with intent, then she'd paused, her throat working hard as she'd swallowed, the only show of emotion as she'd unbuckled his belt. The soft, slapping sound of leather and their quickening breath punctuated the silence as she'd released the snap and unzipped him.

As soon as a bloodred nail traced his fly, he'd gotten hard, then her burning hands slipped under the back of his waistband, gliding inside his briefs. Nails raked his flesh as she curled them over his backside, bringing goose bumps. As she'd pushed down the denim, she'd moved quickly, clearly unable to undress him fast enough.

Then she'd dropped to her knees. Just like that. No warning, no fanfare. No tremulous show about how special this was. Just her cool wet mouth circling him. It had been pure heaven. Hell, too. Desire had seized him like an iron fist, and he'd felt he was down there with the demons, flames licking every inch of him. Angels wings had fluttered around him, and he'd felt lifted up, soaring.

Gasping, he'd tried to widen his stance, to brace himself, but that only made his jeans stretch taut across his legs. Trapped and unable to move, straining to spread his thighs, he stretched his hungry hands down, meaning to stop her. Instead his fingers dived, threading across wind-chilled skin, into lush hair still disheveled from the blustery night. Strands ran through his fingers like water, teasing the spaces between, before he closed his fists, his nails raking her scalp as he brought her mouth even closer.

A sound that was hard to define—of need, hunger and even protest—wrenched from his lips. She was taking his whole length, every inch, her tongue swirling, sending slow jolts to his limbs. A hand had landed on his thigh, tracing his taut muscles, then she'd pushed and he'd fallen like a feather, his back slamming the door behind him. Bending his knees, he'd dropped down an inch, then another inch, desperate to lower himself to her level, where she'd been kneeling; he'd have done anything to get closer to the bliss.

She'd been suckling him, her mouth drawing hard, the pad of her tongue exploring each ridge, taking him deeper than anyone ever had, all the way into the scalding, maddeningly wet tunnel created by her lips. When his sensitized flesh had hit the back of her throat, he'd released a sound he hadn't recognized as his own. Animal and primal, it came from a place previously lost to him…a place no woman had found until tonight.

Freeing his fingers from the tangle of wild, red hair, he'd curled a hand around the doorknob to better support himself. His mouth had gone dry, and he'd licked his lips, desperate to relieve the cottony feeling, but in an instant, it was dry all over again. Staring downward, the pleasure made him want to shut his eyes as he pushed away her hair and smoothed it over her shoulders.

"Take off your shirt," he'd said thickly, then groaned, watching as she'd followed his command. Unhooking her bra, she'd wiggled the straps down her creamy arms, her breasts swinging free, begging for his touch. Then her mouth was on him again, her tongue turning lazy—mercilessly flicking under the head of his penis, worrying the rim, teasing and grazing sharp teeth against him until he was raising his hips, silently telling her to finish what she'd started.

Now, recalling the moment, undeniable pangs claimed his groin, making him shift uncomfortably on the mattress. He wanted her again. She wasn't even touching him, but something liquid was swirling around his erogenous zones. What had he gotten himself into? he wondered as his eyes drifted over the waves of her silky red hair. Against the white of the pillowcase, they looked like wild tongues of fire.

Hours ago, he'd watched as she'd playfully touched him until his release was imminent. He'd held back, not wanting the pleasure to end, but then, she'd tickled him, the feathery touch pushing him to the edge, where he'd teetered.

"Please," he'd whispered, stunned to see his own hand tremble as he reached for her. Gently, he stroked her cheek, then her eyebrows, the pad of his fingers skimming her skin, his eyes glazed with need when they'd locked with hers. "Please…"

When she took him between her lips again, a feeling such as he'd never imagined consumed him entirely. There was nothing in the world but her. Nothing would ever matter but her. He wanted a life with her….

Pat would say his love games had finally gone too far. This was about sex, after all. No hearts and flowers. Nothing but raw need. It wasn't anything he hadn't done with countless other women. Janet and Sheila were just the tip of the iceberg, but his heart had remained untouchable and protected. He didn't even have a past love life. No true romance from high school. No lover who'd burned him, leaving him unable to trust. And he didn't want to start such a history with Cassidy…

Still, he only thought about how fast time was passing. It was Friday, which left only three nights until the court date. After that, he'd never see her again. He felt it deep down in a gut he'd learned to trust as much as his own mother.

Cassidy Case was going to walk. Or run. Her marriage had hurt her too much, leaving her touchy, resentful and convinced people would take advantage of her. Many would, too, just not him. Anger twisted inside him, and Dario silently cursed Johnny Case for destroying her. He'd never laid eyes on the bastard, but Johnny was in the way of everything Dario wanted now—Cassidy.

Too bad the best women often got hurt the most. On the job, he'd seen gorgeous girls practically held hostage by controlling men. Sometimes, the men would belittle the women to drive down their self-esteem, so they'd feel grateful and stick around. It was a sick kind of love. Something Dario had no interest in. Abruptly lifting his gaze, he realized she'd been watching him.

She squinted. "You okay?"

He glanced down at the sheaf of papers in his hand again. "Sure. I'm just thinking."

Her voice hitched in a way he was coming to love. "Me, too." She nodded toward the photocopies he was holding. "Did you finish reading?"

Because he hadn't even started, he couldn't help but smile. "Do you really think I was worrying about Lily Jordan's diary?"

"You do have a one-track mind," she admitted.

"I thought it was two."

"Two?"

"Are you referring to sex or food?"

She laughed. "Sex. Don't you ever rest?"

After the way she'd gone down on him a couple hours ago? "Uh…no." Taking a deep breath, he recalled the fun they'd had ordering take-out food afterward, and how they'd fed it to each other. "Having a babe next to me wearing such a slinky nightgown is a little distracting."

"This old thing?"

The nightshirt was worn, printed with pink poodles which had faded with too many washings. "It makes me hot," he assured.

"You're hopeless."

"So true." Staring at the pages again, he forced himself to pay attention. The photocopies were good, catching nuances of the original, which they'd been able to view briefly at the library. A smile curled his lips once more.

"What?"

He glanced from a mess of drywall in the corner, taking in the crowbar she'd been using to hack her way into whatever lay beyond, then he looked into her heart-stopping emerald eyes once more. They were glittering like the stones they'd spent part of today trying to find. "You," he said simply.

"What about me?"

He'd been thinking of how she'd acted at the library. "The way you were sizing up Janet."

Cassidy swatted him with the papers, and he grabbed her playfully, laughing as he hugged her to his side. "Now, you're really distracting me."

"She wasn't very pretty," Cassidy offered, grinning and settling into the pillows again.

Actually, Janet was a knockout. Tall and willowy, with washy blond hair and dark chocolate eyes. "Not nearly as pretty as you," he said honestly, then smiled. "Not smart, either."

"She has three degrees," Cassidy admitted.

"Maybe we should fix her up with your ex," he suggested with mock seriousness. "Wasn't he a brainiac?"

That made her chuckle. "Can we officiate at the wedding?"

"No. We might accidently catch the bouquet and garter."

She made a show of shuddering. "And then where would our sex life be?"

"After marriage, nobody keeps doing it," he returned. Now, c'mon, behave," he chided, changing the subject. "Did you find anything interesting in the other half of the diary?"

She sighed, her eyes turning dreamy, like a sun-touched sea in twilight. "You already read my half yourself," she said. He'd done so while she showered. "But…" Her voice trailed off and she shrugged. "I thought Lily's love affair with Mark was sweet."

"You're turning mushy on me again. I knew a romantic spirit was hiding inside you somewhere. Which part did you like?"

She shrugged. "How they met at the skating pond."

The two lovers had exchanged letters by courier for

months, and they'd dated in a way that no longer existed nowadays, sometimes accompanied by chaperones. "Lily had a wild life story, too," Dario commented. Like Gem, Lily had made a hard passage from Ireland, hoping to be united with distant relatives in Boston. She'd been earning money for the next leg of the journey when she'd met Mark O'Shea.

"Without parents, and few American connections, I guess Lily never had to explain Mark's unconventional family life."

"It couldn't have been easy to be illegitimate."

"Or to have your mother work at Angel's Cloud," Cassidy continued. "But we still don't know much about Gem's personal life, her relationship to Angelo or who fathered Mark."

Pausing, she shook her head in amazement. "Can you believe how New York was back then? Now average buildings are forty stories high. Some even higher. But just a hundred and fifty years ago, much of the city was still farmland. Carriages would have to pull over and wait for pigs to cross dirt roads."

"The bridge and tunnel people weren't even a concept," agreed Dario.

"The who?"

"People from the Burroughs, New Jersey and Connecticut. The ones who come and go through bridges and tunnels."

She grinned. "Is that what you call them?"

He laughed. "Only when I'm mean."

She rolled to her side and propped on an elbow. "You *are* mean," she teased, her eyes glinting with mischief.

"Want a spanking?"

She considered. "What have I done wrong?"

"Looking as good as you is a crime, sweetheart."

She smiled. "They were so in love," she said, speaking of Lily and Mark again. "Don't you think things must have been easier then? Simpler?"

Than lying next to a contemporary woman who could be this intimate with a man, then walk away? He sent her a long, sideways glance. "Doubtful. Gem and Lily escaped a potato famine on dirty ships in the dead of winter, then landed in countries where they didn't know anybody. At least your folks spoke English. Mine only knew Italian."

"You've got a point. C'mon," she added. "I want to read the rest."

"No spanking?" After shooting her a glance of disappointment, he began scanning the pages. Just as the portion he'd read previously, this was written in Lily Jordan-O'Shea's antiquated English and steady hand. "This section's about the wedding," he murmured, absorbing details about Lily's wedding dress. He passed the sheet to Cassidy.

"And Gem's death," he murmured a moment later, causing Cassidy to set aside the sheet, scoot closer and read over his shoulder.

"Oh, no…" Cassidy murmured. "The wedding was so perfect, but then…"

His eyes followed as she read Lily's words aloud. "…I wish my beloved mama had lived to see my wedding day. Trembling, I wait for my husband tonight, the passion of our first night so near. His steps are on the stairs! Shall I leave a candle burning? Oh, yes! Tonight I wish to see all of him. I wish to know everything about love…"

The very next entry described Gem's death, as if Lily had no time to reflect on whatever had happened. "Such an omen for our first day of marriage!" Cassidy read. "I feel such terror! The sadness of my beloved Mark overwhelms him! In one day, he's gained a wife and lost a mother. Worse, we're to keep mum about the loss of his father, too! We can say nothing!

"Dear diary, only to you can I pour out my heart. Mark's father, N.H., was in the carriage with my ill-fated mother-in-law, but none of the papers mention him, nor the retrieval of his body. As we make arrangements today for Gem, we've no idea what to do!"

Cassidy broke off. "N.H. That's got to be Nathaniel Haswell." She quickly continued. "My beloved is heart-broken. His parents both killed! We're in shock, and now we hear rumors the carriage was sabotaged, but by who?"

Squinting, Dario read on when Cassidy fell silent. Lily described Gem's funeral, and a few months after that, divulged that she and Mark were pregnant. For that reason, they'd decided to stay in Gem's old quarters for a while, where Mark had grown up.

"That was the building behind this one," Cassidy said.

Dario nodded. "It was torn down, but the property's still attached. Now it forms the backyard. The garages are there and the trash cans out back." Dario shook his head. "All the property, front and back, was rightfully Mark's."

Cassidy gasped. "Look…now Angelo gets sick."

"With some sort of flu. I never knew how he died. It sounds like there was an epidemic or something."

"He went quickly, within a month."

"And then Mark and Lily's baby was born."

Cassidy shook her head. "What a horrible series of events. Mark was just starting his apprenticeship with a lawyer, too."

"He had good schooling." Despite her life challenges, Gem had done right by her son. "His dad wanted to help him, too," Dario added, his tone causing Cassidy to lean closer. "Look," he added, his finger tracing the page.

"I told Mark to leave things be," Cassidy continued. "I told him we were strong enough to make it on our own. We were together. We didn't need the Haswells' money. The newspapers reported Nathaniel had gone missing while on a business trip to Baltimore, but we knew differently. His poor body was lost to the East River forever. No one was to ever know the truth. It was bad enough to grieve alone, we felt. Worse, since we loved Nathaniel more than his wife, Isme, and his son, Dirk. Gem's whole life revolved around him. He meant more to her than some husbands do to their wives."

Pausing, Cassidy said, "So, Nathaniel Haswell really was Gem's lover, and Mark was their son." She blew out a stunned breath. "But Lily's not using initials to hide his name now. I wonder why."

"Anger maybe," Dario suggested as he turned a page. "She's fed up, letting emotions override judgment."

Cassidy gasped. "And now Dirk has the nerve to show his face here," she read aloud. "Because Angelo's gone, Dirk's claiming Angel's Cloud is his. He found out Nathaniel was the owner, and since his father's been gone a year now, Dirk believes everything belongs to him and his mother. It's not true, though! I know it, and Mark knows it. We have it in writing. Foolishly, Mark told Dirk he could prove the house wasn't part of Dirk's inheritance.

"I begged Mark not to show Dirk the will Nathaniel left for us. Dirk has no idea he and Mark are half brothers! At least I don't think so. And Dirk's mother doesn't know, either, I'm sure! It's all so terrible. Gem and Mark were Nathaniel's family, not Dirk and Isme, but the truth can only bring grief. I'm sure of it.

"I told Mark we can work hard, raise our family. I can take in sewing as I did before, and we'll find another place to live, possibly with my relatives in Boston. Two years ago, they expected my arrival. Surely, they'll find room for all of us now, especially since the baby's come.

"But Mark wouldn't listen, and now he's ridden a mare to the Haswells' residence to confront Dirk and Isme with the will. Alone, I wait for his return, cradling our dear infant…"

Cassidy paused, whispering, "Unbelievable."

Dario offered a soft whistle. "And you said things were simpler back then."

"Now she's in Boston," Cassidy went on. "These three days I can only sit alone and tremble, reliving those dark hours. Where is my beloved? I wonder. My heart cries out…

"From the rear building, where we lived, I could see nothing that night, so I started to go to the front building, Angel's Cloud, where I could better watch for Mark's return from the Haswells'. With Angelo gone, the place was frightening, though. Empty and cold. Vandals had even broken downstairs windows, and they hadn't yet been repaired. The girls who'd worked there were scattered to the four winds. Neither Mark nor I wished to run such an establishment, of course. Without others nearby, we no longer really liked staying in the back building, either.

"Mark hoped we could sell, though, and create a future for our baby. Thinking I'd wait at the neighbor's house, where I could watch for Mark through a front window, I headed down the passageway between Angel's Cloud and the neighboring house, but when I heard horses, I stopped in my tracks. The hooves were pounding hard, then Mark's boots hit the ground. I'd recognize them anywhere. He must have looped the reins around the post, because before I could call to him, he was running up the front steps, shouting, "You will leave my wife and child alone, sir!"

"Dirk had to be following him, and Mark was making a

stir to warn me. Could Dirk have designs on our darling child? Clutching the infant tightly against my breast, I looked to the right, then to the left, unsure where to run. At eye level, a window was broken, but inside looked murky and dark, and I could see little.

"Shivering in the cold, I prayed the baby wouldn't cry, fearing we'd be discovered. 'Lily?' Mark called just as Dirk Haswell arrived, tied off his reins and ran inside. 'Are you here, love?'

"I didn't answer, nor did he wish me to do so. I knew, for I heard the high keen of warning in his voice. Peering through the broken window, I thought I saw his shadow whirl to face Dirk, as he entered, but it was too dark to be sure, the hole in the window too high.

"'My wife and child aren't here,' he said. 'Nor in the back house.'

"'Good,' replied Dirk. 'For it's with you I must settle accounts, and now they'll not see what I'm about to do! Hand over the false will. You've no right to bring lies to the door of decent people. You're Gem O'Shea's son. And like a whore's son, you're prostituting yourself, claiming to be the bastard of a respectable missing man.'

"Mark would never have confronted Dirk, but he wished to protect and provide for our child. Dirk reached, grasping the will, the parchment ripping. Mark clutched the other half, but then a knife appeared in Dirk's hand, the blade gleaming. It whooshed, slashing air, then plunged. A sharp cry sounded. It had gone into the chest of my beloved! I thought I screamed. Or the baby cried. But we must have stayed silent. Dirk's shadow didn't turn toward me. Mark ran. From some other room downstairs, I heard fighting.

"Then Dirk's voice came again—enraged and bloodthirsty. 'Or maybe what you say is the truth,' he shouted. 'If so, it will never matter. No one will know. No one cares about the son of a whore. My mother has connections. Any one of them could have loosened the wheels of your mother's carriage on your wedding night.'

"Mark's voice sounded weak. 'Is that a confession, sir?' he called.

"'As much of one as a dying O'Shea will ever get. My kind are respectable people, with reputations to uphold.'

"'By killing?'

"'No one cares if a whore dies.'

"'Your father was in the carriage.'

"'All the better. That ends his ceaseless whoring, and Mother and I are left with the philanderer's fortune.'

"'You killed them!'

"'Aye. And my mother knew the plot. We knew of what my father did here, and we knew of you. What did you take us for, O'Shea—fools?'

"I was frozen to the spot. Crashes sounded. Bangs.

"Then Dirk roared, 'Where've you gone, you bloody bastard? Where have you vanished to? I've cut you good! Maybe you're even dead by now! Do you really think you can hide from me? I'll find you, I will! Good God Almighty, I know you're here somewhere. Damnation!' Dirk blasted the air with his curses, and I heard more sounds of his mad search—furniture being tossed, armoires opened, lamps broken. He descended to the cellar and returned.

"'Oh, good, my love,' I thought to myself. 'You've hidden from this wretched scoundrel.'

"'Wherever you are,' Dirk shrieked, 'no man can sustain the wounds I've given you, so die wherever you hid. May no one ever find you, son of a whore!' Now Dirk ran to the foyer again, just a fleeing shadow. Feeling the blood drain from my face, I edged toward the street, wishing to make sure he was gone. In the lamps from the street, and from the light of the moon, I could see half the will in his hand, but it was his eyes that arrested me. They were mad and wild, with a killer's glint. As the paper slipped from his fingers, he didn't even notice. He was that far gone. He stared down at his own hands, which were covered in blood. He was holding the knife still, and blood was dripping from it! Mark's blood!

"He wiped blood on his coat front, then he sheathed the knife, and craned his neck toward the door, as if he meant to go inside once more. I prayed he wouldn't. Clearly, my love, although severely injured, had hidden from him, successfully. Hurry, I thought. Please go. I had to get inside and find Mark. I was so scared. And yet I couldn't call out. I had to think of the baby.

"Thankfully, Dirk mounted. Driving a whip to the horse's flank, he took off at a gallop, and I fled inside. Quickly, I lit a candle. 'Mark?' I screamed. 'Mark?' But there was no answer. The baby began to cry, and I cried, too. We went from room to room, but Mark truly had vanished! He was nowhere to be found! He was as elusive to me as he'd been to his possible killer! Where was he?

"Kneeling, I found blood in the floor, in the center of a room. There was a lot of it…too much…he couldn't have survived! It was as if my beloved had simply vanished. It was impossible! And I know Dirk left alone. But where was Mark?

"I retrieved the ripped half of the will and tucked it into my bodice. For the rest of my stay in that city, I feared Dirk would think of it and return. I was terrified and confused. I tore apart the house…not only Angel's Cloud, but the house we shared…and yet, I found nothing! How could a man disappear into thin air? My husband!

"And who could I tell? Where could I turn? Only Angelo had known of Mark's parentage. For years, Angelo pretended to own Angel's Cloud, to cover for Nathaniel. Only Angelo knew of the will. If I went to the constables, what would I say? That Nathaniel Haswell had been the true owner? That he'd died with his beloved, Gem, on the wedding night of their son? And that he'd left the property to the son with whom he'd had a real relationship, Mark O'Shea?

"No one would believe me. Some men had to know the truth, and yet I didn't know their identities. Besides, they'd never admit what they knew. And so now I could only sit and tremble. For the sake of our baby, I knew I shouldn't tarry another day, but I could not leave. I was blessed to have relatives in Boston who could take us in, but for a month I searched. If he were elsewhere, he knew of my relatives, and could always find me.

"Perhaps he is gone to some hiding place. Perhaps God took him straight to heaven when he was killed by the true bastard, Dirk Haswell!

"Oh, dear diary. You are my only friend. For the rest of my life, I must live with this strange secret. A bastard son, a lost heir, two murders, and my own husband vanished, most probably murdered, as well! And by a man too powerful for a person such as me to ever accuse. Surely, given the time that's passed, my Mark could not be living. Oh, may God protect me, and the only evidence my beloved was even in the world, our tiny infant…"

"Wow," murmured Dario, shaking his head. "There you have it. What a story! That infant was your ancestor, and that part of the will was passed down."

"Mark's still in the house," Cassidy said excitedly, already swinging her legs over the mattress.

Dario grabbed her hand. "Where are you going?"

Her face was flushed, and his heart swelled as he looked at her. She was so gorgeous. Her bright eyes glittered, illuminated by pinpoints of white light. "To find him," she said. "There has to be an entrance on this floor somewhere. Every night, music plays from inside the walls. We've heard it. We know there's empty space in there. Maybe Mark did, too. Maybe Dirk stabbed him, and he made it into a hidden passageway, trying to save his life."

"And died inside the walls? Lily would have known about the passageways," Dario countered.

"Obviously not. Otherwise, she'd have mentioned looking there. But she doesn't even consider there might be hidden rooms. I mean, vice cops knew about panel games, but nice girls wouldn't."

"She lived at Angel's Cloud."

"Not really. She lived in back. I wouldn't be surprised if she never entered the front building. She said she and Mark had no interest in such a business, remember? And anyway, we know Gem tried to keep Mark separated from life at Angel's Cloud, too. He was going to be a lawyer. I mean, he wouldn't want to involve his bride in…"

"Okay. I get your point. And that makes sense. But those bones, if they're really here, are over a hundred years old, so they can wait one more day. I say it's a job for tomorrow."

"No way."

"We have a deal," he reminded her.

Sighing, she slid beside him. "And now you need your sex slave for…"

He wanted to say for their own love story. For what they could share in the present, in the here and now. But then, he and Cassidy weren't going to fall in love. Their romance was ill-fated, like the one about which they'd read. "Just sex," he promised.

She rolled on top of him, her vixen eyes like Gem's, at least judging from the pictures in the Centuries of Sex Museum. "I bet you're a lot like her," he murmured.

"Who?"

"Gem."

"Is that a compliment?"

"Sure. I bet she drove Nathaniel crazy with lust."

"Is that what I'm doing to you?"

"Not yet." His hands circled her waist and he smiled. "Which is why you'd better get busy, Cassidy Case."

"Magee," she corrected.

"Magee?"

"I'm taking my maiden name back."

"Hmm." One thing was certain, she'd never be a Donato. *Cassidy Donato,* he thought, mentally trying on the name and deciding it sounded strange. Another sign they weren't destined to be together. He realized she was staring at him.

"Do you have a problem with my decision to be a Magee again?"

Shaking his head, he pulled her closer. "Given the way you make me feel," he assured, as he threaded hands through her hair once more and brought her mouth to his, "you're a rose by any name."

She laughed softly. "Are you sure *you're* not a romantic?"

14

CASSIDY UNTANGLED HER arms from around Dario's neck, then rolled onto her back in bed and blinked in the darkness. She intuited the night outside—heavy traffic, horns blowing, a glimmer of light through a far-off window—and she calculated it probably wasn't even midnight. When she heard Dario's soft snores, guilt and desire twisted, twining like two strands of the same rope.

Getting her bearings, she whispered, "Monday." Hours ago, she and Dario had made love. They'd shared a tender moment, too, recalling their first night together. Had she really thought he was Luther Matthews? And had she really pretended she was Gem, while Dario thought she was Sheila?

She chuckled, remembering her fear when she'd discovered his badge. When she recalled how he'd tracked her down, his dark eyes flashing, she felt the same strong visceral pull of physical longing that kept driving her into his arms. Half-smiling, she thought of their deal, and felt a rush of relief. If she'd actually found the jewels this week, she wasn't entirely sure she'd have kept her promise—to give up her rights to the property in exchange for the stones.

Johnny Case's past betrayals had hurt her too much. She wasn't proud of it, but she'd felt used, and she'd wanted to recoup her losses. Now it was a moot point. No jewels had been found, only passion. Shuddering, she admitted Dario had imprinted each inch of her body, and as craving filled her, she knew it wasn't going to be easy to return home tomorrow night.

Could she afford to tack a few more days onto her trip? She pictured her store—the empty cases once filled with sparkling diamonds—and just as much as she wanted to stay here, she had an urge to hop on the next plane, renew her lease, restock her inventory and reopen. Would she?

Tonight, time had passed just as quickly as the last three days, and now tomorrow's court appearance was worrying her. No doubt, that's why she'd awakened. Was she really ready to do whatever was necessary to make this house hers? No matter how it affected her lover?

Chuckie Haswell hadn't contacted her this week, and she'd put off seeing Luther, but between Lily's diary, the inventory list in Dario's possession and the half of the will that was still in Luther's safe, Cassidy thought Judge Zhang might rule in her favor once they presented all the evidence to him. Obviously, the will had been written by Nathaniel. His and Gem's murders were solved, too, even if many details would never be revealed.

Emotion welled inside her. After only a week, the house had become a part of her. She didn't know exactly when it had happened, but she didn't want to leave. Dario's parents had high hopes the sale of the old townhouse would pay for Eliana's wedding, and since the property had always been a source of Donato family pride, Cassidy hardly wanted to take that away from them. And what was Beppe going to say when he saw the damage? she wondered. Over the weekend, she and Dario had used a crowbar to break through weak spots in the wall, although they'd only found another crawl space that led to a dead end.

"Don't worry," Dario had said. "Whatever happens in the future, the owner will have to renovate."

"Unless Judge Zhang decides the house is Chuckie Haswell's." She'd paused. "Or your dad's," she'd added. "If he sells to Chuckie, Chuckie will demolish it to build condos." A week ago, she hadn't cared. She'd only wanted the highest price for herself, so she could use the money to reopen her business. Now she saw Luther's point of view. Refurbished, the old townhouse would be amazing. It would make the perfect bed-and-breakfast or antique shop.

"It feels like the last thing left of the old neighborhood," Dario had pointed out, further convincing her it could be a viable retail space. When he'd told her tales about playing here with his sisters while growing up, he'd been as good a storyteller as Granny Fiona. Little Italy had come alive with boisterous families, favorite eateries and narrow streets from which older women leaned in the windows with elbows propped on the sills, gossiping.

Dario had said he hated the new construction near the river. He feared the city's older buildings would eventually be destroyed, the historical districts mowed down, and when they'd traveled to other parts of the city, Cassidy could see why. Houses were being demolished, and the air space was being rezoned for the building of mammoth glass towers. It seemed a crime, when townhouses such as this could be so easily renovated. Cassidy envisioned a Christmas store full of ornaments, maybe a quaint tea shop and her own jewelry shop.

She started mentally decorating it again, and when she got to the top floor and began imagining an apartment, she realized she was thinking about a future for herself and a man she barely knew. She tried to cut off the reverie, but she couldn't. Maybe because Dario wasn't really a stranger.

From their first meeting, they'd fit. With Johnny, there had been months of awkward dates and social discomfort, then countless arguments as they'd tried to accept each other's flaws. Sex had never become as exciting as what she'd hoped.

Maybe she and Johnny just had different personality styles, she thought now. She'd been too inexperienced to see it, but she could imagine a younger woman loving how Johnny took control. She'd reacted with anger, though, always wanting someone more like Dario. He'd never order meals for her, or tell her how to park her car, or what to wear to a party unless it was no panties.

Nor did he have to work on having an equal partnership. He just did it. Besides, sex with him was so powerful that Cassidy knew she'd always be willing to work out relational fine-tuning. In his arms, after lovemaking, she felt a sense of well-being that she'd never experienced before.

"Why haven't you found a permanent partner?" she'd asked him at one point.

"I never found the right one."

His eyes had seemed to say Cassidy was his it-girl, and that he was considering telling her. Her heart had missed a beat, too, and belatedly, she'd discovered she was holding her breath.

Maybe that's when she'd admitted she was truly falling for him. All week, as they'd wrecked the place, she'd thought he was overlooking his father's probable reaction to the mess just to please her, but later, she'd realized Dario was as excited as she. A cop on the hunt. Like her, he'd really thought the jewels might be here, and now, maybe Mark O'Shea's body, too. Her heart swelled when she thought of his support.

Other than Granny Fiona, Dario was the only person to believe in the old stories. During their first years of marriage, Johnny had listened indulgently as Cassidy retold them, but later he'd always sided with her mother, saying Cassidy was obsessed with castles in the air.

The stories were true, though—even if she and Dario hadn't found the jewels. The old house was quiet now, but last night, the music had been ear-shattering. All the tenants had packed bags and left this morning, announcing they were staying with friends until they spoke again with Judge Zhang. On the way out, Brice Jorgensen had even delivered a speech about the tenants' association having its day in court tomorrow.

Where had the music come from? And why had she and Dario heard none tonight? Why hadn't they found the passageway inside the walls? Comparing the architectural plans had rendered nothing useful, only that extra space had to exist in the building's interior, and Dario was as disappointed as she at finding nothing. The dead-end tunnel in the basement had to be checked again, but given the layout, she and Dario had thought the opening more likely to be located on the first floor, so that's where they'd concentrated their energies.

Now she acknowledged how much she was coming to trust him. Definitely, he was different from Johnny Case. More complicated and full of contradictions. Guarded but with sensitivity. Smarter than Johnny, but not a guy who'd need to string letters behind his name to feel intelligent. He was seemingly unambitious but—as it had turned out—climbing fast through the ranks of the NYPD. Modest, too, taking little credit. Apparently, he often landed on his feet. He'd been single, and yet he was a family man, close to his parents and siblings.

At first, she'd assumed he was a philanderer, like Johnny, a man whose ego could only thrive on new conquests. Maybe Dario was more like Nathaniel Haswell, though—a one-woman man who hadn't yet found the right woman. Despite his infidelity to his wife, Isme, Nathaniel had loved Gem, after all.

Seized by an urge, Cassidy stretched a hand across the mattress, wanting to shake Dario awake. At the mere thought of passion, white-hot desire flashed into her veins, then ran like a live wire racing with electric current. Sex only, she suddenly thought. Why couldn't she keep it simple? Why did she have to want more?

Shaking her head as if to clear it of confusion, and determined not to dwell on her past marriage, she blinked once more in the darkness, but still saw nothing. Then she tensed.

Fire?

Rising an inch from the mattress, she propped up on an elbow and stared intently into the dark. She could swear she smelled an acrid, crisp scent, like leaves burning in a barrel. She shook Dario. "Wake up." Rolling over the side of the mattress, she grabbed her jeans and stepped into them. "I smell smoke," she insisted. Thrusting her feet into her shoes, she tugged on a shirt, then lifted the flashlight and ran toward the hallway.

Dario was on her heels, his steps sounding uneven behind her as he put on clothes. Something scraped on wood, probably his phone. "Fire? Are you sure?"

"Yeah."

As they ran into the hallway, they both gasped. Someone had opened the back door and cooler air gusted through it, carrying smoke. Was it one of the tenants? An intruder? Muttering an expletive as they ran toward the yard, Dario flipped open his cell and punched in nine-one-one. Cassidy turned on the flashlight, and when her feet landed on the first of the back steps, she could feel heat burn through her shoes.

She flashed the beam, then grasped Dario's arm as soon as he quit talking to the dispatcher.

"Look!"

Shaking his head, he uttered another curse as he closed the phone and shoved it into his back pocket. In the glimmer of the flashlight's beam, smoke seeped from the basement windows looking eerily yellow, tinged with blue.

"Fire trucks are on the way," he said. "I'm going back out front, to make sure they see the place."

"But can't we—" She cut off her words. Do what? she wondered, panic taking hold as her head jerked around. She saw no water, no buckets, no blankets. Realizing Dario's eye had caught something in the yard, and that he was changing the direction of his steps, she followed. Swiftly kneeling, he lifted a stick and poked a rag as she shined the light downward.

"Gas soaked," he muttered.

Horror ripped through her, and a hand instinctively covered her mouth. She spoke through her fingers. "What?"

"Somebody set the fire."

She pivoted as he rose, and he followed her toward the house. "Is there a garden hose out here anywhere?" she asked, speaking over her shoulder.

"No," he said as they entered the house.

"Who would do this?"

"Maybe it's connected to the arsons I've been working on."

Had his proximity to an arsonist made him a personal target? she wondered as they jogged down the hallway. He'd said very little to her about his cases. "You really think somebody's trying to hurt you?"

"Maybe."

"Who?" she asked again.

"Chuckie Haswell," he muttered.

"Chuckie Haswell?" What could he have to do with this?

"He's a suspect," Dario returned as they entered the apartment. She headed for the kitchen and flung open a cabinet. "As buildings have burned along the river front, Chuckie's been buying the property."

She gasped, thinking back to the previous week as she rummaged under the sink, hoping to find a bucket or pan. Anything to carry water. Had only seven days passed since she'd bought the red dress at the Pierre Hotel, meaning to wow Chuckie...seven days since she'd wowed Dario instead? "I thought you were only concerned with Chuckie because he was trying to get *this* building," she managed, but then she realized Dario was gone.

A moment later, he returned with the crowbar in hand. "Chuckie's buying other places, too," he said. "Anything near the water."

"And you think he's behind the arsons?"

"Maybe."

She tried to shake her mind free. Had she had drinks and dinner with an arsonist? A man Dario was chasing? There was no time to deal with this complication now. "No pans," she managed to say, wondering what she should tell Dario about Chuckie.

"Here." Reaching past her, Dario grabbed two rags, ran cold water over them, then shoved one into his back pocket and handed the other to her. "Just in case."

So far, the smoke was outside, and a shudder shook her shoulders when she considered the possibility of a worsening fire. There seemed nothing they could do to stop it. "Let's wait out front," she suggested.

They were almost to the door when she heard the far off sound of sirens. "They're almost here," she added in relief, her nostrils still flaring from the scent of smoke. Although they'd shut the back door, the fire was surely spreading, and with it, her fear. Suddenly, she wrenched. Her breath stilled, her senses on alert.

Dario half turned. "What?"

"Listen."

There it was again. She'd known she'd heard something! But was it really a groan coming from behind them? "Somebody's in the wall!"

Dario came closer, and she could see the sharpness of his gaze as they darted toward the back door and the smoke. "Hello!" he shouted. "Is anybody in here? Can you hear me?"

A call sounded, faint and faraway.

"How did you get in there?" Cassidy shouted in panic, her hands racing over the walls in the hallway, looking once more for any way inside. "We tried to find an opening all week," she muttered, terror gripping her. How could someone else have gotten in when they couldn't? "Who are you?"

Another call sounded, but she couldn't make out the words. It was a man, though. "He must have come in from outside," she said. "Or the basement. I smelled smoke, but I didn't hear anyone."

As Dario opened the back door again, gusting wind hit her face, and her heart dropped when she saw flames licking the ground. Tongues suddenly shot through one of the basement windows, but when she crouched, she could see no fire downstairs. "Can you get out?" she screamed. "Where are you?"

She thought she heard a voice shout, "In here!" Then maybe, "help," but she couldn't be sure. A loud bang sounded, metal on metal, and Cassidy raised her voice. "He's beating on a pipe. He's downstairs."

Turning in unison, she and Dario fled inside once more. Dario went down the basement stairs first, taking the steps two at a time. "Don't turn on the lights," he warned, "in case any electrical wiring's affected."

As the nearing sirens wailed, flooding her with relief, she shined the flashlight, suddenly glad for the wet rag soaking her backside. Pulling it from her pocket, she pressed it to her nose and lips. "Look," Dario added pointing.

Flames were visible in a far corner of the ceiling, near the windows. Smoke was seeping into the room, stinging Cassidy's eyes. The clanging metal rang out, louder.

"He's right above us," Dario said. "Coming closer."

"If he got in, why can't he get out?"

The hammering intensified. *Help.* Cassidy could swear she heard the word again. "Maybe he's stuck in the dark," she added. Clink, clink, clink. The sounds came faster. Helplessly, they listened as footsteps passed right above them. Quickly, Dario grabbed the crowbar, stepped on a chair and began tearing at the ceiling.

"Wait," she said insistently. "Listen."

Looking frustrated, Dario stopped. Another clink sounded. "It's coming from there," she added, focusing the beam. She ran toward the rubble she'd left days before, but smoke was in the passageway, and she jumped back, coughing. When another clink sounded, she gasped. He's definitely in there! A gust tunneled through the passage, clearing the smoke as Dario stepped past her. Where had the wind come from? There had to be an opening up above. Would the wind fan the fire?

The beam flailing wildly, Cassidy lunged. Somewhere overhead, wood groaned, then something snapped. Metal crashed. "A ceiling beam," she guessed.

"Help!"

The man's cry rent the air. For a second, she could have sworn the voice was familiar, but she knew that was only her imagination.

As Dario pulled the wet cloth from his back pocket and pressed it over his nose and mouth, she grabbed his arm, her heart lurching. "No! We can't go any farther inside!"

"We have to get him out."

"Don't!" she hollered, but Dario broke free, twisting from her grasp.

As his body moved away, she felt as if her heart was being torn from her chest. In the dark passage, the flashlight beam looked murky. Icy fear such as she'd never felt slid through her, but against her better judgment, she kept following. Where, though? Days before, she'd explored this tunnel but found nothing.

For a moment, when the beam no longer penetrated the smoke and dust, panic overwhelmed her. Vaguely, she was aware she was endangering her own life, but she couldn't leave Dario. If he went on alone, she might never see him again…

"Get back!" he shouted.

"No way," she returned, pressing the wet cloth harder against her lips, so she'd inhale less smoke.

As if realizing she wasn't giving up, he yelled, "You're right. It was an overhead beam. I can see a guy under it."

Gripping the flashlight more tightly, she raced forward, until the man came into her vision. He was lying facedown on a mud-and-dirt-caked concrete floor, crushed by a wooden beam that had fallen squarely across his shoulders. "Is he okay?" she managed, coming to stand next to Dario and the man.

As Dario felt the man's pulse and tried to ascertain whether moving the beam would further harm him, Cassidy's heart hammered. Her eyes tearing, she glanced around. "Can we get him out of here?"

"I'm used to dealing with trauma victims," he reminded

her as she craned her head, her eyes scanning the ceiling. Another beam had cracked, and its splintered ends angled downward. Her gaze shifted to the floor. The man was wearing a safari-style hat, jeans and a long-sleeved shirt. She couldn't even see his hair, much less his face.

As her eyes traveled toward the end of the passageway, she gasped. Something sparkled in the dirt. When she focused the beam, the twinkle intensified. Despite the danger, she rose and ran toward the spot, squinting. Thrusting down her hand, she lifted the rock. "A diamond," she muttered, studying the stone in her hand. It was at least three carats.

"What?" Dario shouted.

"A diamond!"

"You're serious?"

"Yeah."

Her heart was hammering harder, beating her ribs and making her breathless when she saw another glimmer, this one emitting red sparks. Her lips parting, she inhaled sharply, tasting smoke and gagging as she dropped to her knees and lifted another stone. "One of Gem's rubies," she whispered hoarsely. It had to be! As her free hand slid over the floor, following the sweeping beam of light, she found another ruby, this one smaller.

Apparently, the man had dropped them. But where had he found them? Suddenly, her hand stilled. Her eyes narrowed, then she moved forward at a crouching run, not caring that she was moving toward the fire. Behind her, Dario's voice sharpened. "Come back!"

She didn't listen. Everything she'd been told by Granny Fiona was true. In less than a breath, her hand closed over a burlap pouch. Probably, the man had dropped it as he tried to exit the passageway.

And now she saw why. "I knew it," she whispered.

Although aware of the danger, she still couldn't stop herself. In ten more paces, she'd reached a hole in the wall, hacked by the man lying unconscious behind her. She poked her head inside, and her eyes widened. A large room lay beyond. In a far corner, steps led upward, probably near where she and Dario had been in the closet, listening to the music.

A rat darted past her feet, making her squeal. Leaping onto a stool, it ran across the keyboard of an old player piano. It must have hit a switch, because deafening sounds of applause and dance hall music filled the air. So, that's where the sounds had come from! Stunned, she could only stare. The room was decorated with old love seats and once-plush chaise lounges, now musty and savaged by rodents and insects. In the center, wooden flooring had been extra space gouged out, and she realized the pouch had probably been inside.

"Yes." Flashing the light beam around the wall she saw discolored squares on the plaster. She gasped, recognizing the pattern. The paintings in the Centuries of Sex Museum had once hung in this room, she realized, recalling how a viewer's vision was drawn from one picture to the next, only to land on Gem's finger, which had pointed at the floor. Right where the stones had been hidden.

Maybe Angelo had put them there after her death. Or maybe Gem herself had always kept them in plain sight, for safe keeping, as the letter had indicated. Whatever the case, over the past hundred years, someone had discovered the paintings, removed and sold them, without knowing they comprised a clue. Perhaps one of the Donatos' ancestors had discovered the room, but preferred to keep it secret, in case another hiding place was needed someday.

As her fingers curled more tightly over the pouch, flames filled her vision. Just beyond the room, her eyes landed on yet another revelation...bones!

Cassidy staggered forward with one hand clutched around the flashlight, and the other around the gems. She shined the beam into a musty corner, then gagged. Pushing the pouch into the waistband of her jeans, she secured it against her belly, pressing the wet rag to her nose once more as she knelt. Through watery slits of eyes, she could see the bones were old. "Mark O'Shea," she whispered raspily, her throat aching from smoke as she reached for a fluttering slip of paper nearby, half buried in rubble. It was the missing half of the will. Handling it with care, she backed away, and was nearly to the hole in the wall when the piano stopped.

Suddenly, it was pin-drop quiet. Then she heard pounding feet overhead. "We're down here!" Dario shouted.

The firemen were upstairs. Turning, Cassidy bolted toward Dario. As he shifted the man onto his back, the man groaned, and when she came up beside him, she recognized the char-blackened face. "Johnny?" she muttered incredulously.

Dario's eyes locked with hers. "This is your husband?"

"Ex." Johnny Case looked exactly as she remembered him, with the same deceptively blond-haired, blue-eyed good looks that had once stolen her heart. Spotting a paper clutched in his hand, she snatched it, her heart aching when she saw it. It was a map, showing the opening to the interior rooms. Feeling more betrayed than ever before, she spoke between gritted teeth. "Where did you get this?"

"Everything you told me," he said between wheezing breaths, "led me to find some old papers in Massachusetts. They were supposed to be donated with Lily Jordan's diary, to the library here, but someone had kept this paper…"

"Meaning to come here and look," she finished for him. "The way you did."

Heavy boots were traipsing through the basement, and now three men thundered toward them, down the passageway. She pointed toward the fire. "In there!" Definitely, she was more concerned about the house than the two-timing traitor she'd once married.

"We need a traction board," Dario yelled toward one of them. "This guy shouldn't move anymore until a hospital checks him out."

As far as she was concerned, whatever happened to Johnny Case, he had it coming to him.

"Cassidy," Johnny began, grabbing her hand as she stood. Yanking it, she pivoted, knowing she couldn't get out of here fast enough. When she looked at his face another wave of fury coursed through her. "How long did you listen to my family stories, knowing you were going to come here and search?"

"It wasn't like that," he pleaded.

But it was. "You bastard," she whispered.

Turning, she jogged toward the end of the passageway and the basement, just as another fireman appeared. "We've got a guy upstairs," he yelled. "Found him out back. He was trying to conceal a gas can and some rags that were in the backyard. Looks like he started the fire. Can anybody here identify him?"

Cassidy barely heard. She was taking long strides up the stairs, and when she hit the upper hallway, she sprinted, brushing past more firemen. All at once, she was aware of her stinging eyes and burning lungs. Needing air, she hit the windy night and quickly doubled, sucking deep breaths into her chest. Tears pushed at her eyelids, and she batted her lashes, trying to hold them back.

Dammit, what was wrong with her? Why was she crying? She was sure she'd gotten Johnny Case out of her system a year ago. He'd used her even more than she'd previously sus-pected, though. He was a specialist in antiquities, and she'd come to his class, telling tales of lost jewels, which he'd used her to find. Had he ever loved her at all? She guessed she'd never really know. Now, she'd never believe anything he said.

The house was hers, though. With the will in hand, and the bones inside, which had to be Mark O'Shea's, there would be no question as to the property's rightful owner. The jewel pouch was still pressed against her belly, and now everything seemed too overwhelming.

Why was life always so bittersweet? Johnny's latest be-trayal was worse than before. The jewels were found, proving her right, since she'd always believed their exis-tence to be more than a pipe dream, but now she was supposed to give the house to the Donatos.

The tears started falling, feeling as hot on her cheeks as the fire, and she gasped as strong arms suddenly circled her waist. A second later, she was brought flush against the warm, solid front of Dario's body. Her head lolled back, and she drowned in the sensation, resting into the groove of his shoulder. Flames engulfed her, this time burning with passion. Had her lover really just saved her ex? "You shouldn't have helped him," she muttered.

Dario turned her in his arms. "I didn't know who he was."

Lifting a finger, he hooked it under her chin and used it to bring her face toward his. She looked into his eyes. "You would have saved him anyway."

Dark eyes flashed with sympathy. "Unfortunately, it's my job."

"You can't simply kill the bad guys?"

"No. But I can make sure he gets as much jail time as possible." He paused. "If you want to press charges."

Her heart squeezed tightly. The bastard had been her husband, after all, and it was tempting to let him off the hook. But he'd used her, and run her financial existence into the ground. Envisioning the empty jewel cases at her store, she managed a quick shake of her head. "I'll press charges," she whispered.

"I'll get my partner on the case," he whispered back.

"Not you?"

"I have other things to do."

She squinted, her emotions shaky as she thought about him leaving her alone tonight. Suddenly, she wanted to hug him even tighter, and tell him to stay. "Not on our last night," she managed. "What do you need to do?"

"Get in bed with you," he said.

She almost smiled. "I'd like that."

Their eyes met and held. "Somebody's got to remind you that you've met one guy who's not a class A jerk."

She could barely bring herself to believe it. "You're not?"

Slowly, he shook his head.

"What about all those girlfriends?"

"Right now, I've just got one."

Dario Donato was the best man in the whole world, she decided as her hands found both his. She twined their fingers, squeezing, and a second later, his searing lips brushed across hers.

"We'll get in bed," he promised before his lips settled on hers again. "But first we're going to have to give statements and deal with the medical examiner," he whispered. "It looks like he's just arrived."

15

"IT's NOT ACTUALLY our last night together, is it?" Dario murmured in the bedroom two hours later, his throat tightening with emotion as he took off his shirt, then tugged Cassidy's over her head. His gaze briefly settled on her breasts as he trailed fingers down her belly to undo her jeans.

"I don't know," she replied honestly, wiggling out of the pants.

For once, her body wasn't distracting him. He was watching her face, instead. Outside, he'd seen her display raw emotion; it was the chink in her armor, and through it, he sensed he'd find a key that would further unlock her emotional world. "You really just wanted sex for a week?"

"Wasn't that the deal?"

Although her mask was in place again, he knew she wasn't as cavalier as she sounded. "Nobody can do what we have physically, and not feel anything, Cassidy."

"Maybe I can."

"I can't."

"Sheila," she reminded. "Janet." She was trying to look unconcerned, but her smile was forced now. "And how many others?"

"Tons. But they don't matter now." Studying her, he was sure they never would again.

She surveyed him, as if from a distance, a knowing expression in her eyes that he was starting to find irksome.

"A week with me has sworn you off all other women?"

"Maybe," he admitted. "And quit looking at me like that."

"Like what?"

"Like you summed me up the instant we met, and haven't been proven wrong yet." He paused. "I like you, Cassidy," he continued. It was an understatement, but she knew what he meant.

"You're speaking in the heat of the moment."

And she'd make any comment to undercut what he was saying about his feelings. "Not really. And you're still half-dressed."

"Not for long."

He wanted to kick himself for starting the conversation, since she obviously didn't want to hear it. "You…feel so right," he pressed on, anyway, his hands circling her waist.

"You'll forget me quickly enough."

"Like hell."

"You're only after the conquest," she ventured.

"Meaning?"

"If I say I want more, you'll lose interest."

"No way."

"Way."

"What makes you so sure?"

"The fact that I'm definitely leaving is the one thing that makes me different."

"Not true."

"What's different then?"

Your hair, your eyes, your face. The fact that he knew he'd never get tired of her, but whatever her effect on him defied analysis. "You keep me on my toes."

"Exactly. And if you knew you had me, that would change."

Biting back a curse, he damned Johnny Case for what he'd done to her. Now that he'd seen the other man, his animosity had intensified. "At least your ex is in a cell tonight."

"Hopefully for longer."

She was prosecuting him. That meant she'd let go of past feelings. Once this evening's events came to light, her mother would start siding with her daughter instead of Johnny, as well, and that would be good for Cassidy. At the station, Pat was questioning Tim Jones, the man the firemen had discovered in the yard. Tall and skinny, with a shaved head, Tim had sported an ominous tattoo around his neck that was fashioned to look like barbed wire. Apparently, at age eighteen, he already had a long rap sheet and some of the arrests had involved arson.

Dragging a splayed hand over his hair, Dario glanced toward the closed drawer of the bedside table, which held the jewels, then he turned his attention to Cassidy again. Love would heal her, he told himself, not recrimination, which was what Johnny had dished out in hopes of better controlling her.

"If it's just sex you think you want," he found himself saying with a reasonableness he didn't truly feel, "then I'll be happy to give it to you."

Now she sounded flirtatious. "You *will?*"

"You bet."

"Only until tomorrow," she reminded.

He nodded, but he knew he'd use whatever he could to reduce her to putty in his hands, including a body she clearly found irresistible. Already, he was imagining pushing her to the limit, making her plead with him, begging for more. Dammit, she hadn't done anything wrong, but they were both being punished, he decided now. Johnny had messed with her mind, and now she didn't trust herself to find something better with another man. It wasn't fair to either of them.

She was so perfect, too. Every inch of her body was mouthwatering, and now Dario was craving her like a dangling sweet treat. "The panties," he whispered, giving up on any talk about emotions, his eyes burning a trail from her face downward, lingering on her breasts before studying a triangle of blue silk. Beneath the patch, he could see a faint outline of bunched curls, and scents just as tangled were rising from her body, making his nostrils flare. "Come hither," they seemed to whisper.

She shot him a coy look. "The panties?"

"Take them off."

"Like this?" His heart hammered as she stepped from his grasp, hooked a long red nail inside the scrap of material and drew it downward. As it slid over her thighs, it looked like a tiny blue wave cresting over creamy skin, and as he watched, he felt his chest tighten. The material was as light as wind, and by the time she tossed it away, he was breathless. Already, he was envisioning touching her, toying with the moist curls she'd just uncovered, which were within reach. Wet, slick and tight, he imagined how she'd feel closing around his finger, how her lips would go slack as she took the pleasure. A pang coiled at his groin, pulling him close, as if by a magnetic force.

"There," she whispered. "Does this work for you?"

Hell, no, he wanted to say. He wanted more than her body. Why couldn't she say something stupid and girlish and flowery, for once? So many other women had flattered him, experienced heartbreak when he'd ended relationships, and now he was on the other side of the fence. "It'll do," he said, the roughness of his own voice surprising him.

"Liar," she said, offering a tremor of a smile. "You love it."

And she was right. He did. As much as he hated to admit it, he'd almost liked seeing her cry earlier, too, since it brought out his protective instincts. While holding her, he'd felt like she needed him, and like he was becoming the man he was meant to be. He wanted her to stick around, maybe even move here. He wanted to talk about it, at least.

His eyes skated over her body. "Haven't you ever started to want more?" he couldn't help but ask against his better judgment.

"Obviously. I married Johnny."

"Screw Johnny. I mean, now."

"Yes and no."

Frustrated, Dario suddenly wanted to hit something, maybe put a fist through a wall. A man could only take so much. Cassidy Case Magee was starting to make him wish he was in the precinct gym, wearing boxing gloves, instead of watching her strip. *That* was definitely unlike him.

"What are you thinking?" she asked.

The million-dollar question. "That usually naked women turn my head."

"I'm not?"

"Sure you are," he returned, knowing pounding a punching bag would never get her out of his system. "But you're going to have to let somebody care about you again someday," he added, closing an inch between them. The instant he molded his hands over smooth hips again, his anger vanished and he was reveling in how she felt—all fine silk, soapy water and polished marble.

"Johnny never cared about me, not really."

So, she understood that. "Other people might." Dario saw people harmed by vice every day—whether by greed, lust or plain old selfishness. "I don't want you to be a victim. Don't let a guy destroy your life."

"Like most women?"

He arched a brow, thinking about how her father had left her and her mother. "Men can be jerks," he agreed. "But my mother did all right." Beppe Donato was the kind of husband who remembered birthdays and sweated his daughter's wedding. Cassidy's ex had been like a steamroller, though. He'd flattened a life Cassidy had tried to build, and even now, the man was unrepentant.

She was studying him, her eyes suddenly glittering like the stones she'd found tonight. "And the someone meant to love me would be Dario Donato?"

It was hard to tell whether or not she was mocking him. "Why not?"

"It seems unlikely."

If Cassidy let him, Johnny Case would move right back into her life and rip it apart again. She had no reason to believe Dario could be different. "Oh, you've got my number."

"The quintessential ladies' man."

"Like I said, there's only one woman right now."

For a long moment, he stared into the liquid slits of her eyes, fringed by dark, spiky lashes, then he leaned to nuzzle her neck, marveling at everything that had come to light earlier. All the jewels on the inventory list had been accounted for—diamonds, rubies, emeralds and pearls.

He'd started to ask Pat to drop by and take the stones to the precinct for safekeeping, but Cassidy had begged him not to, arguing that she wanted to be alone as soon as possible, after the medical examiner left, saying he'd return again in the morning. Since Dario wanted to be alone with her, too, he hadn't been about to argue. Besides, she'd said he could defend them against any robbers who might attack them before morning, which was true. Still, he'd given in against his better judgment, only because he wanted to be back in bed….

Angling his head farther down, he swept his hair against her chest, burrowing between her breasts, then he swirled his tongue around a stiffening tip. Catching the nipple between his teeth, he held it, tugged, got hard when he heard her heart thudding beneath his ear. It hammered wildly as he flicked his tongue. Her hips swayed gently forward, the provocative brush of her belly making him catch fire.

"Touch me, baby," he ordered, groaning as slender fingers threaded through his hair, massaging his scalp. He pulled his mouth to her breast once more, and as the pad of his tongue lapped a distended tip, her other hand traveled lower, scraping his jeans zipper with a sharp thumbnail. Flattening her palm against his bare belly, she glided it lower until he felt pressure where he most wanted it. He gasped, his breath turning ragged as she began exploring him through the denim, stroking the thickening ridge. Within a moment, he was sure he was going to burst the seams. Making an O of his lips, he exhaled a whistling sound, blowing on a nipple he'd lathered with his tongue, soliciting a shiver.

"That's right," he muttered thickly, his eyelids slamming shut as he rose to full height, his hands settling on her silken hip to steady himself as his eyes rolled back in ecstacy. "If you insist on making this our last night together, Cassidy, then—"

His voice cut off as her fingers clenched around him, squeezing his stiffened length. As blood engorged him, fiery liquid heat shot into his lower belly, swirling like a whirlpool. Waves of fire washed over him, and his skin prickled as a guttural male sound of need lodged in his throat. Something inside him took flight. Undeniable yearning claimed his whole being, pushing his hands downward, around her backside.

"Then?" she said huskily.

He'd completely forgotten what he'd been saying. "If you're leaving tomorrow," he repeated, "then you'd better make it good tonight."

"Right back at you."

"It'll be a night you won't forget," he promised.

Earlier, he'd dressed so quickly that he hadn't worn briefs, and now, as she tugged down the zipper, every inch of bliss felt like torture. As the tab hit bottom, Dario gasped once more, bursting through the opening of his jeans, released from the constraints of fabric.

"C'mon," he muttered nonsensically, not even sure what he wanted her to do next, only relieved that he was this much closer to getting what he needed…what he had to have. For a second, he didn't even blame Johnny Case for the way he'd mistreated her, not that he'd ever behave that way. But Cassidy brought out the animal in a man. Dario wanted to tell her, but he couldn't find words to describe the craving. It gnawed at him like an addiction and made him feel wild.

She was pushing his jeans over his hips, exposing a burning erection. "Let's get you out of your pants," she whispered, playing Gem O'shea once more.

"Is this what you want?" he asked throatily, although he knew it was because of her shallow breaths and the shaky tremors in the hopelessly soft hands now banking his bare hips.

As he stepped out of his jeans and kicked them away, her hands were on him again—silk on silk. A breath sucked through her teeth, sharply audible as she fisted torturous fingers around him, gripped tightly, then moved her hand like a piston.

Something raw hit the back of his throat. It felt like sand

or dust. A pang of greed twisted his groin, and he bit his lower lip in agony, or bliss, he'd never know which. Either way, he tasted blood, and to soothe the wound, he licked his lips. In the next instant, they crushed down on hers.

As her tongue dampened like a healing salve, he tried to be gentle, but her touch was excruciating. Savagely, he responded, pulling her head back. Hot lips tempted, then trembled, parting as his tongue darted. Licking as fast as flames, he could swear he saw red-and-orange forks of fire. Blue hues hazed in the periphery of his vision as her tongue glided along his.

Ready for branding, his lips marked hers. Never breaking their kiss, he urged her two steps to the bed. As her back hit the mattress, rough, greedy hands slipped under her knees, and he raised her legs, urging her to part for him.

"A condom?" she asked shakily.

It was too late. Slick moisture covered him as he pushed each greedy inch inside, muttering, "I'm healthy. So are you. I want it this way."

She must have, too, because she only caught the rhythm, moving in synch. Her first orgasm came an instant later, and his mind blanked as nails dug into his shoulders, scratching a path all the way down his back to his buttocks. Her next took longer, and he reveled in every breathtaking second of the wait. She was shivering, shuddering as darkness overtook them.

Love was blending into love. Arms and legs tangled. Taut nipples brushed and tongues meshed. Perspiration was turning their skin slick and they slid over each other as if lathered in soap. He didn't care where he ended and she began…didn't care when he came still buried inside her. Deep down, maybe he wanted to make her pregnant. That way, she couldn't leave him tomorrow. She'd be forced to deal with him forever….

They drifted. He wasn't sure, but they must have slept for some time. Their hips were still joined when he awakened. As she strummed slender fingers down his spine, he began to move again. Every inch of his body met every inch of hers. Time slowed. Only his hips moved. She brought her knees up once more, rocking her in the cradle of his thighs. The whole house was silent, except for sounds that belonged to their shared darkness—soft whimpers, panting breath.

"Is that good enough for you?"

For their last night? No, he thought in protest, letting his hips do the answering, driving harder against her, deepening his thrusts. The pure silk of her legs wrapped around his back then, those shivering thighs bracing against him as her ankles locked near the small of his back. Digging in her heels, she brought him closer still.

Everything went black when he felt her come again. In that instant, a thousand women passed in his mind, their faces flitting in an endless array. Tall, dark beauties in suits. Petite blondes in sports clothes. Trashy temptations wearing fishnet stockings and spike heels. Then he saw Cassidy again, wearing that gorgeous red dress. Cassidy...beneath him now, her skin flowing under him like water.

Gasping, his hips went wild as he exploded. He was lost, coming and coming, sure the heady sensation of release would never end. No one had ever felt this good. Instinctively, he knew no other woman would leave a mark like hers.

When he caught his breath, he whispered, "Tell me you'll change your mind and give us more than a week." When she didn't respond immediately, he covered her mouth, kissing her, and although she'd drained him, he thrust his hips again, as if to prove they should never be apart.

"Maybe we can work something out," she whispered back.

But he wanted everything nailed down right now, all the specifics discussed, a contract signed and sealed. Damn if he'd let this woman walk out of his life, he thought. Still, relief filled him. She was willing to continue seeing him. He rolled, dragging her on top of him and hugging her tightly as her legs dangled down the lengths of his.

As he began to drift once more, he was vaguely aware of the house. It was as if, after finding the stones, the will and what was probably Mark O'Shea's body, the house's hidden recesses had shut down for the night, like a shop closed for buisness. Having no more secret tales to tell, its ghosts had vanished. No skittering feet had activated the old player piano concealed in the walls, as if out of respect for whatever was happening between him and Cassidy. The past was past, for the house and maybe for them. A smile curved his lips as he burrowed against her warm body….

Or pillow, he suddenly thought.

As he rubbed his cheek against something as soft as cotton, he smelled floral-scented detergent mingled with Cassidy's skin. Rolling, he blinked and glanced around. He was alone in bed. It was morning! Grabbing his cell from the nightstand, he opened it, checked the time and sat up. "Eight-fifteen?"

Court was in forty-five minutes. He had to shower and dress. Last night's intensity had knocked him out cold. Now…

"Cassidy?" Her bag was gone. He was on his feet in a flash, his worst fears realized as he strode through the apartment. *She* was gone. Surely, she wouldn't miss court, he thought. Then the probable truth hit him. Yanking open the bedside drawer, he stared inside. The will, the inventory list and jewels were missing. She was going to be in court, all right, making sure his father didn't get the property.

"Damn," he whispered. Had he really expected her to

keep her end of their crazy deal? To give him sex, if he let her search for her beloved stones? It had seemed like an adventure, an inconsequential game with the sexiest woman he'd ever laid eyes on.

"Pat would have a field day with this." Countless women had turned his head, but it had taken Cassidy to airlift him and spin him around until he felt like he was inside a tornado. By rights, she was supposed to give the property to Dario now— or to his father. And of course, she'd decided against doing so.

For a moment, he merely stood in the middle of the room, unsure of what he felt. The deal had been crazy, sure, and her enthusiasm had captured his imagination. Now he felt… wistfulness, maybe. Defeat. He felt the way he did when a perp got away, as if the good guys were losing ground, and the bad guys were destined to win in the end. Johnny Case had so disrupted Cassidy's ability to trust that she'd become untrustworthy herself. She wanted payback, but it wasn't Johnny she'd hurt, it was Dario. And herself.

He sat on the edge of the mattress, wishing her scent wasn't everywhere. Every breath was pure torment. Imprisoned in his lungs, he was sure it would haunt him for years, just the way ghosts had seemed to haunt the house. Damn if the supposed ghosts hadn't turned out to be Cassidy's ex and a bunch of mice. And now, the only thing left of her was going to be the tapes he'd made of their first night together.

The imprint of her head was still on the pillow. White on white, it was only an indented mark, like footprints in the snow. She'd left without a word of explanation. How could she? Lifting the cell, he flipped it open and punched in her number.

"Cassidy," he said when her voice mail activated, "You're gone, but I imagine you plan to see me in court in less than an hour. Since you've got the stones, both halves of the will and the inventory list, you'll have no trouble making Judge Zhang rule in your favor. I'm a big boy. I can take it. But my family's tended this property for years. It was ours. If you found the stones, you were supposed to give the property to us. So, when we see each other in court, let's pretend we never met."

Abruptly, he hit the off button, ending the call. At least he'd salvaged his pride. With Cassidy gone, it was all he had left.

16

DARIO GLANCED TOWARD the courtroom door, not knowing what he'd do if Cassidy walked in. When his eyes caught Eliana's, she hunched her shoulders in an exaggerated shrug. She glanced toward Judge Zhang, then at Dario again, lifting her hands. "Where's Pop?" she mouthed. "Ma was supposed to meet me, but she didn't show. We were going to go over last-minute details about my dress. The hem's too short. It just doesn't look right, and she picked up your tux, by the way."

It was hardly the right time to discuss the wedding. Leave it to his big sister not to notice he was heartbroken. He turned his attention back to Judge Zhang. The events of the past week had been divulged, and now the judge was about to make his final determination about the property's ownership. Usually, the judge took his time, but today the proceedings had moved quickly due to Luther Matthews who was talking at a fast clip. As much as Dario needed to hear every word, and as much as his mind kept straying to Cassidy, he found himself frowning at Eliana. "Did you call Ma's cell?"

"I got her voice mail."

"And Pop?"

"He said they were fine, and on their way, but he wouldn't tell me anything else."

The motions of Eliana's hands communicated her anxiety. Ever since her engagement, she'd started gesticulating in a way that would showcase the rock on her left hand. Now she seemed to have forgotten the ring completely. "I hope they're okay."

So did Dario. His parents were in good health, and while he hated to think something bad could have happened to one of them, they were usually punctual. "You did talk to Pop?"

"Yeah. And he sounded fine."

"You still want me to stick around?" whispered Pat, who was on the other side of Dario.

"Might as well," Dario said under his breath. "We've got Chuckie Haswell in our sights."

"He's got a helluva lawyer," continued Pat, who'd been up all night working the arson case. "I'll give him that much."

Tim Jones had admitted he'd been hired to start fires, not only at the Donato's property, but all over town. When questioned, the middleman who'd hired Tim confessed the payee was Chuckie Haswell. Shortly afterward, around six, Pat had turned up two witnesses who'd seen Chuckie talking to the middleman, and by seven, Chuckie had been arrested. Within the hour, however, he'd posted bail, but that wouldn't matter in the end. With the information they had, Dario figured they'd get a conviction.

Still, Chuckie had the nerve to enter the courtroom and continue arguing that the very property he'd tried to burn last night was rightfully his. Probably, in his twisted imagination, he'd convinced himself it was. That meant he had the right to do whatever he wanted with it, including destroy it. Johnny Case had turned out to be even more devious. Despite the statement Cassidy had given the police last night, Johnny claimed she'd told him the property was hers, and that he could let himself in to search it.

Pat whistled softly. "Cassidy's not even here."

Dario could have kicked himself. On his way to the court-house, he'd told Pat the whole story over the phone, and of course, Pat had told Eliana. His partner and sister were as nibby as the gossiping women in their old neighborhood. "It was a week-long thing," Dario muttered, wishing his chest didn't feel quite so tight. A part of him wanted to leave the courtroom right now, find Cassidy, and demand an ex-planation. Last night, she'd said they could work things out, but then she'd disappeared.

He tried not to berate himself, but he should have known she was lying. He was a cop, supposedly an expert in deviance. Why hadn't he guessed she was using him all along?

"You let her rip apart Pop's property?" whispered Eliana in disbelief, shaking her head. "He's going to kill you. The woman must have really done a number on you, little brother."

"Mmm-hmm," he said under his breath. Briefly, he shut his eyes, and his mind filled with images of her. "She was supposed to give us the property," he reminded, "if she found the jewels."

Eliana snorted. "And you believed that?"

Yeah. He had. But had Cassidy really just played him? Pushing away his emotions, he shrugged. He wanted to call her, but his pride wouldn't allow it.

"She must be gorgeous," offered Eliana.

"Sexier than Sheila Carella," agreed Pat.

"Like I said, it's over," Dario muttered, and now Cassidy was the last thing he wanted to discuss. She was probably on a plane by now, or in South Carolina unpacking. She'd left Dario and let Luther Matthews do all her remaining dirty work. He was making a good job of it, too, as if he couldn't get the property signed over to Cassidy fast enough. He'd even brought a museum guard, pictures of the jewels, and a handwriting expert to testify to the will's authenticity. Not to mention the inventory list, which was really the property of the NYPD.

How had she accomplished so much in such a brief amount of time? Had she even thought of him during that time? Of how he and his family would be affected by her claiming the property? Of how hurt he'd feel in the end?

But no…her only thought had been for herself. She was as selfish as her ex. And Luther Matthews. Every few seconds, the man's eyes were darting toward the door, as if to say there were a million places he'd rather be.

"Here," Luther said, pacing in front of Judge Zhang's bench. "As you can see, we also have the complete will, written by Chuckie Haswell's ancestor, Nathaniel Haswell. Clearly, the property was a gift to Gem O'Shea. Because they died together, she was never able to take possession, but it was definitely meant for her, and in turn, for her son."

Pausing, Luther shot Chuckie a long look. "A man most probably murdered by Dirk Haswell."

"That's absurd," countered Chuckie. "You can hardly believe Lily Jordan's diary."

"Maybe not," returned Luther. "But the will has been authenticated." Gem O'Shea's jewelry, which was inventoried by the New York Police Department over a century ago, has been retrieved, also, and the judge has pictures. Everything has been accounted for. Surely the bones found this morning must be Mark O'Shea's."

The medical examiner had returned to finish last night's job just as Dario was leaving the house. In the interest of truth, Dario had passed along the information. Just because Cassidy had burned him, didn't mean he was going to turn the tables and do the same to her.

"On behalf of the tenants association," Brice Jorgensen put in, "I'd like to say that we're glad to finally have the matter cleared up. Obviously, something very strange was happening in that building. Now, whatever the outcome, we hope we'll be able to stay in our homes until our leases are up—"

"Duly noted, Mr. Jorgensen," said Judge Zhang.

"Judge—" Pat dragged a hand over his buzz-cut red hair. "Once more, I feel compelled to point out that Mr. Haswell was arrested this morning on charges involving the attempted arson of the property in question."

"They're trying to frame me in order to get my property," Chuckie snapped. "It belongs to me. I assure you I'm being set up by the police! Officer Donato's father is the one who—"

"Careful, Mr. Haswell," the judge interjected. "Accusing law enforcement officers of wrongdoing while in a court of law isn't advisable." He turned to Luther. "So, Mr. Case did not make it to town, as expected?"

"Ms. Case. And yes, she did…" Pausing, Luther sent Dario a glance, making Dario wonder how much he'd been told about the affair. Whatever the situation, Luther probably knew the truth regarding Cassidy's real feelings for Dario, if she had any. "Ms. Case couldn't make it this morning. She sent me on her behalf, however, and the papers are in order, as you can see. I'm hoping we can have a speedy determination, since it's a very busy day for me."

"Wait a minute," interjected Chuckie. "I admit I was arrested this morning, but the behind-the-scenes machinations regarding this property have been unbelievable. Ms. Case came to town last week, all right. She called and asked to meet for drinks at the Pierre Hotel. When I arrived, she was dressed to the nines, in a bright red dress and spike heels. The works," Chuckie clarified.

Dario's body tensed as he registered the betrayal, now realizing he'd never wondered where Cassidy had been the night he'd tracked her to the hotel. He'd been so blown away by how she'd looked in the dress that he'd only asked in passing.

"She said the Donatos were a wild card," Chuckie continued. "She said she didn't care about the museum's interest in the property, either, in spite of what Mr. Matthews is saying now. She wanted money. Just like me, she wanted the best business deal, and I was impressed. She promised she'd sell to me if I helped her stake her claim. Like everybody said, she wanted inside the house, to look for the jewels, which she found, but she didn't tell me about them when I met her. She told me she wanted inside the building for sentimental reasons."

He flashed a sharklike smile. "But that woman doesn't have a sentimental bone in her body. It was all about getting what she wanted. She'd do anything for it, too. Drinks led to dinner…"

Judge Zhang considered. "And then?"

Chuckie looked torn. "And then dinner led to her room upstairs."

"That's a lie," Dario couldn't help but mutter, suddenly hating the weakness Cassidy Case Magee had revealed in him. He was hardly proud of the anger flashing along his nerves, but when he imagined a slimy weasel like Chuckie Haswell pawing Cassidy, he felt positively sick.

"How do you know?" asked Chuckie.

"I was there that night."

Chuckie was loving every minute. "Before or after me?"

Dario shook his head in disgust. "You're an animal, Haswell."

Chuckie threw up his hands, as if to say this was only

further proof the NYPD was out to get him. Dario barely noticed. He was still trying not to imagine the worst— Cassidy clinking champagne flutes with Chuckie, hanging on to his every word, undressing him in her room at the Pierre, just the way she'd undressed Dario.

He thought back, but he could remember no trace of the other man in the room that night—no scent of cologne, or sight of a lost sock or tie. Definitely, he hadn't smelled a man on her. But then, the red dress had completely captured his attention.

Vaguely, he was aware Judge Zhang was speaking to him.

"Are you sure you don't wish to retract your statements, Officer Donato?"

Hell, yes, he wanted to say. He wanted to retract the whole past week. Instead, he'd corroborated the truth—testifying the stones had been found on the property, as well as the other half of Nathaniel Haswell's will. Abruptly, he shook his head, knowing what determination the judge would have to make. "No, sir. Everything I said is true." And by virtue of that, he might as well have signed over his pop's property to the woman who'd used his body for a week, then vanished.

"All things considered, I'm naming Cassidy Case the sole proprietor of 67 Anthony Street," said Judge Zhang. "All tenants will remain in residence until the end of their leases, in accordance with New York law."

Eliana gasped, and without a word, Dario slid a hand under her elbow and began steering her from the room. "We'd better get out of here," he muttered. "I can't vouch for what I'll do to Chuckie Haswell in a one-on-one. Luther, either."

"Ditto," said Pat, who took up the rear as the three headed down a center aisle and into the hallway.

"Meet you outside," Eliana said. "I've got to find the little girls' room."

"Me, too," said Pat.

"You might get arrested," warned Eliana.

"Thanks for the tip. I'll use the little boys' then."

Dario kept going, wanting to avoid Chuckie and Luther, but mostly because he needed air. Using his shoulder, he pushed through brass revolving doors, and then the air hit him hard. While it was sweater weather, the wind felt gusty and carried the first sharp, acrid taste of winter. Just as he sucked a breath deep into his lungs, he could swear he smelled her. Her scent pooled, eddying low in his belly. He turned.

"There you are!" she exclaimed.

She was right behind him. Anger surged when he saw her face, and vaguely, he thought she had no right to look so damn beautiful—her eyes narrowed against the wind, her cheeks pale. Just by surprising him, she was making him see red. He'd been here, after all. But where had she been?

"Did you talk to him?" she asked breathlessly.

"Who, Luther? Chuckie? Oh, yeah," he said acidly, not bothering to let her answer, his annoyance intensifying when he saw the feigned, innocent expression. "You look like you've seen a ghost," he added, and suddenly, he guessed she had. "So, you didn't plan on running into me again, did you?"

"Of course I did. I was looking for you. What's going on?"

As if she didn't know. "You didn't get my message?"

"What message?"

So, she was really going to play dumb. "Court's over, doll. You got everything you wanted. The stones. The property. And if you hurry, you might catch your friend, Chuckie Haswell, before he goes back to jail to keep your ex-husband company."

She blinked as if he were a stranger. Before he thought it through, he'd grasped her shoulders. Almost immediately he emitted a soft, telltale breath, almost a gasp, his fingers loosening their grip. Suddenly, he was both stroking her sweater and damning himself for it, knowing he couldn't afford to let her reopen the wound she'd gouged in his heart. Against his will, he ran a hand upward, along the side of a smooth, silken cheek. Windswept hair across the back of his hand—red on white, like a rose on a sheet— and it felt as astonishingly soft, just like a petal.

"I tried to get here," she said weakly, still seemingly breathless, as if to prove she'd run all the way here.

"But you didn't quite make it, right, Cassidy?"

"Look," she began. "I—"

"Whatever you did, I don't care," he murmured, and he really didn't, not anymore. But he had to kiss her again. Just once. Angling his head closer, he paused before their lips brushed. Her breath was mingled with his, carrying a mint scent. He hovered, committing the sensation to memory, knowing he'd never feel it again.

"Sex for a week," he whispered, his voice gravelly. "That was the deal, right? And you played it well, Cassidy. Didn't you? All the way to the hilt. You're a real pro. In the end, you put Gem to shame—"

She tried to step back, looking as if she'd been stung, but he tightened his grip, holding her fast. "Chuckie said he enjoyed that gorgeous red dress every bit as much as I did, and Luther argued your case brilliantly."

She was shaking her head. "No! I only told Luther to keep the—"

He used a finger to silence her. "I want to remember you the way you really are."

"How's that?"

"Sexy as hell. And totally out for yourself."

"That's not true," she said, shaking her head.

"I won't forget the way you pretended to be upset about Janet and Sheila. Meantime, you were meeting Chuckie… Luther."

"You can't believe that."

Now she was going to deny the obvious, exactly like Johnny Case. "Your ex screwed you over," he continued, "and now, you're passing along the goods. But don't worry," he said, his voice lowering, "I can take it. I see this every day at work. What goes around comes around. Call it what you will. Divine Karma. Tit for tat. Whatever the case, I want you to know…you're the best—" He trailed a finger down her cheek. "I enjoyed every minute we spent together." Nothing would detract from that.

"You've got everything wrong."

"That's what Johnny said last night, wasn't it?" He flashed a smile that didn't meet his eyes. "And I guess you learned that from him, too."

"You think I was with Chuckie?"

"I know you were. But you can ask your friend, Luther. I'm sure he'll fill you in on the details when you pick up your precious stones."

"I'll do that," she managed to say.

"Meantime," he began, leaning another inch toward her lips, "this is goodbye."

He kissed her then, and beneath his, her lips felt cool and firm, parted more in surprise than passion. Slowly, he increased the pressure, already feeling the heat course between them. If one more second passed, instinct would take over. Already, he felt compelled to pull her against him, wrapping his arms tightly around her waist. He wanted to rip off her clothes, unbutton her jacket, reach inside, and strip off whatever was beneath. Instead, he broke the kiss abruptly, pivoted and headed down the courthouse steps.

For a moment, he heard nothing. Then high heels. She was running after him. Right before she reached him, he hit the lowest step, raised his hand to hail a taxi and glanced over his shoulder. Something in his expression stopped her in her tracks. Her own eyes were gorgeous, a jewel-like green that sparkled with uncertainty. Hair blew wildly around her face, the red strands whipping her cheeks. Her jaw slackened, and her lips parted as if she was about to speak.

He didn't let her. "Stay away from me," he said as a cab pulled to the curb. He got in, slammed the door and gave the address of his apartment in Battery Park, which he hadn't seen in a week. It was an apartment that, thankfully, would carry no reminders of Cassidy Case Magee. She'd never even been inside it before, just as he'd never seen the interior of her home in South Carolina. This seemed further proof that the week had been only a mirage. A passing indulgence. A sexual encounter taking place in a moment out of time.

He didn't look back.

"You are not even my son," Dario's mother chided a week later, in the hallway of the church where Eliana was getting married. Wearing a grim expression, as if to say all her children were married now, except for her wayward, youngest son, she brushed at the shoulders of his tux, smoothing imaginary wrinkles.

"This could be you, going down the aisle, Dario," she continued. "But no. You have to follow in the footsteps of Angelo. Thank God—" his mother crossed herself "—that terrible place has finally left our hands for good. Now, maybe you'll find a nice girl."

Taking advantage of the narrow window, Dario leaned

quickly and kissed her cheek, hoping doing so would make her change the subject. "You look beautiful, Ma." And she did, dressed in a gold dress, similar to those worn by the bridesmaids.

"Humph. Don't distract me. Maybe your luck is about to change. Maybe you won't send away another girl who was going to be my daughter-in-law."

Dario groaned. "Cassidy Case wasn't going to be your daughter-in-law, Ma."

"Magee," his pop corrected. "And that's not how it seemed to me when she came to meet us last week," his pop said, sidling next to his mother.

"She snowed you two, just the way she did me," Dario offered gruffly, although he knew it was lie. Later, he'd discovered he was in the wrong. Cassidy had been late to court because she'd been trying to strike a compromise with Beppe. While Dario had been sleeping, she'd been busy approaching his folks with a plan to start a commercial venture in the townhouse, comprised of small boutique-style shops.

They'd reached an agreement to manage the property jointly, too, and she'd hoped to work out an arrangement that might help the museum, also. Luther had double-crossed her, arguing for her to get the property, when she'd asked him to make sure Judge Zhang understood she wasn't intent on keeping it. Later, after it was hers, and she'd refused to sell to Luther in fury, it had become clear that he'd really had her best interest at heart, and Dario guessed she'd forgiven the curator.

Now, no one knew what would happen. Cassidy's plan had been a better proposition than if the Donatos had been awarded the property, and then sold, since the house would have continued to produce revenue for years to come. In addition to showing how the venture would pay for Eliana's wedding, Cassidy had talked to his folks about keeping space available for her living quarters, which would provide in-house security, as well.

The impromptu meeting had run on too long, then Dario's folks and Cassidy, traveling in separate cabs, had gotten stuck in traffic. Now his parents were convinced Cassidy had meant to include Dario in the deal, and that she'd imagined living with him, once she was in New York, with an eye to marrying him.

Of course, that's what his folks *would* think. They loved him. Good Italians, they wanted their kids married off. And as far as they were concerned, every female in Manhattan had been chasing Dario since birth. Cassidy hadn't, though. He was the one who'd tracked her down and inserted himself into her life while she was trying to heal from a relationship.

His stomach flip-flopped when he recalled the look of hurt on her face. He'd left four voice mails during the week, hoping to apologize, but she'd never returned the calls. Anyway, she was back in South Carolina now. A lawyer had contacted Beppe, saying Cassidy had changed her mind. The deed was Beppe's, in accordance with what she'd called "an undisclosed deal between myself and Dario." Now the Donatos could do whatever they wanted.

Legally, it had been accomplished overnight, leaving Dario's mind reeling with if-onlys. If only he hadn't brought up Chuckie or accused her of lying. But he had, hadn't he? In the end, he'd been the one without any trust. Always, when he awakened now, he'd imagine she was naked beside him, then he'd recognize it was only a lingering dream.

"I'll see you inside," he said abruptly to his mother. "I'd better line up with the other ushers, and Eliana needs you more than I do right now, Ma."

"I already said goodbye," his mother said, tearing up. She stretched on tiptoes, kissed his cheek, then kissed his father. "It's time for me to go in. I'll see you gentlemen at the altar." She quickly patted Dario's shoulder before starting down the aisle.

At least the past week had been a madhouse, Dario thought, as he pushed open the door to where the ushers were lining up, his father close behind him. His chest got tight when he saw Pat. "Hey, buddy. You're next in line, after Eliana."

"Not until spring. Karen just set the date."

"Congratulations."

The next few minutes passed in a haze. The week really had been crazy. Eliana's dress hem had to be lengthened at the last minute, and one of the bridesmaid's shoes had been dyed the wrong color. He must have been completely out of it, he realized, seeing a man from their social circle among the other ushers. He could have sworn he wasn't a member of the wedding party, but then, he'd been so caught up with Cassidy....

As his turn to walk down the aisle neared, he glanced at his father, who was preparing to give away Eliana. As Pat preceded him, to walk with Karen, Dario couldn't help but wonder if he was ever going to join the ranks of his married friends. Probably not, he decided. He didn't even want sex at the moment, not unless it was with Cassidy.

Eliana's wedding planner, a woman who'd done little more than graciously take orders from Donato females, nodded at him. Telling himself to ignore his own soured love life, since it was his favorite sister's big day, he stepped through a door, into the hallway. A second later, he was facing the long, white runner, and was stunned at the sea of smiling faces looking his way. Crooking his arm, he forced himself to smile toward one of Eliana's childhood friends, Melissa Keating, whom he'd be escorting.

"Cassidy?" he said aloud, half believing his mind was playing tricks.

She looked stunning in the bridesmaid's dress, a floor-length gold gown that made her upswept red hair dance like flames. His eyes left her face only for a moment, seeking his sister, but she was nowhere to be found, of course. She was behind him, waiting to walk down the aisle herself. So, his favorite big sister had trumped him on her very own wedding day. This explained the extra usher. *I'll be damned.*

Cassidy was surveying him, her gaze wavering with uncertainty until he put out his arm. The second hers slipped into the crook, peace filled his heart. It was risky, but he couldn't help but say it. "Welcome home."

"Good to be back."

It was that simple. The rift repaired. And as they walked to the altar, he knew he'd be next in line, after all, and the last of his crowd to marry. When they'd almost reached the pulpit, his eyes widened. He could swear Gem O'Shea was seated in the front pew, right next to his mother, and then it occurred to him that it had to be Cassidy's mom. Given his lack of priors, Johnny Case was headed for plenty of community service, instead of jail, but it was probably enough to make Cassidy's mom see the light about her daughter's relationship. Finding the jewels had changed everything. Cassidy had been right. And leave it to his own ma to set about matchmaking.

"My folks must really like you," he whispered before they parted at the altar.

"Not as much as *you* like me," she returned.

The service went by in a flash. As much as Dario tried to attend to his sister's vows, he couldn't wait for the ceremony to be over, so he could hold Cassidy again. As much as he liked his new brother-in-law, he was gaining more than a brother today. Cassidy was in his life again, and he was fantasizing about how her mouth would feel. Forget everyone, he decided. He was going to find some hidden nook in the church....

"What made you change your mind?" he asked once they'd traversed the aisle once more and he'd grasped her hand, pulling her through the front door and down a sidewalk. Seeing that the back door of an empty limo was unlocked, he opened it and urged her inside. Soon, the driver would arrive, to take them to the reception, but they had a few minutes.

"Sex for a week was pretty good," she murmured, seemingly noting the tinted windows as she snuggled next to him, "and the plan I proposed to your folks was brilliant, if I do say so, myself. I've forgiven Luther..."

"No more talk about other guys."

"Jealous?"

"Like I said, you turned the tables on me. Sure I am."

"Show me."

His mouth was on hers in a flash. As a hand rustled the hem of the gown upward and glided it high on her thigh, his tongue thrust possessively between her lips. Arching, she gasped in response, clearly missing their passion as much as he. He urged her on top of him. The gown bunching around her thighs, she straddled him, and he inhaled sharply as his hands grasped her ankles. Her legs were bare, as smooth as glass when he began gliding them upward on her calves, then her thighs.

"I need you," he whispered. Inside. Deep.

"I need you, too," she whispered against his mouth.

"Really?"

"Uh-huh," she managed breathlessly, the words coming on a soft pant of excitement. "Which is why this sex for a week thing got me to thinking."

"Funny," he muttered, heat flooding his groin, "because I can't think about anything right now."

"Not even me?"

He shook his head. He could think only about her hand, which was gliding between them, burrowing in the folds of his slacks. He darted his eyes around, then pressed a button and secured the only unlocked door. It was risky, but he had to have her. Leaning his head back on the plush leather, he gazed intently into her eyes, and hers burned back at him, the green irises blazing. Then her mouth brushed his, a spark of fire, and her hand massaged him, driving him wild with the touch he'd been so sure he'd never feel again.

"Cassidy," he begged, overwhelmed that they were together. "I want…"

Her kiss silenced him. "I know."

She wanted it, too. With a quick glance through darkened windows, she urged the slacks down on his hips, then poised above him. Sucking a breath through his teeth, he glided his hands higher…then higher…and gasped audibly when he felt her silky backside. No panties.

"You've forgiven me for not trusting you?" he asked.

"Have you forgiven me?"

"Yeah."

"Then ditto."

"Rose and Brice got together."

She smiled. "But Johnny got off the hook."

"Sort of." Now he was smiling back. "Wearing an orange jumpsuit and collecting litter in your hometown will probably make him look less appealing to the girls he chases."

She laughed softly. "True."

"Chuckie will probably do time."

"Good." She surveyed him, and something in her eyes made him think about Gem's last night. Somehow, it seemed fitting they were sealing their love in a carriage of sorts, even if, unlike Gem and Nathaniel, they were going to live and prosper.

"Like I was saying," she continued in a deep murmur, lowering herself, her wet, slick warmth surrounding him, making him cry out, "when I thought about sex for a week, I got to thinking."

He could barely find his voice. She was so beautiful, and the thrusting, rhythmic movements were making his pulse race. Tightening his arms around her waist, he hugged her close, burying his face against her chest and whimpering, "About?"

"Sex for a lifetime," she answered, threading splayed fingers into his hair.

His throat felt raw. "When do we start?"

Her arms wrapped around his neck, and her hips rocked even more deeply against him. When they were completely joined, she went very still. Suddenly, he lifted his face and found her eyes. "We already have," she told him gently.

"Then love me, Cassidy Case Magee," he returned.

She began to move again, her hips sending shudders through them both, and as she did, as if it were really their own wedding day, she whispered, "I do."

* * * * *

*Silhouette® Romantic Suspense
keeps getting hotter!
Turn the page for a sneak preview of
Wendy Rosnau's latest* SPY GAMES *title*
SLEEPING WITH DANGER
Available November 2007

*Silhouette® Romantic Suspense—
Sparked by Danger, Fueled by Passion!*

Melita had been expecting a chaste quick kiss of the generic variety. But this kiss with Sully was the kind that sparked a dying flame to life. The kind of kiss you can't plan for. The kind of kiss memories are built on.

The memory of her murdered lover, Nemo, came to her then and she made a starved little noise in the back of her throat. She raised her arms and threaded her fingers through Sully's hair, pulled him closer. Felt his body settle, then melt into her.

In that instant her hunger for him grew, and his for her. She pressed herself to him with more urgency, and he responded in kind.

Melita came out of her kiss-induced memory of Nemo with a start. "Wait a minute." She pushed Sully away from her. "You bastard!"

She spit two nasty words at him in Greek, then wiped his kiss from her lips.

"I thought you deserved some solid proof that I'm still in one piece." He started for the door. "The clock's ticking, honey. Come on, let's get out of here."

"That's it? You sucker me into kissing you, and that's all you have to say?"

"I'm sorry. How's that?"

He didn't sound sorry in the least. "You're—"

"Getting out of this godforsaken prison cell. Stop whining and let's go."

"Not if I was being shot at sunrise. Go. You deserve whatever you get if you walk out that door."

He turned back. "Freedom is what I'm going to get."

"A second of freedom before the guards in the hall shoot you." She jammed her hands on her hips. "And to think I was worried about you."

"If you're staying behind, it's no skin off my ass."

"Wait! What about our deal?"

"You just said you're not coming. Make up your mind."

"Have you forgotten we need a boat?"

"How could I? You keep harping on it."

"I'm not going without a boat. And those guards out there aren't going to just let you walk out of here. You need me and we need a plan."

"I already have a plan. I'm getting out of here. That's the plan."

"I should have realized that you never intended to take me with you from the very beginning. You're a liar and a coward."

Of everything she had read, there was nothing in Sully Paxton's file that hinted he was a coward, but it was the one word that seemed to register in that one-track mind of his. The look he nailed her with a second later was pure venom.

He came at her so quickly she didn't have time to get out of his way. "You know I'm not a coward."

"Prove it. Give me until dawn. I need one more night to put everything in place before we leave the island."

"You're asking me to stay in this cell one more night...and trust you?"

"Yes."

He snorted. "Yesterday you knew they were planning to harm me, but instead of doing something about it you went to bed and never gave me a second thought. Suppose tonight you do the same. By tomorrow I might damn well be in my grave."

"Okay, I screwed up. I won't do it again." Melita sucked in a ragged breath. "I can't leave this minute. Dawn, Sully. Wait until dawn." When he looked as if he was about to say no, she pleaded, "Please wait for me."

"You're asking a lot. The door's open now. I would be a fool to hang around here and trust that you'll be back."

"What you can trust is that I want off this island as badly as you do, and you're my only hope."

"I must be crazy."

"Is that a yes?"

"Dammit!" He turned his back on her. Swore twice more.

"You won't be sorry."

He turned around. "I already am. How about we seal this new deal?"

He was staring at her lips. Suddenly Melita knew what he expected. "We already sealed it."

"One more. You enjoyed it. Admit it."

"I enjoyed it because I was kissing someone else."

He laughed. "That's a good one."

"It's true. It might have been your lips, but it wasn't you I was kissing."

"If that's your excuse for wanting to kiss me, then—"

"I was kissing Nemo."

"What's a nemo?"

Melita gave Sully a look that clearly told him that he was trespassing on sacred ground. She was about to enforce it with a warning when a voice in the hall jerked them both to attention.

She bolted away from the wall. "Get back in bed. Hurry. I'll be here before dawn."

She didn't reach the door before he snagged her arm, pulled her up against him and planted a kiss on her lips that took her completely by surprise.

When he released her, he said, "If you're confused about who just kissed you, the name's Sully. I'll be here waiting at dawn. Don't be late."

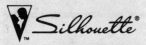
Silhouette®

Romantic
SUSPENSE

Sparked by Danger,
Fueled by Passion.

Onyxx agent Sully Paxton's only chance of
survival lies in the hands of his enemy's daughter
Melita Krizova. He doesn't know he's a pawn in the
beautiful island girl's own plan for escape. Can
they survive their ruses and their fiery attraction?

*Look for the next installment in the
Spy Games miniseries,*

Sleeping with Danger

by Wendy Rosnau

Available November 2007 wherever you buy books.

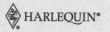

HARLEQUIN®
INTRIGUE®

WHITEHORSE MONTANA

Love can be blind...and deadly

On the night of her best friend's wedding, Laci Cavanaugh
saw that something just didn't seem right with Alyson's
new husband. When she heard the news of Alyson's
"accidental" death on her honeymoon, Laci was positive
that it was no accident at all....

Look for

THE MYSTERY
MAN OF
WHITEHORSE

BY B.J. DANIELS

*Available November
wherever you buy books.*

HARLEQUIN Romance

New York Times bestselling author

DIANA PALMER

Handsome, eligible ranch owner Stuart York knew
Ivy Conley was too young for him, so he closed his heart
to her and sent her away—despite the fireworks between
them. Now, years later, Ivy is determined not to be
treated like a little girl anymore…but for some reason,
Stuart is always fighting her battles for her. And safe in
Stuart's arms makes Ivy feel like a woman…his woman.

Winter Roses

Available November.

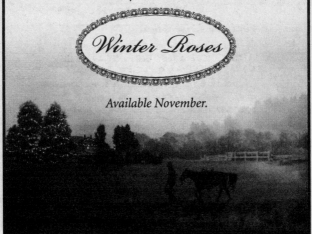

REQUEST YOUR FREE BOOKS!

2 FREE NOVELS PLUS 2 FREE GIFTS!

HARLEQUIN®

Blaze®

Red-hot reads!

ATHENA FORCE

Heart-pounding romance and thrilling adventure.

History repeats itself...unless she can stop it.

Investigative reporter Winter Archer is thrown into writing
a biography of Athena Academy's founder. But someone
out there will stop at nothing—not even murder—to
ensure that long-buried secrets remain hidden.

ATHENA FORCE

Will the women of Athena unravel Arachne's powerful
web of blackmail and death...or succumb to their
enemies' deadly secrets?

Look for

VENDETTA

by *Meredith Fletcher*

*Available November
wherever you buy books.*

HARLEQUIN®

Mediterranean NIGHTS™

Not everything is above board
on Alexandra's Dream!

Enjoy plenty of secrets, drama and sensuality
in the latest from Mediterranean Nights.

Coming in November 2007...

BELOW DECK

by
Dorien Kelly

Determined to protect her young son,
widow Mei Lin Wang keeps him hidden
aboard *Alexandra's Dream* under cover of
her job. But life gets extremely complicated
when the ship's security officer, Gideon Dayan,
is piqued by the mystery surrounding this
beautiful, haunted woman....

HARLEQUIN®

Blaze™

COMING NEXT MONTH

#357 SEX BOMB Jamie Sobrato
Elle Jameson can wield a .38 as fiercely as a makeup brush. But there's not a big demand for her eclectic skill set. Then Christian Navarro appears to recruit her to a secret spy agency. A chance to use her talents *and* a superhot guy to train her? She is so there!

#358 DEAD SEXY Kimberly Raye
Love at First Bite, Bk. 1
Hairdresser Nikki Braxton has had it with dating losers. So when she falls desperately in lust with sexy cowboy Jake McMann, she's thrilled. Jake is the real deal, a man's man. Too bad he's also a vampire....

#359 DANGEROUS... Tori Carrington
Extreme
When undercover agent Lucas Paretti agreed to infiltrate the mafia, he never dreamed he'd have another chance with his first love, Gia Trainello. Or that his still unbelievably sexy Gia would be the new Lady Boss of the family he's vowed to bring down...

#360 WILD CHILD Cindi Myers
Sex on the Beach, Bk. 3
Sara Montgomery needs this vacation in the biggest way. But getting unplugged from the cell phone and laptop is proving tricky. Luckily for her, hottie surfer guy Drew Jamison arrives as the perfect distraction. Who can think about work with this kind of temptation?

#361 FEELING THE HEAT Rhonda Nelson
Big, Bad Bounty Hunters, Bk. 1
Bounty hunter Linc Stone always gets his man. But when irresistibly sexy Georgia Hart joins him, insisting on helping him track down her louse of an ex-boyfriend, Linc can't help thinking he'd like to get his woman—*this* woman—too. Into bed, that is...

#362 TALL, DARK AND FILTHY RICH Jill Monroe
Million Dollar Secrets, Bk. 5
"There's always dirt." That's female P.I. Jessie Huell's mantra. But when she uncovers a serious scandal involving Cole Crawford—her long-term crush—will she be so quick to reveal it? Especially when it might ruin her shot at finally bedding the gorgeous TV producer?

www.eHarlequin.com

HBCNM1007